HANDMADE HAPPENSTANCE

HANDMADE HAPPENSTANCE
MARMALADE AND MAGIC™ BOOK 2

MICHAEL ANDERLE

This book is a work of fiction. All of the characters, organizations, and events portrayed in this novel are either products of the author's imagination or are used fictitiously. Sometimes both.

Copyright © 2022 LMBPN Publishing
Cover by Fantasy Book Design
Cover copyright © LMBPN Publishing
A Michael Anderle Production

LMBPN Publishing supports the right to free expression and the value of copyright. The purpose of copyright is to encourage writers and artists to produce the creative works that enrich our culture.

The distribution of this book without permission is a theft of the author's intellectual property. If you would like permission to use material from the book (other than for review purposes), please contact support@lmbpn.com. Thank you for your support of the author's rights.

LMBPN Publishing
PMB 196, 2540 South Maryland Pkwy
Las Vegas, NV 89109

Version 1.01, June 2022
ebook ISBN: 979-8-88541-621-4
Print ISBN: 979-8-88541-622-1

THE HANDMADE HAPPENSTANCE
TEAM

Thanks to our Beta Readers
John Ashmore, Rachel Beckford, Kelly O'Donnell, Jennifer Carter, Malyssa Brannon

Thanks to our JIT Readers

Wendy L Bonell
Dorothy Lloyd
Jackey Hankard-Brodie
Zacc Pelter
Dave Hicks
Diane L. Smith

Editor

Lynne Stiegler

CHAPTER ONE

Jemma Nox groaned when she woke up. The heat was out again in the small house she and her father shared. Tad Nox had gone to work for the day and had, no doubt, noticed the lack of heat when he woke up. *Another thing to add to the long list of things to do—heater repairs.*

The last snow of winter had fallen in early March in Kalhoun County, Tennessee, coating the mountains in a thin sheet of white that the sun did not work very hard to melt. Those who lived in the Eastern Appalachian Mountains were used to receiving snow as late as mid-April, with many fair-weather days between. "False spring" was a common occurrence in the area.

Soon, however, True Spring would arrive in her full glory, and the pine trees that covered the mountains would not be the only green anymore. After everything else came back to life, the place would look a lot less forlorn and haunted.

People in Tennessee and the surrounding states avoided places like Kalhoun County and the small town of

Solomon's Cross at all times, let alone a winter holiday or a summer vacation. If anyone did stumble upon the town, they would leave as soon as they could, certain the small hamlet was the kind from which stories about witches and ghosts came.

They weren't wrong. Solomon's Cross was not what it seemed to be for both good and bad reasons.

Most of the people in town were kind-hearted, but they had their prejudices and liked keeping insiders in and outsiders out, thanks to a long history of trouble with certain kinds of outsiders. Even stray cats were shooed out of town as soon as possible unless they quickly proved themselves to be useful by killing a good number of mice or befriending a local trucker.

On the other hand, the town had a past with strange folks inhabiting the more secluded spots. Rumors aplenty had been born. That was to be expected in a town with a population of only three thousand people, who grew bored when there wasn't much gossip to be passed around.

When there was a shortage of "this woman's husband slept with this other man's wife" and "this couple's child ended up in jail again," the people resorted to talking about the old woman who lived at the top of the mountain and the town's murky past.

For most of its existence, Solomon's Cross hadn't shown up on most maps. Putting it into a GPS took the driver to a church several hours away from the town. It wasn't until the driver arrived in Kalhoun County, where they could ask directions to Solomon's Cross, that they found the small mountain town.

Its downtown area was one street with one diner

everyone ate at, a hardware store, a bank, a post office, a grocery store, and a clothing shop. The latter could not be called a department store and was run by an old woman who was out of touch with the modern fashion trends.

Just outside of Kalhoun County was Johnson City, which was much easier to find with or without a map. Awareness of Solomon's Cross' existence, however, had changed quite a bit during the holiday season after Jemma and her father moved to the town. That was attributed to the recently re-opened Gran's Rest, a bed and breakfast on top of one of two mountains looming over the town. The B&B was owned by Eloise Brickellwood, who, as many said, was older than the town. Maybe as old as the mountains.

The town had fared well as a result of new travelers stopping in for the holidays. Business had slowed after Christmas and the New Year, but with the promise of warm weather and the snow soon to melt, outsiders had placed reservations weeks in advance to secure a spot.

It was now safe to assume that with a well-designed website and a good amount of traffic both there and into Solomon's Cross, the town was firmly on the map. The occupants, though wary at first of Gran's Rest reopening, were much appeased when their places of business started doing much better.

The workers at the local diner, Harv's Hamburgers and Hotcakes, quickly set aside their "we don't like newcomers in here" attitude and put on smiles for visitors. The residents of the town who regularly frequented the diner were glad the coffee was fresh more often, and the food was more carefully cooked, with fewer overcooked burger patties and undercooked pancakes. The soda was no longer diluted with water, and they started offering two different cuts of fries and added a fourth milkshake flavor to their menu.

Jemma thought about all these things as she made her way up the mountain to Gran's Rest. Several months previously, when she and her single father moved here, she had viewed the town as other wary outsiders would. It had once been too quiet and dark for her liking. After she met Mama B and her best friends the McCarthy siblings, things changed. Now she liked the town and wished to help make the place more appealing to visitors.

That could start with her job as head groundskeeper at Gran's Rest.

The strangeness could become endearing with the right marketing. For instance, there were many odd yet endearing things about her employer.

It was a warm day despite snow still being on the ground, so Jemma had chosen to ride her bike up the mountain. Since the ground had been too cold to work, her groundskeeping tasks had been limited for the past couple of months. Riding her bike up the mountain would help her build up muscles.

When she arrived, Jemma leaned her bike against an old shed she had recently given a new coat of paint and went toward the front doors of the cabin-like structure that was Gran's Rest. She smiled and nodded at a middle-aged couple occupying a newly repaired swing on the porch. They drank post-breakfast coffee and looked over the grounds.

Jemma went inside and found the hall with the front

desk vacant. The adjoining den and dining room were occupied by the housekeepers and the three maids Mama B had hired to keep the place orderly and clean. Jemma greeted them with smiles too and went into the kitchen, where she found the cook cleaning up from breakfast. She swiped a couple of leftover waffles, not minding that they were cold, and a cup of coffee. "Seen Mama B yet today?" she asked the middle-aged woman who was employed as the breakfast cook.

The cook shook her head and continued wiping down the counters as the dishes dried. Jemma glanced out the window, which overlooked the back portion of the grounds. A slope led down the mountain. The garden just outside the back door looked dismal since nothing had yet grown back. When the garden began blooming again, Jemma would have her work cut out for her. She was looking forward to it.

As she'd hoped, Mama B was *not* sitting on the stone bench near the back window. Jemma stopped short, hearing noise from overhead—the clacking of a keyboard and muttered curses. Jemma shook her head, grinning, and muttered, "It's Mama B on that damned computer again."

Finishing off her coffee and eating the last bit of waffle on her way up the stairs, Jemma sought the bed and breakfast's owner in her quaint wood-paneled office-library combo. In the narrow hallway, bathed in the golden morning sunlight, Jemma almost ran into another one of the maids, who carried an armful of linens she was taking down to wash.

"Mornin', Jemma," the young woman greeted her. Since

she was taking college courses remotely, the maid worked at Gran's Rest in the mornings and evenings.

"Mornin', Liza," Jemma returned. She would have normally engaged the employee in conversation, but she could hear Mama B's deep sigh from the room at the far end of the hall. Jemma passed the maid and entered the room. There, she found that Mama B was indeed at her large oak desk, bent over a massive computer. If Mama B hadn't been so old, Jemma might have thought the computer had been pulled out of ancient times and hooked up to electrical wiring that hadn't been tampered with in over twenty years. One of these two things was true.

The room was darker than the rest, because even though it had a large window overlooking the grounds, Mama B had a heavy curtain pulled across it. Stacks of books littered the room, resting on the overstuffed olive-colored chairs with glossy wooden backs or on a sofa that hadn't been dusted in years. Jemma made a mental note to come back and clear some things off.

This room was the one place none of the maids, the housekeeper, or anyone else who worked here was allowed to enter. Well, that and the cellar. Jemma, of course, was an exception.

She made another mental note to ask her father to build some shelves so the stacks of dusty books could regain a semblance of dignity.

Mama B didn't notice that Jemma had entered. The girl went to the window and pulled the curtain back so she could see the grounds. The sunlight made the thin layer of snow glitter like diamonds. Many improvements had been made to Gran's Rest in the last three months. The tiered slope had been cleared, and they were just waiting for the snow to go away before they could begin using it for entertainment purposes: small get-togethers for the locals or those visiting the area.

With the help of Jemma's father, Tad Nox, who worked for a fiber optics company, Wi-Fi had been installed. It wasn't the fastest, but it was enough for Mama B to use her massive Ice Age computer. Jemma was used to smartphones and laptops. She did her online schoolwork on her laptop at Gran's Rest during breaks. Mama B's choice of computer bugged Jemma. The woman told Jemma she had "gotten it out of storage," but Jemma wasn't sure what that meant since, as far as she knew, Mama B only had a tiny attic to store such things in.

These improvements had led to Gran's Rest doing well enough that its owner could start paying off the bills. The installation of the Wi-Fi, however, had one downside: Mama B was exposed to the world wide web, and then a whole new side of her was exposed to her favorite employee.

The old woman regularly sat in front of the hulking gray machine. Mama B wasn't easily flustered. When dealing with anything other than foolish people, including technology, Eloise Brickellwood had the patience of an oak. She also wasn't afraid of new things, as Jemma had feared when the computer was brought into the library. Jemma was sure Mama B wasn't capable of real fear. The problem was, Mama B had never had much use for technology, which hadn't been helped by being a recluse for a few decades.

Jemma still didn't know why Mama B had kept herself

separate from the town and closed Gran's Rest for more than thirty years, but she did know that the Information Age had sort of passed her by.

And then a teenager came to work for her, Jemma thought as she made her way to the desk. "What is it this time?" Jemma asked the old woman.

It was only then that Mama B noticed she had entered, and her head snapped up. Her face was as deeply lined as an old oak tree, but the dark brown eyes peering from it were full of vigor and life. Her expression was frazzled, and the loose strands of her wavy, gray hair poking out around her head matched it. Mama B was bowed with age, and anyone who saw her on the grounds saw a hobbling old lady.

Jemma knew a very different version of the woman. Mama B was far from agile and athletic, but she had a determined will that made her formidable—even physically at times. Jemma glanced at the gnarled cane leaning against the wall near the desk and imagined all sorts of circumstances in which Mama B had used it to defend herself. And that was without magic, another thing the people who came to Gran's Rest didn't know about.

Again, Jemma was the exception.

"Damn computer!" Mama B hissed. She sighed and leaned back. "Help an old lady out, why don't you?"

Jemma rounded the desk and peered at the screen. Her brows lifted. "Mama B! You haven't paid property taxes yet?"

Mama B scowled. "Well, no. I haven't ever paid 'em!" She said that as if it were obvious. As if paying property taxes was a ridiculous notion. "Your father said I better do it since this place is a business again, though."

Jemma agreed with her father but didn't voice the thought. Mama B grumbled on. "My claim on this land goes back before any fool came 'round tellin' me I gotta pay some uppity folks for the privilege of ownin' what's mine." Jemma knew Mama B had lived here for a long time but wasn't sure how long. Whatever the timeline was, she was sure Mama B had a right to feel the way she did.

But Gran's Rest had more attention on it now from people outside of Solomon's Cross and Kalhoun County. They had to cover their backsides.

"Besides," Mama B proclaimed, throwing her hands in the air and scooting away from the computer a fraction, "I've done more for the people of this county than any living soul." She lowered her voice. "Save one."

Jemma knew that to be true as well, though she paused when Mama B added, "Save one." She assumed the old woman was referring to another holler witch or a former close friend who was no longer here. Here as in Solomon's Cross, though here as in alive was a possibility too.

Witches and covens, she thought. *I'm still wrapping my mind around it.*

Since the ordeal with the boo hag, Jemma had continued training with Mama B, but she liked taking breaks. She enjoyed the work needed around the property more. The ordeal had almost cost her father's life, and she hated thinking about it.

Since the reopening of Gran's Rest, Mama B had made it a point to take care of all the other responsibilities, including employing townspeople like Jemma's friends, the

McCarthy siblings. That was a higher priority than paying her property taxes, or as she called it, "Givin' them governmental bloodsuckers the scraps from my table when they're better-used givin' to the people I know!"

Jemma attempted to maintain a neutral expression and not show her mixed annoyance and amusement. When setting up her internet, Tad and Mama B had argued at length over the use of tax dollars. Mama B didn't like taxation, but Tad believed it could be helpful. Jemma hadn't formed an opinion. To her, Mama B's old ways were too far behind modern times for her liking, but then again, it was the woman's "old ways" that had saved her, her friends, and her father's life. She couldn't discredit them, she often reminded herself.

"I did some tax work for my father after my mom left," Jemma told Mama B. "Maybe I can help." She pulled over one of the overstuffed chairs and plopped down to find that the computer had been overloaded with pop-up ads, downloads, and half a dozen porn bombs. "You've got to have at least a couple of viruses on this thing, Mama B," Jemma remarked dubiously, for she doubted the ads for sex toys, the porn bombs, and the potato casserole recipes littering the screen were a result of Mama B's searches. The old woman didn't need an online recipe to aid her in making the best food Solomon's Cross had ever tasted.

Poor computer's been abused and can't handle working anymore, Jemma thought as she closed tabs and moved dozens of downloads to the trash bin. Mama B watched her with a sharp, annoyed expression. "Nothin' works! Everything's too slow," she declared. She was neither flustered nor fearful, just perturbed to her core.

Jemma sighed. "Give me a minute, Mama B. I'm going to sort everything out." She spoke with more confidence than she felt, but clearing out Mama B's computer was like clearing out a garden full of weeds. If Jemma focused and didn't get flustered, the work could be done easily and without much trouble.

However, a basic computer safety crash course for Mama B had to be added to her task list. *Internet safety lessons, clean out Mama B's office, heater repairs,* Jemma listed to herself. She removed a few hundred bookmarked pages and files with names consisting of a series of numbers and letters. Assuming all of it was trash, she got rid of it. And if any of it was important, well, ignorance was bliss.

"Oh, no! Jemma, don't delete that," Mama B interjected as Jemma clicked on one of dozens of open windows. She had kept the online tax form site open and was closing unnecessary windows.

"Okay, okay!" Jemma responded. Mama B took the mouse from her. Jemma glowered at her employer. "I won't get rid of it, but you need to let me do this."

Mama B huffed and leaned back in her chair. Jemma peered at the screen to see what was so important to the old woman about the open window. Jemma's brows rose. What she saw on the screen were paragraphs so long she had to scroll to reach the bottom, consisting of an argument between Mama B and User42678, who had apparently decided to keep their name to themselves as they trolled.

Jemma's eyes widened as she read the contents. It was a review website for hotels, bed and breakfasts, and vacation rental places. Gran's Rest was one of the topics started by

User42678. With detailed descriptions of dilapidated cabins haunted by the ghosts of killed children and mangy, rabid cats running all over the grounds, the troll seemed to be looking for a way to discourage anyone from going to Solomon's Cross' main attraction.

Jemma sighed. "Mama B, this internet troll has never been here. He's just trying to get a reaction." She scrolled down. "Which you definitely gave him."

Mama B's eyes had gone wide. "There are trolls on the internet?"

"Well, they're not real trolls…" Jemma started. She almost added, "Wait, are there real trolls?" but she didn't bother. Life was confusing enough these days, given the element of magic and supernatural creatures being part of it. Mama B had never mentioned trolls, but the expression on her face told Jemma they were real. "It's just some guy in his basement, trying to make people mad because his life sucks," Jemma explained.

"Well, that's the dumbest reason I've ever heard," Mama B replied.

Jemma skimmed Mama B's response, but her eyes snagged on the end of it and widened. "Mama B!" She couldn't help sounding alarmed.

Mama B's long-winded response ended with an invitation to the "snot-nosed lil' shit" to come to her home and "say it all to my face!" Subsequently, she had provided her address. Of course, Jemma knew Mama B owned Gran's Rest, which anyone could get off the internet, but providing the address told the internet troll she lived there, too.

"God," Jemma sighed, leaning back and closing her eyes.

"Okay, Lesson One, Mama B." She opened her eyes again. Mama B looked at her innocently. "Never, *ever* give anyone your personal information online."

"But I have to for the taxes..." Mama B protested.

"That's different!" Jemma almost threw her hands in the air. She was about ready to give up. She took a deep breath and hovered over the message between Mama B and User42678. Before Mama B could protest, Jemma deleted the post, including the message with the address.

"Jemma dear, why did you do that?"

"I am quite serious, Mama B. That wasn't cool," Jemma replied.

Mama B's brows rose. "Cool? I'll show him what's cool!" She reached for her cane.

"What are you going to do, bash him through the computer?" Jemma asked dryly.

Mama B faltered. "Well, that won't work. Why can't he give me *his* address?"

Jemma straightened and folded her arms across her chest. "Well, for one, he's been trolling long enough to know *not* to do that. And think about it. If he gets your address and phone number and other information, he could steal your identity."

Mama B frowned. "Well, nobody can do that. He probably doesn't even look like me."

Jemma didn't have enough energy to explain that identity theft didn't mean User42678 had to *look* like the oldest woman in Kalhoun County.

"Come on, Mama B. Let's get these taxes done." Jemma had a feeling they would be here for a long time unless some miracle arrived and took her away from it.

Finally, the old woman relented, and Jemma made good progress on getting the computer stable enough to begin the tax-paying process. She had been so focused on the ordeal that she hadn't heard an old truck rattling up the road. The truck, owned by the McCarthys, had probably been driven up the mountain by Val.

Hearing the truck come to a stop and the engine go silent except for various creaks and groans, Mama B raised her head. Her brows furrowed. "Strange. Neither o' them works today."

Jemma knew that to be true. Easter and Val went to school during the day and worked on weekends and some evenings if they could. Val came by more often since Easter, her health improved after the boo hag had been dealt with, had auditioned for the spring play at Solomon Cross High. Jemma hadn't yet heard if she had been given a role, but if she had, Val would be around Gran's Rest a lot more frequently than his sister.

Jemma paused when she heard the front door open on the floor below. Footsteps sounded on the stairs, and a moment later, Val slammed into Mama B's office. He almost *flew* in, he was going so fast. He knew he wasn't supposed to be in here, which meant that whatever news he'd brought, he thought they needed to hear *right now*.

Jemma's head snapped up from the computer when he entered, and she took in his trembling, thin frame, pale skin, and haggard expression. "There's more boo hags! A whole mess of them!"

CHAPTER TWO

Jemma sprang to her feet, alarm filling her expression. Her whole body was as taut as an arrow that was about to be released. Val was too flustered to get anything else out. Mama B also rose, a little slower than Jemma had. She was alarmed too.

It's been four months since we dealt with the first boo hag, Jemma thought. *Why the fuck is it—or they—coming back now?* She had done everything in her power to stop the nightmares about the boo hag experience, both in her waking life and when she was asleep. Just when she had started feeling like she might have a normal life back, Val had burst her bubble.

"What?" she asked, hoping she had heard him wrong.

Valentine McCarthy was unable to explain. Footsteps running up the stairs and then down the hall caught Jemma's attention. Seconds later, Val's older sister Easter skidded to a halt just outside the door and peered in. She was panting from her run from the truck. She stalled, her eyes traveling over the room and taking in the contents:

the scattered stacks of dusty books, the giant computer, and the window overlooking the back garden. She also noted who was in the room. It was then that Jemma remembered neither of the McCarthys was supposed to be in here, even though they were her friends and Mama B trusted them with special information.

"Now, now. Settle down," Mama B interjected before Jemma could make Val explain his declaration. It would have been in vain. Mama B shuffled over to the boy and helped him sit in one of the upholstered chairs. He was trembling so badly he didn't realize what was happening.

Mama B *tsked* and muttered, "Everything's gonna be just fine, child. Settle down, son." Jemma gazed at Easter. The McCarthy siblings were her best friends, and aside from her father and Mama B, they were her favorite people to spend time with in Solomon's Cross. She grew excited every time she heard the rattling of their truck and saw their faces. This was especially true now that Easter looked better every time Jemma saw her.

Since the boo hag had been gotten rid of, Easter's health had vastly improved. Color had come back to her complexion, and she had put on weight now that she could eat full meals and no longer fought nausea all the time. She had also had a fair amount of hair growth, but it had come in patchy and lank, so Easter had made the stylistic choice to keep it buzzed and wear hats.

Today, it was a stocking cap. Easter was dressed in black and wore a cape about her shoulders. Jemma thought the get-up was strange, but then she remembered Easter's audition for the high school's spring play.

She must have gotten a part.

Jemma set aside her thoughts and any questions she had for Easter about school and the play to return her attention to Mama B and Val. The young man had been given a glass of water, and it trembled in his hand as he attempted to gulp it down. Jemma hadn't seen Mama B leave the room to fetch it, so it seemed to have appeared out of nowhere. She didn't bother to ask, being far more concerned about boo hags.

Easter strode over to where her brother sat and placed a comforting hand on his shoulder. Val just stared down into his cup. Easter spoke more calmly than her brother had, but Jemma could see the fear and alarm in her dark eyes. She swallowed hard and told them, "A concerning number of young children from our area of town have suddenly taken sick. Too suddenly. Not flu-suddenly. They're all showing signs of wasting conditions like what I went through."

She paled. The memory of the side effects caused by the boo hag's torment was enough to put her in an unpleasant state of mind. "Honestly, we don't even know if it is a boo hag, but all of them fell sick around the same time. Seven, I think? That's how many we know about. Actually, we don't know if what is causing the sickness is supernatural."

It seemed like Easter was trying to downplay Val's statement. Jemma couldn't blame her. After all Easter McCarthy had been through, it made sense that she wanted to pretend it couldn't happen again. That the boo hag they had managed to get rid of had been the only one to ever exist. *But what if,* Jemma thought, *that boo hag's ability to do what it did for so long gave others the courage to do that same?*

The thought chilled her, but she would not shudder in front of Mama B and her friends.

At last, Val spoke again. His voice was tight and a little rough. "No one believed me before." His eyes snapped up to meet his sister's as if to rebut her last statement. "But I am certain that whatever is making those kids sick is something spooky, even if it isn't a boo hag."

His expression hardened. "Which I'm not dismissing as a possibility. I mean, what else could it be?" Before any of them could answer, he went on. He spoke as if the words had been building inside him since he came into the room, and he needed to burst. "Those kids were fit and healthy only a week ago. Nobody gets that sick and…*drained* that fast without a clear cause. Ebola or some shit maybe, but that's not it."

"Where are the children now?" Jemma asked.

"They have all been taken to the hospital in Johnson City where I went for treatments," Easter replied.

"Do they have an answer for the sudden sickness?" was Jemma's follow-up question. Easter started shaking her head before the sentence was out of Jemma's mouth.

"They said the same thing they told me: they don't know what it is." Easter sighed and looked at Val. "On top of that, Val has been spending a lot of time with the kids, and he isn't sick."

Jemma's curiosity increased. "Who are these kids you're so close to, Val?"

Val and Easter exchanged knowing glances. Something sorrowful came over their expressions. Val's eyes filled with tears, and Easter had to step in to explain. "It's hard to talk about because not many people understand where we come from."

Jemma's expression and voice softened. "Try me."

"Well, for one, you know where we live." Jemma nodded. The McCarthys lived on the edge of Cider Creek, which was the poorest part of Solomon's Cross and indeed all of Kalhoun County, as well as the five adjoining counties. It was a series of mobile homes arrayed along the bank of Cider Creek, a stream that came from much farther up the mountain.

"Cider Creek isn't any different than other places of extreme poverty," Easter explained gravely. "Many of the children are not well-tended, either because their parents are working every odd job they can get, or they're drunk or high off their nut." Although Jemma and her father had almost been down that path, it hadn't gotten that far. Still, Jemma remembered people from her last hometown who had lived in a poorer area. Some of the kids she used to go to school with had parents who were, as Easter put it, "high off their nut."

"The kids roam about like a pack of strays," Easter went on. "They get bored, of course, and the older they get, the more likely they are to steal or damage whatever they want. Without their parents around, they don't have to care about direct consequences."

She glanced at her brother before adding, "So, to protect his beloved truck, Val has spent the last few years befriending this pack of kids." A small smile crept across Easter's mouth. "He teaches them how to fish, gig frogs, run trotlines, and have fun out in the timber around Cider

Creek. It keeps them out of trouble, gives 'em all something to do, and well, it makes them happy."

Jemma shared Easter's smile. "I'm happy for you, Val."

Val just nodded, as unhappy as he could be.

Easter sighed. "Val's been up in the wooded hills around Cider Creek recently since it's gotten warmer out. He's been setting simple snares."

Val lifted his head slightly. "Yeah. I wanna get into fur trapping, but I can't afford the kind of high-quality traps I need, so I've learned a lot about reading tracks and game trails." He shrugged. "I was teaching some of the kids what I'd learned."

"They were all out and about last weekend, and that was when Val noticed something was wrong," Easter added.

Val nodded, a little stronger and able to carry on the story. "All the kids were walking slower, then one of them said he was tired and fainted a moment later. We stopped and turned back. He came to all right, but he was real weak, and his face was all pale and his eyes were glazed over." Val shuddered.

"Then he started having trouble breathing. All the kids started to feel bad. I heard from a few parents that some of them weren't eating, either. I wouldn't have been too concerned if it had been just a couple of 'em, but the whole street? Well, it's spooky." He swallowed hard and added, "Reminded me of Easter when it started with her."

Mama B had listened intently as Easter and Val told their story. After they finished, she stayed quiet, looking instead at Jemma.

Jemma had been training long enough to be of help to Val and Easter, but...

I'm hesitant to go after this, she thought. *I have enough on my plate.*

She had her online school and finishing her junior year, her work at Gran's Rest, which was only going to pick up in the coming weeks with the arrival of warmer weather and more visitors, and on top of all of that, there was her father.

Since the events of last fall, the trust had been broken between father and daughter. Tad hadn't put any restrictions on Jemma. No curfews or anything like that, but he asked more questions. She didn't lie to him any more than she had to. Witch training was a complicated extra-curricular, but all Tad wanted was for his only child to fit in with the rest of Solomon's Cross' teens. *I've got Easter and Val. What more do I need?* Jemma often thought when Tad suggested she go to school events or parties.

Tad Nox liked Easter and Val, and he supposed it was better than having Jemma hanging around rougher people. AJ Kilmer, for example. Jemma's thoughts returned to the matter at hand. *What if this is just a matter of kids being dumb enough to eat some varmint Val taught them how to catch?* But the doctors at Johnson hospital would have figured that out.

In addition, Jemma doubted one boo hag could be tormenting so many at once. Whatever was causing this sickness, it wasn't one miserable creature working on her own. This thought didn't comfort Jemma. The silence went on for a little too long, so Mama B finally piped up, "Well, I think the situation is a great next step for Jemma's training as a holler witch." Her tone was cheerful.

Jemma shifted, unsure of how she felt. Easter eyed her, then glanced at Mama B. "Are you sure?"

Mama B nodded. "Well, of course. An investigation won't hurt, anyhow." She smiled at Easter. "And you can help Jemma."

Easter's eyes widened. "I-I don't know about all th—"

Mama B waved a dismissive hand. "None of that, child. Hush. I am afraid real magic will be too much for your recovering constitution, Easter dear, but if you went with Jemma, you wouldn't have to use any magic." She shrugged. "Just collect information."

Easter was as unconvinced as Jemma. Val, on the other hand, wore a relieved expression. "Well, I'm glad we can at least start doing something about it." He stood, a little steadier than he had been minutes before. "We'll head home and see if we can talk our folks into letting us go to Johnson City tomorrow to check in with the kids." He looked at Jemma, his expression pleading. "We can give you a ride if you think you can get your father to agree."

Jemma glanced at Mama B. The old woman's expression offered no indication of her feelings, so she shook her head. "I have some stuff to finish up here." It wasn't a lie. They had taxes to finish, as well as a slew of things to do around the bed and breakfast and grounds before the snow melted.

Val's shoulders slouched and he looked defeated. Jemma hated the way it made her feel. Guilty. It had been her constant companion since her mother left, and it now crushed her heart and lungs at the one look from Val. She wanted to give him hope, but how could she? Knowing a bit about magic didn't make her an expert or able to take on whatever the kids had wrong with them.

But then, she thought, *who else can help? If I don't, I'll regret that I didn't at least try.*

"Think about it, and call us if you change your mind," Easter called to Jemma as she followed her brother out of the room. Jemma and Mama B were again alone. Jemma heard Val's truck start and back out of the gravel drive. Jemma sensed Mama B's sharp stare on her. When she turned, she didn't let the woman speak first.

"I have misgivings," she confessed. What Jemma had been thinking, she couldn't bring herself to say to Val and Easter. Mama B, however, might understand. "My training is taking a lot of time, and going after boo hags or whatever the fuck it is this time is only going to take more." She sighed. "I'm almost seventeen. I've got a year and a half-ish of high school left and not a lot of time left to think about college and what I want to do in life. I have to think about my future and decide what to do before long."

Mama B's expression softened. "I understand, dearie. You children have too much pressure on you these days." Jemma dropped into the nearest chair. Now felt like a good time to pout. She'd been thinking about it for weeks. With fewer distractions and being able to focus on school and work, Jemma had begun contemplating if she wanted to make groundskeeping, of all things, her future. Or, she was good at science and liked it. Did she want to do something with that?

Mama B stood as Jemma considered and came to stand before her. She offered Jemma a warm, steady hand. "You need to accept that your future changed forever when you moved here, Jemma dear, and even more so after you encountered a boo hag." Mama B patted her hand. "I can't say anything for sure. I was never much a seer and never trusted their sort anyhow. But Jemma, you need to get rid of the idea that your life is going to be as simple and straightforward as graduating, going to college, and having a nine-to-five career. You might as well abandon that idea."

For a moment, Jemma felt only indignation. How could Mama B say that with so much confidence? She was tempted to give in to the belief that it was Mama B's "old ways" that had her saying such things. The more Jemma thought about it, however, the more clearly she saw the truth. Still, her anger came out when she spoke.

She pulled her hand out of Mama B's. "I don't have to accept living in a crumbling home all alone and jarring herbs for my whole life."

The older woman's eyes flickered with hurt. Jemma instantly wished she hadn't said those words. Mama B, however, didn't get angry in return. She only looked at the floor and shook her head slowly. "You will have to learn how to accept your new calling, Jemma." She lifted her head, and their eyes met. "You cannot deny that things have changed."

She was right. Everything had changed when she went after the boo hag. Well, long before that. Not even with moving to Solomon's Cross, but when Jemma's mother Delilah had left them three years before. "I'm sorry," Jemma heard herself say. She sighed. "I guess I'm just scared and confused."

Mama B reached for her hand and tried to give her a

reassuring smile. Neither was much comfort to the younger woman. "I know, Jemma. I know very well what you mean." Her words and the look in her eyes had so much weight that Jemma wondered once again about Mama B's past. She wanted to know everything from what year she was born to how she had become a witch and all the scary things she had fought. She knew Eloise Brickellwood was far more than a very old former midwife and herb-whisperer-genius.

Mama B's voice was solemn, and her expression was grave. "Your eyes are open to a reality few get to encounter for real, girl. You can't close 'em until you're ready to close 'em forever. Simple as that."

To Jemma, it didn't feel simple. She gulped. *So, in other words, I'm a witch until I die.*

CHAPTER THREE

Just before dusk, Jemma rode her bike back down the mountain. The sun had shone all day and melted much of the snow around Gran's Rest, but there were still piles of it among the trees on either side of the long, twisting mountain road. Jemma referred to the road as the Great Snake, even though everyone else in Solomon's Cross considered the road up to Gran's Rest fairly straight in comparison to others in the area.

Jemma arrived home as the sun sank below the horizon. The shadows lengthened and thickened, and it got a lot colder after the sun went down. Jemma pulled on the sweatshirt she had tied around her waist and plopped down on the steps of the front porch. She had a key but wanted to wait until her father was home. She had a call to make anyway.

"Hello?" Easter answered.

"Hey," Jemma started. She hesitated before adding, "I think I've changed my mind."

Jemma could hear the relief in Easter's voice. "Thank God, Jemma. Val hasn't said a word since we left. I'm really worried about him."

Jemma was concerned as well. She remembered the lengths Val had gone to to help his sister months ago. He cared about these kids, and Jemma didn't want to know what he would do by himself without their help. She knew he wouldn't give up, so she couldn't either.

"Being with the kids is the first thing he's had to himself, ya know?" Easter told Jemma. "Other than working on his truck, of course. It's a thing for just him, something he doesn't have to share with me."

"I understand," Jemma replied. She was an only child and didn't understand the dynamic of interacting with a sibling, but she understood having something to herself. She and her father had shared much, especially after her mother left them. The witch training, even though she was uncertain about it, was just for her. "What about you, Easter? Do you have anything for yourself?"

Easter's voice brightened. "Well, yeah, actually. I got a part in my school's production of *Macbeth*. It's probably going to be a shit show because the director doesn't know what the hell he's doing, but it's something. It's not a major role, just one of the three witches." Jemma remembered Easter telling her earlier in the week that the school's theater director was a former student who hadn't gotten into his favorite theater school and had thus stuck around his hometown to direct high school plays.

"Still," Jemma replied, "it's a part."

"Yeah." Jemma imagined Easter was smiling. "I've

always liked theater, but after I got sick, I didn't have the energy to memorize lines, let alone go to rehearsals and all that."

Jemma grinned, happy her friend was doing better. "Let me know when the play is going to be put on. I want to come see it."

"Of course." Easter laughed. "And I'm glad I have a couple of real witches I can borrow cues from for my acting." Jemma tensed, thinking about her training and the investigation she would soon be part of. Easter's voice was solemn when she spoke again. "I feel bad about it, though."

She hesitated. Jemma prodded, "Why?"

"Well, I'm going to be at school after classes are over for an hour or two every day, which means I can't spend as much time with Val and help him with his…case."

Great, Jemma thought. *We're already calling it a case.* She didn't say that, however, since she wanted to console her friend. She used her cheeriest voice. "Don't worry about it, E. We'll figure it out. Besides, Val will have me. I'm basically an older sister too, right?"

Easter laughed. "I'm not sure Val sees you that way."

Jemma didn't ask what she meant but said instead, "I'll see you tomorrow. Tell Val so he doesn't worry anymore."

"I will," Easter replied. "Thanks, Jem. You're the best."

She hung up. Jemma was left alone to watch the twilight fade into night. She'd have to think of an excuse to give her dad. She was not sure how he'd feel about her going after boo hags again.

Just then, headlights shone on the pavement. A moment later, Tad's truck rolled into the gravel drive and crunched to a stop. Jemma stood as her father's tall form appeared from the driver's side. She heard the truck door shut just before he called, "Jemma, why on earth are you waiting outside for me? It's cold as sh—" He stopped, not wanting to curse in front of his daughter—who wouldn't have cared.

Tad's cheerful voice made the troubles of her day melt. He came up and pulled her into a tight hug. "Sorry it took me so long. I picked us up a couple of burgers on the way here." By a couple, he meant there were two for each of them.

After burgers were consumed and Jemma had heard far more about how hard it was to get guys to come out and fix fiber optic cables running up the mountains than she ever cared to learn, Tad leaned back, smiled, and asked, "And what about your day, Jem? Better than mine, I hope."

Not better. Not by a long chalk, and tomorrow might be worse. Jemma forced a smile. "I had to help Mama B file an appeal for her property taxes."

"Ah, so that's the look of dread I see on your face." Tad laughed and sipped from a bottle of ginger beer.

One of Jemma's disadvantages was that she couldn't keep her true thoughts and feelings from showing up on her face. She was glad that her father had come up with an excuse for her. "And we're not even done. I have to help her finish another day." She gave a brief summary of the day's events before Val and Easter showed up. She hesitated before asking, "Mama B gave me the day off tomorrow." It was true. If anything, Mama B wanted Jemma to go to Johnson City more than anyone else except Val. "Easter and Val invited me to go to Johnson City so Easter can have a checkup. Can I go?"

Tad's brows rose. "Checkup? Isn't she a lot better?"

Jemma shifted. "Yeah, it's probably the last one." She hoped her father wouldn't see the lie, so she insulted it a bit more. "Val has some sick friends staying there as well he wants to visit." Again, a truth. Jemma wanted to lie as little as possible after everything that had happened in the past several months. They had each promised the other to be more honest.

"My only concern is that Val's rundown truck won't make the trip," Tad told her after finishing his ginger beer.

"It'll be fine. Val works on that thing every spare second he gets," Jemma assured him. That was also true. Whatever spare parts Val could find in junkyards or other people's garbage piles, he stored in a shed by their trailer home and used for his truck when required. "If something happens, I'll call," she added.

Tad nodded. "All right. I suppose it's fine, then."

Jemma smiled. "Thanks. I've got to be honest with you, Dad. I'm kind of excited to see a city again." Johnson City was far from large, but it would look like one since it had more than one street in its downtown area. Regardless, it was out of Solomon's Cross, and that was enough to excite Jemma.

Tad leaned forward and folded his hands together on the checkered tablecloth. Jemma stilled, noting hesitancy in his eyes. "Jem, there's something I wanna talk to you about."

Jemma swallowed. Things had been a lot better between her and her dad recently, and she was scared that whatever he was going to say might undo that. A tentative smile formed on her father's lips. "I'm not saying I'm going to, but what would you think about me starting to date again?"

This was the last thing Jemma had been expecting. She tried not to laugh. "Well, I guess that would be fine. But who are you going to date in Solomon's Cross?" Jemma hadn't seen one woman of her father's age who wasn't either married, divorced four times with a couple of kids, or weird enough for Tad. Granted, he had his peculiarities too. Jemma thought about one woman who recently started working in the hardware store in town. Jemma was pretty sure the woman wasn't married, but she had a girlfriend.

Tad laughed. "I don't have anyone in mind, Jem. I just wanted to make sure you wouldn't think it was weird if I *did* meet someone."

Jemma had to think about it for a second. "I mean, I'm not keen on having a stepmother anytime soon, but hey, why not? Sure. Do what makes you happy, Tad." She often substituted "Tad" for his title.

"Maybe I'll try one of those 'swipe right, swipe left' dating apps you kids use these days," Tad replied with a wink and a grin.

Jemma groaned. "Oh, please, no." She rose and deposited their burger wrappings and the Styrofoam takeout box in the garbage can. Tad chuckled, promising he would do no such thing. Jemma made her way out of the kitchen and up to the loft that served as her bedroom. The thought of her father going out on *dates* was very strange, even though he and her mother had been divorced for over three years.

I suppose he deserves to be happy. If he finds someone, I'll be happy for him, Jemma thought. She just hoped she wouldn't be seeing a new woman on her father's arm anytime soon. She believed that if it would help her father move on from Delilah, her mother, it might do him some good. Jemma also knew, however, that when Tad Nox fell in love—be it with a woman, art, or an obscure Japanese noir film series—he fell hard and fast.

Jemma rolled into bed a little while later, hoping to engage in a long, dreamless sleep before the drive to Johnson City the next day.

Val and Easter arrived mid-morning the following day. Tad was working from home and offered them a breakfast of pancakes, eggs, and orange juice in his usual cheerful manner, but upon seeing Val, Jemma knew they had to be off.

"Not today, Dad," Jemma told him as she pulled open the back door of the truck and climbed in.

Easter smiled at him from the passenger side. "Some other time, Mr. Nox. Thank you."

Tad waved a hand, annoyed with Easter calling him "Mr. Nox" instead of "Tad." "Be safe, kids. I'll see you this evening, Jemma. Call if anything goes wrong."

Val and Easter exchanged glances.

"I will. I'll be home by nine," Jemma told her father. As Val pulled the truck out of the drive, Easter glanced at Jemma over her shoulder. "Does he know what we're doing?"

Jemma shook her head. "He doesn't know boo hags might be involved. He was talking about the truck breaking down."

This was usually when Val patted the dash and assured his passengers that his "ol' girl" would make it just fine. When he didn't, Jemma's concern flared. Val's face was pale today, and he gripped the steering wheel like it was a life raft.

Jemma wasn't feeling so good herself. She hadn't dreamt about boo hags the night before but had still awakened with a sense of unease. Mama B's words the day before about not being able to ignore her destiny still moved around in her mind. *My life is changing, and I keep wanting to ignore it,* she thought. *Why can't I just have burgers with my dad in the evening and go riding around in a rustbucket with my friends during the day?*

Easter's voice broke through Jemma's thoughts. "Geez, Val, take turns a little smoother, will you?"

Jemma was jerked to the left as the truck swung around a particularly sharp curve.

"Sorry," Val's voice shook, and he gripped the steering wheel tighter.

He's a nervous wreck about the kids he's befriended, Jemma thought, feeling sorry for him again. Despite Val's apology, he accelerated down the mountain. He was desperate to get to Johnson City and wasn't aware of how fast he was going. The speedometer bobbed up to an alarming number. Jemma knew it was sometimes broken, so she wasn't sure if eighty-five was their true speed. It sure as hell felt like it.

Jemma caught a glimpse of Easter's wide eyes in the mirror as the older McCarthy sibling pulled out her big-sister voice. "Val! You're going to kill us!"

"Sorry," Val squeaked again. He slowed down, but Jemma noticed his shoulders and hands remained tense. They managed to get to the bottom of the mountain without anything more than a hard jolt over a deep pothole and Val swerving to miss a squirrel darting across the road. Under normal circumstances, he wouldn't have thought twice about hitting it by accident. He was on edge.

They entered Solomon's Cross, and since the speed limit was low, they made it through without incident. The state route road was smoother and had fewer curves. Jemma once again became lost in her thoughts as the mountains and farms blurred past. They cycled between what Mama B had told her the day before, impending dread at seeing the sick kids and possibly figuring out there were boo hags at work, and her father maybe starting to date again. The acceleration of the truck once more pulled her out of her thoughts.

"You need to pull into a gas station soon," Easter told her younger brother.

Val continued to stare out the front windshield. "We'll make it. We don't have time." He wanted to get to the hospital to check on the kids.

Easter frowned. "No, Val, we won't make it. I need to

use the bathroom, and you need to fill this rust-bucket. Otherwise, we'll get stuck and be of no help to anybody."

Reluctantly, Val pulled into the next closest gas station, which, unlike the only gas station in Solomon's Cross, had more than two pumps and a full indoor store, along with a bathroom. While Val filled the truck, Easter went inside to relieve herself. She returned shortly, also having purchased a chocolate bar for herself, Jemma's favorite gummy candy, and a peach-flavored sweet tea for Val. Val murmured his thanks but didn't seem interested in his favorite drink.

He was so distracted that he almost walked away from the pump without taking the hose out of the gas tank. "Gotta go to the bathroom too," he murmured before darting into the gas station. Jemma was as anxious as Val to get to the hospital, but she was grateful to have a moment alone with Easter.

Easter turned in her seat to face Jemma, who sat in the back with the unopened bag of candy in her lap. Easter glanced at the bag and then at Jemma's face. "Something's on your mind, Jem. What is it?"

Jemma hesitated but decided that if there was anyone she could talk to about what Mama B had said the day before, it was Easter McCarthy. She told her friend about the conversation that had led her to change her mind and call her about coming to Johnson City. "I knew Mama B had said something," Easter stated.

Jemma nodded. "It's just scary, is all. I'm not sure I want this...*calling* she says I have. I only started with this witch shit because I was trying to help y—" She stopped short, not wanting Easter to feel like this was her fault.

Easter's face adopted a resigned, somewhat glum look,

but she didn't appear to be hurt. Jemma sighed. "Just feels like my future has been decided for me, ya know?"

Easter was too kind to give Jemma a speech like, "You're the only one who can help, so you should," or "Think about someone other than yourself for once," so she settled for taking Jemma's hand. "Think about everyone you've helped so far, Jem." She mustered a small smile. "Me, Val, your dad. A bunch of others probably if that...*thing* had stayed around much longer."

Jemma tried not to think about "what ifs," but sometimes she wondered what would have happened if the boo hag had kept tormenting Easter. Her friend would have eventually died, and the boo hag would have had to move on. Would the creature have then turned to Val? Without being dispelled, it could have gone through any number of people in Solomon's Cross. Slowly, but with deadly effect. Jemma shuddered.

"Isn't that worth something, helping people?" Easter asked, breaking through Jemma's thoughts.

Jemma considered, then nodded. Easter was right. There was still much to figure out, but having saved Easter's life and spared others from the boo hag curse was worth something.

Feeling chastened, as only Easter knew how to do gently, Jemma decided to put away her dread. They were just going to take a look at the kids; that was all. Nothing was certain yet. A moment later, Val climbed back into the truck, muttering about there being a line to the bathroom, then turned the vehicle on.

As he pulled out of the gas station and onto the main road, Jemma continued to think about what Easter had said. It certainly put everything into perspective. Still, the idea of having a "calling" picked out for her burned.

They reached Johnson City Medical Center half an hour later. The building was tall, white, and non-descript. It was smaller than many Jemma had seen, but Johnson City wasn't large, so it made sense. It was also the only hospital for at least fifty miles, which meant anyone who had a major emergency had to come there. Fortunately, Val had driven the rest of the way at the legal speed, so it was early afternoon when they arrived.

Val hurried in ahead of the two girls. When Jemma and Easter entered, they found Val talking to the woman at the front desk. Her brows were raised, and her eyes were narrowed in suspicion. "Slow down, young man, and tell me who you're here to see."

"Th-there's seven of them. K-kids," Val stammered out, tongue tripping over his words.

The woman, who looked to be at least fifty, glowered. "You're going to have to give me a name and a good enough reason for me to give you a room number."

"Or I can just go to the children's wing and find them myself!" Val declared, and his sweeping gesture almost removed the papers and pamphlets lining the desk.

"Val…" Easter started, pulling at his arm. "Calm down." She stepped in front of her brother and apologized. The woman seemed more annoyed now that there were three teenagers standing in the front office. "We know at least one of the parents is here. We'll call real quick." She pulled out her phone and, consulting Val, punched in a number. While it rang, Jemma looked around the lobby. It was empty of people except for the woman at the desk. Everything looked dingy and gray. The seats lining the wall in the seating area were worn and faded and a few decades old. A TV was on and playing some midday game show where old people could win boats for vacations to Mexico.

Jemma's eyes strayed away from the TV and down the hall, where she saw a couple nurses walking into a back room. Easter finished on the phone and hung up. "Ms. Martha Green is with her daughter Sharina in the children's wing and says we're welcome to come back," Easter told the woman at the front desk.

The woman, having heard some of the phone conversation, grunted and told them a room number. The three of them took the elevator and wound down several halls before arriving at the right side of the children's wing, where an entire hall had been set aside for seven children. Easter told Jemma their names as Val nervously looked into each room. Sharina Green, Robert "Bobby" and James "Jimmie" Oldfield, who were twins, Margaret "Margie" Bowden, Lawrence Jean "LJ" Marbary, and finally, Sarah and Rosanne "Rosey" Keele. The one thing they had in common was that their parents liked nicknames.

Jemma wondered why an entire hall had been set aside but soon figured it out. "The doctors are still trying to figure out what the hell is going on," Easter murmured to Jemma as she looked into one of the rooms. LJ, Easter pointed out to Jemma, was hooked up to a respirator. The same was true of the other six kids, as Val very soon told the two girls. None of them could breathe on their own, Jemma realized, horror filling her.

Another reason the seven children were isolated was that the doctors believed they had something contagious. *Or they're all being attacked by supernatural creatures,* Jemma thought. Stating that wouldn't help, though. Not to men of science.

At the far end of the hall, a woman wearing a faded green blazer and jeans stood outside of one of the rooms. She had a tissue under her nose and sniffled. Under her eyes were puffy red bags. She had been crying for a while, it seemed. Jemma didn't blame her. Inside the room, a little girl no older than six lay on a hospital bed, hooked up to a respirator like the rest of them. The girl's eyes were closed, and she was asleep.

The woman's clothes told Jemma she had tried to come to the hospital looking professional but didn't have the money for business casual attire. Val and Easter recognized and approached her. "Ms. Green, thank you for letting us come visit," Easter told the woman when they reached her.

Seeming to notice she wasn't the only one standing in the hall for the first time, Ms. Green turned. "Oh, the McCarthys. Thank you for coming." She sniffled again and forced a smile. "Some of the other parents have been in and out, but I've only got Sharina, and Sharina's only got me. I can't bring myself to leave."

Sharina must be her daughter's name, Jemma concluded.

In a low voice, Ms. Green shared with Val what the doctors had reported to her while Easter and Jemma looked into the room and listened in. "The kids are struggling to breathe because lesions have opened in their throats and mouths."

Val's eyes went wide.

Ms. Green's voice was choked when she added, "In some of the lesions, they have found tumorous growths. Not in all of 'em, mind you, but..." Her words trailed off, and her eyes filled with tears. Sharina, it seemed, was one of the children subjected to the additional torture.

This wasn't good. Jemma felt sick to her stomach. This didn't sound like normal boo hag torture, even if the cause was boo hags. Her heart thumped hard, and her agitation about her "calling" faded a little. *I am mad because my future is set in stone, but some of these kids won't have a future*, she realized. She was unable to tear her eyes away from the poor dark-haired girl inside the room. Even with her eyes closed, Sharina looked a lot like her mother.

"May I go in?" she asked Ms. Green.

For a second, Ms. Green hesitated since she did not know Jemma. Then, realizing that Jemma had come with the McCarthys and must be a close friend of theirs, she forced a small, sad smile and nodded.

Jemma stepped into the room alone. Easter and Val watched from outside. Val swallowed hard, knowing Jemma was going in to find out if she could sense the presence of something foul and magical. As soon as Jemma was under the flickering fluorescent light, she felt something familiar in an "I've had nightmares about this" way. Jemma tried not to show her apprehension since she was aware that the girl's mother was watching her.

It smells like the dark presence of a boo hag in here, she thought. Like something rotten but not distinct, like it was underwater or covered up. *Like a boo hag is hiding in the wall, watching and waiting to come out when it's dark.*

Just then, Sharina Green's eyes opened. She sat up, looking groggy. Her eyes were gray, but Jemma knew it wasn't the natural color of her eyes. She opened her mouth to say something like, "Hi, Sharina. I'm not going to hurt you," but she didn't have time to get the words out.

One look at Jemma, and the little girl screamed.

CHAPTER FOUR

Jemma froze, not knowing what to do. Spring forward and tell the kid to stop screaming, that she was all right? She didn't have time to react. The child's cries had caught the attention of two nurses and a doctor, who arrived on the scene. "Ma'am, you're going to need to step out into the hall," one of the nurses told Jemma.

Jemma couldn't move. The horrid odor of the boo hag, which apparently only she could smell, grew stronger as Sharina continued to shriek. Her crying started to make her choke. The nurse gave Jemma a slight push, and she snapped out of her daze. "Y-yes, of c-course," she stammered as she stepped into the hall.

Easter's and Val's faces reflected their horror and shock. "It's not like Sharina to freak like that," Val told Jemma breathlessly. "She's the most level-headed of all the kids."

At first, the child's mother seemed flustered, but then she placed a shaking hand on Jemma's shoulder. "Don't worry, child; it's not your fault. Most children who don't feel good will cry out when they see an unfamiliar face. Sharina is just scared, that's all."

Jemma hoped that was the reason, but she couldn't help thinking the boo hag had sensed her presence and the magic within her and had reacted by hurting the child. As Ms. Green's hand slipped off Jemma's shoulder, another doctor approached them. His dark brows furrowed in concern. "I need the four of you to step away from the door, please." He spoke tersely.

He went into the room and conversed with the young doctor while the two nurses worked to calm Sharina down. After the conversation, which was held in low tones so the teenagers and mother of the patient couldn't hear, the first doctor left. The two nurses calmed Sharina down. Ms. Green tried to enter, but the second doctor frowned and asked her to wait in the hall.

Ms. Green huffed. It was *her* daughter, after all, but she did as he requested and waited. A little while later, the nurse soothed Sharina to sleep. *That was close,* Jemma thought. *There sure as hell is something wrong in there.* She glanced down the hall at the other rooms. In how many of these other rooms would she sense darkness and danger? She didn't have the time to go and find out since the second older doctor came back into the hall, looking annoyed at the four people waiting for him.

"The four of you shouldn't be upsetting my patients," he told them sternly as he clutched paperwork to his chest. Jemma eyed him, thinking how much she didn't like him despite having just met him. *Well, not even met,* she thought. *I don't even know his name.* Her eyes strayed to the name tag on his white coat. *Dr. Falksworth.*

Val's expression hardened. "We're not leaving, Doctor. We know that little girl."

"Please, Dr. Falksworth. That's my daughter," Ms. Green implored. "I just want to talk to her. She knows me. She won't scream when she sees me."

Doctor Falksworth's face soured further. He sighed after a moment of considering the four of them, his eyes narrowing on Easter and Jemma in turn. Neither of the girls said a word. They rested the longest on Jemma, which made sense since she had been the one in the room when Sharina screamed. The doctor motioned for Ms. Green to step into the child's room, but he prevented the others from entering. "Stay where you are."

Val looked ready to punch the older man, but he stopped himself when Easter tugged his sleeve in a silent command to stand down. Jemma couldn't hear what the doctor told Ms. Green, but she had the feeling that however good a doctor the man might be, he was doing a piss-poor job of hiding his disdain for all of them.

She caught pieces of his sentences. Snide things like, "She needs basic care, Ms. Green. Cleaner clothes. A bath more often." Jemma stiffened. Was the doctor truly insinuating that Sharina's poor health was a result of growing up around stupid hill folk? "Look," the doctor continued, folding his arms over his chest, "we don't get folks from Solomon's Cross often, so whatever's being passed around your people is from there. Best you get a medical professional closer to your area to—"

"This *is* the medical place close to our area!" Val spat as he stepped into the room. Easter pulled him back when Doctor Falksworth cast them a glare.

He thinks the kids are dumbass hill folk who've gone and gotten sickly, Jemma thought. She was just as furious as Val.

Doctor Falksworth began telling Ms. Green about the overall condition of the children and the symptoms they shared. Of course, Ms. Green already knew all this, and Jemma could see it took every ounce of her patience to listen to the doctor. Falksworth's sneering attitude, Jemma concluded, was offered to cover that he didn't know what was wrong with Sharina or the other children. *That might scare him,* Jemma thought. Still, it didn't justify his rude behavior.

Easter leaned close to Jemma and whispered, "I didn't have him when I was here, but the rest of the doctors are just as dimwitted and prejudiced."

Telling the doctor that boo hags were the problem wasn't going to help. He'd just look at her like she was as crazy as the rest of them.

Jemma was drawn out of her thoughts again when she heard Doctor Falksworth tell Ms. Green, "I can confirm that all the children have above-average levels of heavy metals in their blood, which can cause a number of health problems."

"Please explain more," Ms. Green pressed, brows furrowed in deep concern and confusion. Her eyes kept flitting between her sleeping daughter and the tall, dark-haired, dark-eyed man standing before her.

Doctor Falksworth hesitated for a moment, then admitted, "The symptoms we're seeing, Ms. Green, are severe and alarming. They're…well, unprecedented. Can you tell me anything about the state of mining and logging in Kalhoun County?"

"Well, yes," Ms. Green started. "Neither the logging nor the mining has been a major industry in years. Decades, even." Though clearly flustered by the situation, the woman spoke calmly.

Hearing this, Val and Easter pressed in. Val lifted his chin as he inserted, "At least we've never poisoned our land with coal mining or any other heavy industry."

Doctor Falksworth's brows rose, and his eyes betrayed that he thought they were ignorant of what was really going on. It wasn't beyond the realm of possibility, she had to admit. There were some things Easter and Val thought about their town, things they thought made it special, that Jemma didn't agree with. Solomon's Cross was like most small mountain towns with odd histories and a past that included making a profit off the land. Once, logging and mining had been industries in the area, but they had ground to a halt in the last seventy years.

There was a spiteful look in Doctor Falksworth's eyes when he turned back to Ms. Green, ignoring Val. "My office has reached out to the state about this, Ms. Green. I assure you we're doing everything we can. The state directed us to the Eastern Tennessee Rural Advancement Association."

ETRAA. Jemma had never heard of it. Looking at Ms. Green, Easter, and Val, she could tell they had never heard of it either. The name was probably as long as it would take to get someone down here to do something about this.

As if Doctor Falksworth's mention of the ETRAA alone was like summoning some evil spirit, a nurse hurried up to the doctor. "Mr. Stomphord has arrived and is asking to see you, Doctor."

Falksworth's brows furrowed, and he cast Ms. Green a dubious look. "So," Val drawled, "is that the ETRAA rep?" Doctor Falksworth nodded and sighed as he turned to go to the lobby. Ms. Green and Val exchanged looks before following him.

Easter and Jemma took a second longer because they were staring in bewilderment at one another. Once they reached the lobby, they found Doctor Falksworth shaking the hand of a tall, wiry-looking fellow wearing a gray suit with matching pants and a purple and black diamond-patterned tie.

Jemma surveyed him with disinterest at first, but when she read his nametag and saw the organization he represented, her curiosity returned. *Weird timing,* she thought. *The ETRAA rep shows up just as Doctor F starts talking about him.* The ETRAA rep had wispy gray hair and a petulant face he tried to make look pleasant with a too-wide, toothy smile.

It was evident that Doctor Falksworth was peeved because his four questioning visitors had followed him despite having to take separate elevators. The ETRAA rep's eyes slipped past Doctor Falksworth and landed on Ms. Green. He smiled, and Jemma thought his teeth were too big. He extended his hand. "You must be one of the mothers of the children Doctor Falksworth has told me about. I cannot imagine the distress you have been put through. Have no fear. I've come to lend a helping hand in whatever way I can."

Meaning, under whatever stipulations you come up with, Jemma wanted to retort. Mr. Stomphord looked weaselly. "Of course, no one at the ETRAA is responsible for the condition of the children, but we want to be good neighbors and see if there is anything we can do to help."

Easter and Jemma exchanged wary glances. *What a strange thing to say,* Jemma thought. *No one was thinking it was your fault, Mister.* Stomphord's eyes roved to the three teenagers, and Jemma realized how stiff she was. She uncrossed her arms, dropped them to her sides, and tried to appear relaxed despite feeling anything but.

"What do you mean by 'neighbor?'" Val demanded, not wasting time.

"Now, now. You three shouldn't even be here—" Doctor Falksworth started, trying to shoo the three teenagers away again. This time, Ms. Green came to their rescue.

She gave the doctor a cool glance. "These kind people live in Kalhoun County, and Val is as good as family to my Sharina, so anything anyone wants to say to me can be said in front of him."

Doctor Falksworth and Mr. Stomphord eyed Val with no small amount of annoyance. For a moment, both seemed to forget Easter and Jemma were there. Then, Doctor Falksworth, looking awkward, suggested they all go into his nearby office. The group followed him into an adjoining room, which Jemma quickly decided she didn't want to be in. The lighting was dimmer in here. The walls were gray, and there wasn't a single window or shred of light aside from the flickering yellow bulbs above. *What is this, a jail cell?* she thought. Doctor Falksworth sat behind a desk, but the rest remained standing.

"Well… 'neighbor' is a loose term," the ETRAA rep stated, turning to Ms. Green even though Val had asked the question. It was clear he was attempting to backpedal. He straightened and forced a fresh smile. "In an effort to enhance the quality of life of all people in Eastern Tennessee, including Kalhoun County, the ETRAA had begun surveying and collecting samples on the mountain heights all over the county, including Kalhoun's Crest."

Jemma narrowed her eyes. Everything he was saying sounded scripted. She kept her mouth shut so he could continue. Jemma wasn't sure where Kalhoun's Crest was, but Easter leaned close to her and whispered, "It's the peak that overshadows most of Solomon's Cross. The mountain across from Mama B's."

Mr. Stomphord noticed Easter whispering to Jemma and cleared his throat. He glowered at them, clearly annoyed by the interruption. Jemma didn't care. Company men sniffing for minerals without people knowing about it was never a good thing.

Jemma knew that well despite being just a...*teenager.* It was the presence of the young people that seemed to disturb the two grown men the most, so they kept most of their attention on Ms. Green. She was the most vulnerable of them all, given the state of her daughter, but she was also a mother. She was the most determined to get answers.

She just doesn't know where the hell to start, Jemma thought. *I don't think starting with a crash course on boo hags is going to sit well with her.* Jemma was of the mentality that one shouldn't cause unnecessary fear.

Mr. Stomphord seemed to sense the growing hostility and suspicion from Ms. Green, Val, Easter, and Jemma. His smile faltered, but he maintained his cheery, business-like voice. "I assure you, the ETRAA is only looking out for the good people of Kalhoun County and the surrounding areas." His smile grew. Jemma wanted to slap it off his face after he added, "Our people are your people. Our families are your families."

She and Easter exchanged glances in which they agreed his words were bullshit.

"Though the doctors have found traces of heavy metals," Mr. Stomphord continued, "we at the ETRAA can prove no heavy metals have been mined or dug up by our operations." He shrugged. "So it can't be we who are responsible."

Ah, so that's where his earlier comment came from, Jemma thought. The ETRAA rep's explanation sounded like over-compensation to her.

Easter spoke for the first time. "The heavy metals are only part of the concern here."

Mr. Stomphord seemed to notice her for the first time. He slid on an oily smile. "Young lady, there is no evidence that the ETRAA has done anything untoward, but I suppose as a gesture of good faith and our goodwill toward the people of Kalhoun County, we will gladly help take care of the financial burden caused by the children's illnesses."

Off the bat, it didn't sound bad, but Jemma looked at Ms. Green's face and saw that the woman wasn't fooled. She could smell what this shitheel was stepping in with. Mr. Stomphord gave Ms. Green another grin, but she spoke before he could go on. "Look, I don't need help with the medical bills. I'm not on TennCare, so the state is covering the hospital bills. For the other children, too."

Jemma thought of the families in Cider Creek and how

it was possible some of the children hospitalized here didn't have parents who cared to visit them at the hospital, let alone had nice insurance plans. She thought back to Mama B's opinions on taxes, then her father's. The taxes from a place like Gran's Rest *could* help the families with sick children here.

She understood Mama B not wanting to pay for land that was already hers, but the children?

She thought about the expression on Sharina's face just before she screamed and decided to do what she could. She looked down, finding her hands had clenched into fists.

Mr. Stomphord was unfazed by Ms. Green's statement. His smile vanished, and he returned dully, "I am aware of that, ma'am, but I am also aware that you work two jobs to take care of yourself, the aging uncle you've left at home, and your daughter."

His smile reappeared, but it was far more unpleasant than the previous ones he had produced. "Every minute you spend in Johnson City is a minute you aren't working either of your jobs." He leaned back. "We at ETRAA can help with that and make sure you don't have to worry about money through Sharina's recovery and beyond."

Jemma got tenser. Was the ETRAA rep really suggesting Ms. Green just go home and not worry about it while these two buffoons figured everything out? And how the hell did he know Ms. Green worked two jobs and had an aging uncle to take care of?

Ms. Green's eyes shuttered in surprise, then her expression hardened. Jemma could see she wanted to tell the man to go hang himself with his necktie. On the other hand, the offer was tempting. From her own experience, Jemma knew full-time school and a full-time job could be exhausting, and she didn't have two people depending on her. Extra help from the state would be nice.

More than nice. It could change her life for the better. Still, unease stirred within her. She almost interjected, but Mr. Stomphord held out his card to Ms. Green. "We want to be a friendly neighbor, but we can only help if people are willing to be friendly back."

Jemma almost groaned. Here they were again, assuming the people living in the mountains were unfriendly and closed off from the rest of the world. Some of them were that way, but given how quickly Ms. Green had shown Jemma kindness, the mother wasn't one of them.

Ms. Green eyed the card. Jemma could tell that she, Ms. Green, Val, and Easter were on the same page. The card represented some kind of devil's deal. Without thinking, Jemma reached out and took the card out of Mr. Stomphord's hand. "Ms. Green is going to have to think about it."

As Jemma took the card, her fingers brushed his, and a new sensation entered her. It was the same nauseating wrongness she had sensed in Sharina's room as well as when the boo hag had crumbled into nothing months ago.

It took everything in her to push the sickness away and not show his touch had affected her. *What the hell just happened?* she wondered with no small amount of alarm.

Mr. Stomphord didn't seem to notice, but he held onto the card a second past politeness before letting it go. With a tight-lipped smile and eyes brimming with smoldering anger, he said to Ms. Green while looking at Jemma, "Of course. I don't want to be insensitive. Again, just trying to help."

With the card firmly in Jemma's hand, she began to recover. The nausea went away, and she got steadier. Mr. Stomphord turned to Doctor Falksworth and said something she didn't hear. She leaned close to Val and Easter and, in a low voice, told them, "I'm ready to go back. I have enough information now."

CHAPTER FIVE

Well, I learned a lot more than I thought I would, Jemma mused as she walked out of the hospital. Val and Easter hurried to catch up with her. When they passed the front desk, the woman behind it scowled, then looked after the teenagers with a confused expression.

Jemma didn't notice. Her heart was hammering, and her thoughts buzzed like a full beehive, and yet, there was more to learn. If she had stayed, maybe she would have figured more out, but after touching Mr. Stomphord's hand...

She just couldn't wait to get out of there. The nausea had abated, but that dark feeling flitting over her senses was difficult to banish.

Jemma heard Easter mutter to Val, "Well, that was fucking weird."

They reached the truck, and, looking around, Jemma spied a van with ETRAA written on the side. The full name was painted under the acronym. She noticed there was a man sitting in the passenger seat. He had a hard expression and steely eyes that hadn't missed the three teenagers hurrying out of the hospital. He peered at them, and his eyes narrowed.

Feeling more uneasy, Jemma climbed into the back seat of the truck. Easter and Val also got in, but before he closed his door, Val demanded, "Jemma, what information did you get 'enough of?'"

Jemma put a finger to her lips for him to be quiet. Val snapped his mouth shut and followed her line of sight. He saw the van and the man inside, who was still watching them. Jemma didn't want to appear distressed or be overheard. Val and Easter closed their doors, and Val started the truck.

As Val pulled out of the parking lot, Jemma looked back one more time. Mr. Stomphord had just walked out of the medical center and was staring after the truck. He didn't seem to know Jemma could see him. She saw a different version of the ETRAA rep than the man she had met twenty minutes earlier. A greedy smile was pasted to his lips, and his hands were clenched around a file—the file Jemma remembered seeing Doctor Falksworth getting from Sharina's room. Sure, files all looked the same, but this one had a name—Sharina's, probably—written at the top in green Sharpie.

Why had Mr. Stomphord been given a patient's private file? Why *was* there a file? All medical data was digitized these days. Had the doctor printed out the information for the meeting? Cursing under her breath, Jemma told Val they needed to get back. "As fast as *legally* possible," Easter interjected as her brother turned onto the main road.

"Jemma, tell me," Val pleaded as soon as he was on the highway. "You look green around the gills."

Jemma explained the sensation she had experienced when she'd entered Sharina's room right before the girl woke up and screamed. "I felt the same damn thing when I took that card from Mr. Stomphord. I touched his fingers for a fraction of a second and felt the same thing. It was… strong. Really fucking strong." It had been less than a second. Jemma wondered what kind of horrible effect he would have had on her had he shaken her hand.

In the rearview mirror, Jemma's and Easter's eyes met. Easter's face was full of dread and horror. "The same feeling you had when the boo hag died?"

"When it crumbled and disappeared, you mean," Jemma corrected.

Until this point, Jemma had considered the boo hag dead, as in not coming back to haunt her. Ever. But she could be wrong. The thought made her heart sink.

She expected Val to take the revelation worse than Easter, but he just gripped the steering wheel and declared, "I knew something spooky was going on. I *knew* it!"

Easter laid a hand on his shoulder. "And we believed you, though being at the hospital did a lot to boost our confidence in your story, brother."

Val muttered something under his breath that might have been, "Nobody believes what I say until they see it with their own eyes." Jemma couldn't quite make out his words, though.

The next moment, Val drove through a red light and received honks from all sides. Fortunately, he had driven through it when there wasn't opposing traffic, so they didn't get into an accident. "Val!" Easter cried anyway.

Shaken and oblivious, Val glanced sideways at her. "What?"

"Did you not see the fucking red light?"

Val faltered. "Well…no, I d-didn't."

Easter insisted he pull over and let her drive, but Val reminded his sister that she didn't have much experience on the twisting roads and sharp turns around Solomon's Cross. "I'll be more careful, I promise."

It was a fight to keep Val from going into full-on panic attack mode for the whole trip. "I just can't stand it. Can't stand seein' those kids that way, and those shit-eating men they call doctors…" His words trailed off. He was no longer as pale as death but flushed with anger.

Jemma understood how he felt, and the greedy look she had seen on Stomphord's face had made her stomach twist more.

Val managed to stay on the road. The truck rocked back and forth, hitting potholes Val would normally have missed. He was still distracted. Easter and Jemma hung onto their doors for dear life. The setting sun and the truck's dim headlights didn't help matters.

"We're going to Gran's Rest first," Val told them. "Before any of us go home." Easter and Jemma agreed that was the best course of action. When they saw Mama B, they could get a better handle on the situation. Easter, however, told Val she was hungry.

"We can stop at Harv's. I won't be long, I promise, and it'll be faster than asking Mama B to make something for us," she told him. "Besides, Mama B isn't going anywhere. She'll be there when we arrive."

Val was eager to get to Gran's Rest but relented. He and Jemma remained in the car as Easter went inside to get burgers and drinks. Jemma wasn't sure she wanted to eat since the aftereffects of touching Stomphord still lingered. She didn't feel like she had to throw up, but she didn't want to push herself by eating either.

After fifteen minutes, Val cursed. "What the hell is taking her so long?" There weren't many cars or trucks parked in front of the diner. The busiest hours, dinner time between five and seven o'clock, were over. Just as Val was about to go inside, Easter reappeared. She had their burgers and drinks in hand, but she was clearly frightened.

She climbed in. "What the hell happened?" Val demanded.

Easter hesitated, then explained. "I saw something weird in there. Four guys dressed all nice like businessmen were sitting in a booth in a corner, looking at papers. Nothing about them told me where they were from or what they were doing, but I'd never seen them before." The McCarthys knew everyone in Solomon's Cross, so Easter seeing men she didn't know was worth noting.

She passed a burger to Val. "Lottie pulled me aside while the burgers were bein' made and told me they've come in every day for a week. 'Then they drive off, and none of us knows where they go,' she told me." Lottie was one of the waitresses who worked every day of the week. She might as well have lived at Harv's. If she said the men had come in every day, they had.

"They don't sound like the type of visitors who come

into town because of Gran's Rest," Jemma commented. She wondered if the businessmen were somehow connected with the mineral activity Mr. Stomphord had mentioned. "Whatever it is, even more reason to get up to Gran's Rest."

Val restarted the truck, which he had turned off to save gas while Easter was inside the diner. He parked at the top of the hill a little while later, and his sister and Jemma breathed sighs of relief. Jemma climbed out, glad she had managed not to lose her cookies during the trip.

The lights inside Gran's Rest glowed warmly through the windows. The three jumped out of the truck and made their way to the front door. Jemma suggested they enter calmly so they would not confuse or disturb any guests or staff inside. They did the best they could, but when they entered, it only took Mama B glancing at Jemma before she ushered them into the kitchen.

"Sit down, child. Sit down." Jemma obeyed and slumped into a chair in the breakfast nook where the staff members normally ate or took breaks. Mama B didn't say another word as she shuffled about the kitchen, preparing some tea for Jemma.

Val and Easter watched the old woman with puzzled expressions but didn't ask questions. They fidgeted enough to tell Jemma they were eager to tell Mama B about their day. The brewing tea produced a scent that began to clear Jemma's head and settled her knotted stomach. Once it was brewed, Mama B poured her a cup. "Thank you," Jemma murmured before lifting it to her lips. She didn't like tea, but with a touch of honey and Mama B's hand, it could taste perfect.

She sipped the hot liquid, and after she swallowed, she

felt much better. Jemma looked into the cup after noting its flavor. "Is there hash oil or something in this?" Jemma asked before she thought. In the grips of her struggles with her mom leaving three years ago, Jemma had dabbled with street drugs for about five minutes before deciding they were the last things in the world she needed.

Easter's and Val's brows rose, and Mama B shook her head. "I'll tell you more about it later. Right now, we need to figure out why that Dirty Spirit is back."

Jemma gently set the teacup down. "How did you know?" Mama B often just knew things, which had bewildered Jemma. She was quite used to it now, however, and the awe had worn off.

Mama B positioned her fists on her hips and looked gravely at the girl. "I could smell that haint's stink on you the second you walked in the door. Now, finish your tea, and we'll go somewhere a little more private."

There were a few guests in the adjoining salon, enjoying the warm fire before going up to their rooms for bed. After Jemma finished her tea, dregs and all, she, Easter, and Val followed Mama B upstairs to one of the unoccupied bedrooms. Mama B sat in a chair beside the empty hearth while Easter and Jemma sat on the four-poster bed. Val sat cross-legged on the floor.

Easter started by explaining that they had gone to Johnson City Medical Center and visited the seven children. She described the respirators, then seeing Ms. Green and her daughter. She then turned her eyes to Jemma so she could describe what had happened when she'd stepped into the girl's room. "It felt horrible," she stated after giving Mama B the details. "The girl woke up and screamed. It was an angry scream, though. Not scared."

Mama B confirmed Jemma's suspicions. "The boo hag, if that's what's possessing her, sensed it was a witch, and she reacted angrily. The child probably didn't even know you were there." Mama B shook her head, looking sorrowful. "Poor child's mind musta been taken over."

Val's face paled. He looked sick. Sharina, even though she was six years old, was his friend and like a little sister to him. All the kids had been taken under his wing. Jemma wondered if he felt like he had failed by not being able to protect them or see the signs ahead of time.

"Then the doctor came," Easter continued. She gave a brief description of Doctor Falksworth and the arrival of Mr. Stomphord. Mama B's eyes narrowed when she heard the plan Stomphord had proposed to Ms. Green. "Greedy company men looking to take, take, take. Hang 'em all!" Fearing Mama B was about to get onto a soapbox, Jemma interjected and described the final part: barely touching the ETRAA man's fingers and feeling like she was going to vomit.

"Ah! *That's* what I smelled on you, child." Mama B looked alert and alarmed, then concerned. The old woman glanced at Val on the floor, who looked like he was about to burst into tears. He had been holding his emotions back since they'd arrived, but he was about to break. Jemma wasn't sure how she could help him hold it together.

Mama B's expression softened. "Ah, child, do you mistake my concern for me thinking the children won't be okay?" She shook her head, dispelling any such fear Val might have had. "With Jemma's help, I am almost sure I can get those smart-aleck white coats to sort out those poor young 'uns."

Relief washed over Val's face. There was still concern in his eyes, which would remain until the ordeal was dealt with. *Here we go,* Jemma thought. *Just when I thought my life was going back to normal.*

But those kids needed help.

Easter spoke up. "You still seem concerned, Mama B." Her brow furrowed, and her eyes flitted between her brother and the old woman. "Why?"

Mama B stared at the floor for a long moment while rocking in her chair. At last, she sighed and lifted her head. The look in her eyes was sorrowful and far away, as if many painful memories weighed on her mind. "Maybe it's best not to talk about that right now. It's a long story, and it's getting late."

Val, Easter, and Jemma shook their heads. Val leaned forward, voice firm. "None of us are going home until we know what is going on."

Mama B sighed once more. "Very well. I'll begin as close to the beginning as I can."

CHAPTER SIX

Since the guests had gone to bed, the teenagers and old woman went back down to the main level and settled in front of the hearth in the parlor. Mama B made them each a cup of tea. Jemma sensed she did that to delay the inevitable. It was possible that she hadn't told her story in a very long time. It might be hard for her.

At last, Mama B sat down and began. "It started a long, long time ago." She sighed. "A lot longer than I care to say."

Jemma recalled how many who lived in Solomon's Cross spoke of knowing Mama B since they were small children. Mama B herself had stated that she had brought the parents of the adults living in Solomon's Cross into the world. Once a midwife, she was now far more. The town still called her a witch. She was, but not in a sinister way.

"My two sisters and I traveled for some time before we reached Solomon's Cross. Mind you, they weren't my actual sisters, but rather, my coven sisters."

Easter's brows furrowed. "There's a difference?"

Mama B nodded. "Yes. Rather than being sisters by

blood, they were my sisters because we often cast spells in tandem. We were magically bound. Their names were Josephine Doire and Vesna Soucek."

Jemma's eyes widened. She recognized the name "Doire." The previous owner of the house she and her father lived in was Mabel Doire. Was she a relative of the Josephine Mama B had known?

"Anyway, like I said, we traveled for some time before we came to Solomon's Cross. This was before there was even a Kalhoun County." Mama B paused, considering how much to share.

Jemma gave her a look as if to say, "The whole truth or none of it."

Mama B had said those words to Jemma. "We soon discovered there was rich life and magic in the area, so it seemed like a fine place for three practitioners of the Art to settle." Mama B shrugged. "The people here weren't openly hostile to us, which was a surprising and good thing in those days."

Jemma wondered what time Mama B was referring to, but she didn't ask. Mama B was still speaking. "They weren't hostile *yet*, anyway. That came later." A sense of foreboding could be heard in her voice. "Josephine and I had no trouble deciding to live here. Vesna, on the other hand, feared something that had chased her out of Eastern Europe before she met Josephine and me. She did not want to stay, but in the end, we convinced her to."

In the journal Jemma found in her house, she had read many entries about a young woman escaping some threat in Eastern Europe before coming to Solomon's Cross. Had the author of the journal been Vesna Soucek? All this time, Jemma had assumed it was Mama B.

She wanted to know about the threat Mama B spoke of, but the old woman continued before any of them could ask questions. "It wasn't long before we began working freely with the magic and making a true home for ourselves here. There was so much magic. It was unbelievable how much there was. Eventually, we discovered why."

She paused to sip from her tea. Deeply interested, Jemma, Easter, and Val leaned forward in their seats. Jemma had forgotten about her tea, which had gone cold on the end table beside her chair.

"There was—and still is—a great concentration of magic within Solomon's Cross. We found out this was the case because long before Solomon's Cross existed, perhaps even before humans walked in this world, there was a great sealing and trapping of all manner of dark things."

Jemma stilled, remembering how they had sealed the boo hag. She couldn't begin to imagine what sealing and trapping "all manner of dark things" entailed. *Probably a really powerful witch or many of them,* she thought. And that had occurred *here*...in Solomon's Cross. A chill darted up her spine. The faces of both Easter and Val told her they had similar reactions.

Mama B's expression remained grave. "This concentration of magic sealed beneath the ground is under what is now called Kalhoun's Crest."

Jemma's head whipped to Easter and Val, who occupied a sofa. Their alarmed gazes met hers. The ETRAA rep had mentioned Kalhoun's Crest. Jemma gulped. Was the work the ETRAA doing connected with the magic trapped beneath the mountain overshadowing Solomon's Crest?

The apprehensive expressions of her listeners did not escape Mama B's notice. She continued without asking about them. Perhaps she already knew, or she felt she didn't need to. "The abundance of magic, bound up in the life there, was part of what kept everything sealed inside the mountain. While it was resilient, it wasn't invulnerable, and our free use of the available power cracked the seal." Mama B's hand shook around her cup of tea. "It was just a tiny crack; we didn't even know we'd caused it until it was too late. What had been trapped beneath the ground for millennia emerged, and our small coven had our hands full for years. We had to destroy, reseal, or drive off the haints who crawled out of the darkness. It was a lot of work for only three of us. After the haints came years and years of fending off boogers and dark witches. They came to the surface like sharks scenting blood."

With these last words, Mama B shuddered. She sat before a fire, but the memories made her cold. Easter, seeing Mama B's reaction to her story, brought over a blanket. "Thank you, dearie." The old woman gathered herself and continued.

"When the dust finally settled, we realized we could never leave this place. We feared long-term consequences would follow from what we had done. We couldn't leave the people of Solomon's Cross to be tormented by what slipped through the crack and do nothing about it.

"There was also the fear that if the dark things from inside the sealed mountain ravaged the small town we lived in, what was going to stop them from going farther out into the world?" Until this point, her eyes had been fixed on the fire, but now they drifted to meet Jemma's, Easter's, and Val's in turn. "We didn't know how deep the darkness ran."

The storyteller shifted and set aside her teacup. Folding her hands in her lap, she continued, "That was another thing Vesna Soucek didn't like. She disliked staying in one place for long. I never learned why, but Josephine and I guessed it had something to do with whatever had chased her out of Eastern Europe."

Jemma wished she had the journal with her.

"Josephine and I did our best to convince Vesna that she could have a good life here." A small smile crept across Mama B's lips. "Jo and Vesna took husbands and had children." Jemma thought about the photo album she had found with the journal. There had been pictures of many children inside it. *Was Mabel Doire one of them?* she wondered.

"What about you?" Easter asked, eyes sparkling. "Did you marry, Mama B?"

A look of sadness came over Mama B's features. "I did not, though I did fall in love." The sadness in her eyes grew. She did not explain, and her listeners did not push her. "I was only Eloise Brickellwood back then. Not yet Mama B." She chuckled. "I was a beauty as well. I never married, but many wanted me to."

Jemma thought about the World War Two veterans who had come home to Solomon's Cross. She wondered how many of them had sought Eloise as a wife. For some reason, she had denied them all.

"I didn't want to marry when Kalhoun's Crest might

break open at any moment," Mama B stated, her grave expression back. "Eventually, it wasn't haints or witches or boogers that brought everything to an end." She paused once more, weighing her words carefully.

The anticipation in the room resulted in Jemma, Easter, and Val leaning forward in tense silence. "It was men looking for minerals."

Alarm shot through Jemma. Sharing a look with the McCarthys told her they were turning the same questions in their minds that she was over. Men like the ones who worked for the ETRAA? Did the high amounts of metals in the bloodstreams of the children in the Johnson City hospital have anything to do with what lay under Kalhoun's Crest? She reached for the tea, hoping it would keep her from getting sick again. It was cold, but she didn't care.

"It took all of our cunning and calling in every favor from the people of Solomon's Cross to keep the companies from digging into the mountain and opening Pandora's box," Mama B explained. Val's remark about Solomon's Cross not having a mining or logging industry made more sense to Jemma now.

The old woman forged ahead. "Lord knows how many of the people in Solomon's Cross were unhappy about it. It was then that they decided we were sinister witches who would gobble their children up after fattening them with candy."

Jemma nodded. It made sense. "They got scared and reacted in anger."

The sadness in Mama B's eyes remained as she dipped her head in confirmation. The worst part, it seemed, was still to be told. "You see, until the men looking for minerals came in, the three of us—Josephine, Vesna, and I—were well-respected among the people. I was a midwife, remember, and made all sorts of herbal concoctions to help the sick. It didn't seem to be a problem until...well, until we got blood on our hands." She paused once more, and this time, one of her listeners didn't stay quiet.

"What happened next?" Val prodded.

"There was a...falling out, we'll call it," Mama B answered. "The hostility between the vengeful corporations and those within Solomon's Cross rose to dangerous levels." Mama B fidgeted with an old fringed throw pillow. When she looked up and held Jemma's gaze, her eyes brimmed with tears. "The violence resulted in the death of Vesna's children."

Easter and Val gasped. Jemma heart thudded faster. Sighing, Mama B leaned back as if telling the story had exhausted her. "The death of Vesna's children signaled the end of the coven. She blamed us, me most of all, for staying and causing the whole mess." Mama B looked down at her hands as if looking for the blood of the innocent people she hadn't killed but had, in part, been responsible for.

"Vesna's heartbreak and bitterness swelled until it drove off her husband, who drank himself to death shortly after. Josephine and I feared Vesna might do something drastic in her grief, so we made the difficult decision to seal her off from the Art lest she do something terrible."

"I'm guessing she didn't take it well," Val inserted dryly.

Mama B shook her head. "She was enraged but impotent, so she left Kalhoun County, cursing our names. We never saw her again."

Mama B took a handkerchief out of her pocket and wiped her eyes. "The ordeal nearly broke poor Josephine. She and Vesna had been much closer than Vesna and I were, you see. She decided her part in all of it was done. The mountain was safe now, and it only required one to maintain it. I agreed to stay and keep my magic."

All alone, Jemma thought. *She's been keeping a great darkness at bay by herself for many years.*

"I didn't have a family like Josephine did," Mama B continued, "so I didn't have as much to lose. It was best for me to stay anyway since I had the strongest voice among the people, having brought many of them into the world and all."

Jemma didn't want to diminish what Mama B had done for the people of Solomon's Cross, but she wondered if her justification stemmed from a sense of guilt. "Josephine stayed in Solomon's Cross during the 1980s and 90s, when things got a little better for black folks, at least economically. Josephine's grandson talked her into moving to Knoxville with him and some of her other family. She agreed." Mama B looked at Jemma. "She left her home to her daughter Mabel."

Easter and Val sensed that this statement held some significance for Jemma. "Mabel owned the house my dad and I live in now," Jemma explained.

"Small world," Easter murmured.

"No," Val corrected. "Small town."

The story weighed on Jemma's shoulders. She wondered how much more of a burden it was for Easter and Val. They had lived here their whole lives. What was it like for them to learn there had been a great darkness trapped near their town this entire time? And that one person, Mama B, who people talked shit about for being a witch, had protected them.

"That's why I've been here all this time," Mama B stated with a resigned sigh. "I had always lived on this mountain opposite Kalhoun's Crest, so I could see anything fishy going on. Once the rumors started flying about why Josephine and Vesna left town, the people became suspicious of me. Gran's Rest closed, and I was left alone on the mountain. Sometimes, Mabel would visit me, but I think she wanted to get away from the whole ordeal. She had seen what happened to Vesna's children."

Jemma couldn't blame her.

"It's true that I've grown lax in tending the Art and making sure everybody with bad interests stays away," Mama B admitted. "And now things are being stirred up again. Greedy men will always creep in here like the dirty cockroaches they are." Mama B offered a small, dismal smile to her listeners. "I'll need your help to get it done."

Easter and Val nodded without hesitation. "Of course we'll help, Mama B," Easter answered.

"Anything to get those kids back and make sure they aren't hurt again," Val chimed in gravely. He seemed calmer now that he knew what was happening, but perhaps he was just processing the story.

Jemma's mind reeled. She didn't think she would be able to sleep tonight with all that now weighed on her mind. What a day it had been. She hesitated to answer, feeling like an outsider to this world. *I've only come to this town in the last seven months*, she thought. *It's not like I've lived here my whole life like Easter and Val or most of it like*

Mama B. She didn't have the deep connection to Solomon's Cross the rest of them did.

She lifted her head and forced herself to say, "We'll do whatever we can."

Mama B nodded. "We can tackle this tomorrow." The old woman rose. "For now, the three of you need to get home."

Jemma whipped her head to the clock on the mantelpiece and saw that it was fifteen minutes past eleven. She looked down at her phone and found it was dead. "Shit! My father's gonna kill me. He's probably called and texted me, like, ten times." She remembered promising to be home by nine o'clock.

Easter and Val stood. "We'll take you home right now," Val told her as they made their way to the front door. They walked out into the darkness of the night. Normally, Jemma wouldn't have minded the drive from Gran's Rest to her house after dark, but the story she had just heard played over and over in her mind. The darkness added to her unease. The occupants of the truck were silent as they drove to the house. Jemma didn't doubt Easter and Val would talk the story over on their way home.

Easter and Val said their goodbyes to Jemma, thanking her again for going with them to Johnson City, then drove off into the night. Jemma made her way inside. All lights were off except the one in the kitchen. She heard her father's steady snoring from his room on the first floor and breathed a sigh of relief. She was glad he hadn't stayed up for her.

When she entered the kitchen, looking for something to eat before bed, her relief departed. Her heart sank as her eyes landed on a handwritten note on top of her schoolbooks. "Shit, I missed a test today. I thought I would be back in time to take it."

She picked up the note.

We need to talk.

Filled with dread, Jemma made her way to the loft, hoping she could get some sleep before facing her father in the morning.

CHAPTER SEVEN

Tad was up before Jemma.

When she awoke, Jemma could hear him down in the kitchen, shuffling around. She thought about pretending to be asleep for longer, hoping he would go to work before she got up. However, she would have to face him sooner or later. *Might as well get this over with,* she thought with an inward groan as she swung out of bed.

When she entered the kitchen, Tad turned. For a moment, it looked like he was going to give her his normal cheery morning smile, followed by a, "How'd you sleep, Jem? Fight off any monsters in your dreams?"

Jemma didn't talk about her nightmares with her father anymore, but when she was little and afraid of monsters under her bed, Tad would tell her to just, "Fight 'em all off in your dreams." When she awoke the next morning, Tad would ask her how many monsters she had killed. He still asked nearly every morning. This morning, though, Tad wasn't in the mood for banter.

"Ah, you're awake. Sit down so we can talk." He offered

her a toasted bagel with cream cheese and a glass of orange juice while he put a couple of spoonfuls of sugar in his coffee.

Reluctantly, Jemma pulled out one of the chairs at the dining table. After she sat down, she pulled her knees up to her chest. Tad drew out the chair opposite her. "We need to have a serious conversation about school, Jem. You missed another test yesterday."

"I know," Jemma answered, not looking at her father. Her eyes roved around the kitchen, noting there were dirty dishes in the sink and the trash bin was overflowing. With both of them out of the house so much, the housework had slipped. Perhaps after they talked about school, Tad would bring up the fact that she hadn't done her chores in a few days.

"Why were you gone so late?" Tad asked his daughter.

Jemma decided two things. One, she didn't want to lie to her father and two, she didn't want to tell him everything she had learned. It was a lot for her, and she wasn't ready to share it with him yet. "We went to Gran's Rest after we got back from the hospital and there was...work to do." It was the truth. Mostly. She just didn't bother to mention *when* they had arrived at Gran's Rest. "Time slipped away, Dad. I'm sorry. And my phone died. I promise it won't happen again—"

Tad put up a hand. He sighed, looking bereaved as he stared at the checkered tablecloth. "You're doing all right in school, Jem, and this is the first test you've missed in a long time. That's not the problem I have."

Jemma's brows furrowed. "Then what is it?"

"I've talked with your teachers. They've all told me

you're passing, but the work you're putting in is…substandard for you. They're concerned, and rightly so. I am, too. I want to know what is going on."

Jemma shrugged. "If I'm passing, that's what matters, right?"

Tad sighed again. "What matters is that my daughter isn't doing as well as she normally does and doesn't seem to have a reason for it." Concern caused his brows to draw together.

Jemma knew the full explanation would include explaining her supernatural double life, which would not help matters. With everything she had learned in the past couple of days, Jemma wasn't even sure how much school mattered to her anymore. If her calling meant staying in Kalhoun County for the rest of her life, what the hell were straight As going to do for her? She didn't need to pass every chemistry and math test to be a witch. Every time she thought about it, she wanted to give up.

On top of that, if she worked with Mama B, Easter, and Val on this new "case," as the McCarthys called it, school would have to be put on the back burner for even longer. She didn't think her dad would let her.

As she thought that, Tad straightened and said, "I've decided you're going to take a break from Gran's Rest until you've gotten your schoolwork straightened out." He shrugged. "Maybe you just need to decompress."

Jemma's heart sank. If she couldn't go to Gran's Rest, how the hell was she supposed to work with Mama B and the McCarthys? Mama B didn't like leaving Gran's Rest. Jemma wasn't sure why, and she was curious. She remembered Mama B coming down the mountain to the house. It had been a strenuous and terrifying experience for the old woman.

"I can see you struggling, Jem, and maybe it's more than just school and work. If you need more time before you can tell me, I understand." Tad gave her a reassuring smile.

It might take all the time in the world before I'm ready, Jemma thought, defeated. At least her father was being understanding. She couldn't blame him for his concern, considering she kept him in the dark.

"For now, I need to know you're doing something about your future," he added.

My future? I don't even know what my future is going to hold. Well, I do. Kind of. But I don't know if I want it. She thought about Vesna and Josephine, who had eventually decided they didn't want to be holler witches anymore and moved on.

Why couldn't she have the same option? Then she considered that after Josephine and Vesna had left, Mama B had been alone. She probably didn't want to be the last witch of Kalhoun County forever.

Sighing, she nodded at her father. Her plans for the day were ruined, and although she was angry, she could tell her father wasn't going to back down. He remained calm but firm in his resolve. Tad stood. "I have to get ready for work now. You will stay here while I'm gone. If you want, we can talk more about it when I get home." He offered a subtle invitation. "If you want to tell me what's going on, you have the whole day to think about what you want to say."

Jemma doubted that would happen. It would take the whole day to process yesterday's events. Instead of arguing with her father, Jemma texted Easter. The girl understood and promised to call her after school.

Jemma spent the day doing schoolwork, as she had promised her father she would. She took the test she had missed the day before and submitted it. By the time late afternoon rolled around, she had completed all the work necessary for the day and then some.

Her phone rang around four o'clock. It was Easter.

"Hey, Jem," Easter greeted when Jemma answered. "How are you doing?"

"Well, I definitely feel grounded."

"I'll go up to Gran's Rest soon and tell Mama B what happened," Easter told her. "Val and I were supposed to go up anyway."

"Thank you," Jemma replied, relieved that Easter knew she hadn't told Mama B. Jemma had considered calling Gran's Rest but concluded that either her father had already told her employer or Easter would. Besides, Jemma didn't want to admit to Mama B that she had fallen behind in school.

Even though I didn't, she thought. Jemma couldn't fault her father or her teachers for their concern, though. She now lacked the passion for subjects she had previously excelled in, and it showed.

"How was your day at school?" Jemma asked. She could hear the engine of Val's truck in the background.

"It was good," Easter returned. She sounded cheerful, which Jemma was glad for. "Rehearsals are well underway for the play, and Val and I went for a bite at Harv's after." She lowered her voice, even though Val could still hear her. "Val wanted to see if the men Lottie says hang around there every day were there."

Interest heightened, Jemma asked, "Were they?"

"Only one of them was," Easter answered, "and he was on the phone the whole time. I heard him talking about samples his men had collected and how he was bringing them back to the lab as soon as he was done eating. He talked about it as if the lab was close by, but I don't know what he meant. There isn't any laboratory for any kind of testing in Solomon's Cross."

Easter paused, and Jemma heard the muffled sound of chewing. After she swallowed, she went on. "Then he said something under his breath into his phone. I couldn't quite hear it, but it was something like, 'These dirty mountain hicks better keep their noses out of our business.' Then he laughed and said a bit louder, 'I suppose if I eat at their diner every day, they're bound to ask questions. You know they only got one diner in town, Frank?'"

"Who the hell is Frank?" Jemma asked.

"No clue," Easter answered. "But he thought it was awfully funny, and I didn't. What was weirder is that I kind of forgot I was staring, and he looked up and caught me. His eyes got all mean-like, so Val and I packed up our food and hightailed out of there. We just left about five minutes ago, and then I called you."

Jemma was eager to be out of the house to work on the case with this new information. She groaned inwardly. "Let me know what you learn," she told Easter.

"Will do. Goodbye."

An hour later, Jemma heard the crunch of tires on the gravel drive. Her father was home. "I guess I'll just have to make the best of however many days Dad plans to keep me away from Gran's Rest," she murmured to herself before going to the door.

That night, Tad didn't bring up anything other than school. "Did you get that test done?" Jemma told him she had, and they had dinner together. Then he suggested they play a couple of games. For several hours, Jemma didn't think about being grounded or anything witch-related. She and her father settled down to play one round of chess, which he won, then a few games of slapjack after Jemma insisted they needed something requiring less brain work. Those games she won since she was faster than her father.

He went to work in the morning, and for the next several days, Jemma experienced a strange mixture of boredom, anxiety, and brief moments of relief and excitement. With nothing else to do, Jemma flew through her coursework with ease. She had gotten used to having a lot more to do during the day, so having only schoolwork meant she got through it a lot quicker than she wanted to. By noon, it was finished, and she was left to wait and wait and *wait* for her father to return. Then there would be pizza and a board game before bed.

The bright spot in her day was when Easter called after finishing school. "We have a date for the play!" she announced on Wednesday.

Jemma was glad to hear the happiness in her friend's voice. "April tenth! I hope you can make it, Jem."

"Me too." Jemma sighed. "He should let me out of the house by then, right?"

"I sure do hope so," Easter returned. "I'm glad I've got this play to distract me since I can't see you. Not that hanging out with Val isn't great. It's just, well, he's my brother, and I see him all the time."

"Yeah, I get that. I should be able to come to your play. I really want to." Jemma thought about something else. "Actually, my dad is quite the Shakespeare buff. Used to quote it all the time. He might want to come with me."

"The more, the merrier," Easter replied.

She hung up shortly after, leaving Jemma to the silence of her house. *I wish I had a dog, at least.*

The conversation with Easter allowed Jemma to remember her father talking about the play *Macbeth* years ago. He always laughed at the three witches' lines. "Ironic," Jemma murmured to herself as she went to her father's bookshelf in the living room.

Like everything else Tad Nox touched, it was a mess. Books were stacked to the very edge of the shelf, with other stacks behind the ones in front. Series had their titles in different places. It looked like Tad had thrown his books straight out of the packing box onto the shelf. *That was exactly what happened,* Jemma thought. Even though they had been living here for over six months, she still felt like they hadn't really moved in.

Jemma often thought it felt like someone else's home. After hunting around, she pulled out an old leather complete edition of William Shakespeare's works. Turning to *Macbeth*, she read the first lines spoken by the witches at the beginning of the play and wondered which ones Easter had to memorize.

> "1 Witch. When shall we three meet again?
> In thunder, lightning, or in rain?
> 2 Witch. When the hurly-burly's done,
> When the battle's lost and won.
> 3 Witch. That will be ere the set of sun.
> 1 Witch. Where the place?
> 2 Witch. Upon the heath.
> 3 Witch. There to meet with Macbeth.
> 1 Witch. I come, Graymalkin!
> 2 Witch. Paddock calls.
> 3 Witch. Anon!
> All. Fair is foul, and foul is fair.
> Hover through the fog and filthy air."

Jemma looked up and through the window, noting how gray it had become outside due to dark clouds. Rain threatened. In the distance, thunder rumbled. She sat down in the nearest chair and read the lines again. "Fair is foul, and foul is fair. Hover through the fog and filthy air." Before coming to Solomon's Cross and meeting Mama B, she wouldn't have thought twice about what she'd read. It was just a story. But now that she knew witches were real, the words held more weight.

She shuddered and reassured herself, "It's just a story." She closed the book and placed it back on the shelf, yet could not stop comparing what she'd read to real life. There were three witches in the play, and Mama B had been one of three. Perhaps it was a common occurrence. One thing was certain. Jemma planned on being ungrounded by the time Easter's play came around.

Tad returned home a couple of hours later, and the night proceeded as Jemma had expected. The next day was the same, except this time, she felt like she was going to go crazy. Her anxiety built at the thought of other people climbing up to Kalhoun's Crest, whether they were prying corporations or kids looking to explore. She worried about the children from Cider Creek staying in Johnson City under the care of doctors who, one, didn't know what they were up against, and two, didn't seem to care.

I should be out there helping, Jemma thought as her irritation rose. *Not stuck inside.* She wondered what Easter and Val were up to. Easter reported every day but had yet to form a plan with Mama B about what to do. Were they waiting for her? Could they do anything on their own? *Do I want them to do anything without me?* Jemma wondered. On the one hand, she was glad she didn't have to face her calling head-on right now. On the other, she felt like she was missing out and not just on something adventurous. She was missing an opportunity to figure out what her future would be.

Every day, she thought about voicing her frustrations to her father. *But how?* she wondered. The whole thing sounded insane.

Despite her anxiety and boredom, for a few moments sprinkled throughout the day, Jemma caught herself enjoying simple pleasures as she had not done in the past several months. Having been so preoccupied with work at Gran's Rest, school, and luring boo hags into traps, she'd had little time to herself. She read more of *Macbeth* and played video games she hadn't previously pulled out of the moving boxes. When it stopped raining, Jemma went for a walk to the end of the road.

When she caught herself in these moments, she sighed with relief. *I'm glad I can still just be myself when there's nothing to do,* she thought. Being able to enjoy simple pleasures that didn't involve her calling allowed her to feel more clearheaded. Jemma stopped short as this thought came into her mind, and guilt and anxiety flooded in. *Here I am, enjoying a walk, and those kids are sick almost to death in the hospital.*

She walked back to her house and the sky darkened at the same time as her mood. *I need to find a way to escape for a moment,* she thought, wanting to forget her calling. As she reached the gravel drive leading to her house, her phone rang. "Hey, Easter."

"Hey, Jem. It's Val. My phone died, so I'm using Easter's."

"Oh, hey, Val." She had barely talked to Val during the whole week, other than exchanging text messages. She could tell he was calling to ask her about something.

"Hey, so Easter and I came up with an idea. We wanna check Cider Creek for heavy metals. We know you can't come with us, but you're good at chemistry and all that, so we thought we'd ask you to tell us how to do it."

Jemma brightened. "I'll write it down and send it to you. Shouldn't be too hard."

"Thanks, Jemma." Val hung up, and Jemma went inside to consult her chemistry books.

I'll report our findings, Val texted in response to the instructions.

That night, while Jemma and Tad were eating dinner, her phone *dinged* with another text message. It was from Val's number.

ETRAA lied.

"No shit," Jemma murmured.

Tad's brows rose, and Jemma thought he might rebuke her for her language. Instead, he asked, "What is it?"

Not wanting to appear she was hiding anything, she told her father as much of the truth as she could. "Val and Easter went to check a water source near their house for metals. Science experiment."

"And?" her father prodded.

"They found plenty of heavy metals," Jemma replied. *Which means that not only to did ETRAA lie, but the kids got the heavy metals from the stream as a result of mining activities on Kalhoun's Crest.* A chill skittered up her spine at the thought. Somewhere up the mountain was a breach. Jemma wondered how long it had been open. She couldn't wait to find out.

Tad's eyes filled with interest. "Science experiment? Sounds fun."

"Yeah, Val and Easter asked me to send what I know about checking for metals in water."

Tad smiled. "That's why you need to do well in school, Jem. You can help others that way too, not just by pulling weeds up at Gran's Rest all the time." He winked and rose from the table. Jemma knew he didn't mean to downplay her role at Gran's Rest, but the misunderstanding made her uneasy.

Her thoughts turned back to Val's text. He had just sent another.

Kids musta waded in the water just enough.

Leave it to kids to wade in the water during the winter, Jemma thought. *It must have caused the haint's tainted presence to drive the heavy metal into their bodies. I'll need to talk to Mama B and see if she knows anything about haints in relation to water.*

She paused, looking up from her phone while turning new information over in her mind. *If we follow the creek up the mountain, we'll find where ETRAA is and where the breach is.* Jemma typed that into her phone and sent it to Val.

We were thinking the same thing.

We promise not to go without you…but please get ungrounded soon.

Jemma knew Val would do his best to keep his word, but she wasn't certain how long he could hold himself back.

In the midst of her thoughts, Jemma had a revelation. The journal! It might have something about corporations going up the mountain and digging around for minerals.

She rose and told her dad she wanted to finish a project, then asked if they could play games tomorrow. Tad smiled and nodded, leaving his daughter to climb into her loft and pull the journal out of her closet. She had reflected long and hard over the journal's contents before, spending much time trying to decipher the cramped, tight handwriting.

Now that she had a fuller view of the story, it might be easier.

Jemma knew it was Vesna Soucek who had written the accounts within since there were many entries describing an escape from somewhere in Eastern Europe from "the Enemy," whoever that was. Jemma was now sure that Vesna had kept her former location in Eastern Europe a secret for a reason. Everything else in the journal, from herbal remedy recipes to descriptions of machinery, was very detailed. It wasn't like the author, as far as Jemma could tell, to leave out details.

Had Vesna Soucek been afraid the journal might fall into the wrong hands?

Regardless of her reasons, it seemed that Mabel Doire had found it and kept it in her house, along with the photo album. Months ago, Jemma had sorted the entries chronologically and found the dates ranged between 1940 and 2011. *That was strange,* she thought. *Mama B said Vesna left long before Josephine, and she left in the nineties.* Had someone else added to the journal after Vesna left? Perhaps Mabel Doire had had a hand in it, or another family member.

Jemma leafed through the pages once more, her eyes having adjusted to the cramped writing. Now that she knew what she was looking for, the words were easier to distinguish. She stumbled across a faded date that looked like August 1951. Jemma remembered other dates she had seen in the journal from the same year.

Her eyes flitted over the pages until they landed on the first line of a paragraph in the middle of a page.

There's so much magic here. Much more than I've felt in any other place. E, J, and I all feel it.

Jemma paused, supposing Vesna used "E" and "J" to refer to Eloise and Josephine. Apparently, the writer was concerned with running out of space in the journal. *Or she was trying not to give more away than she must,* Jemma added.

After reading the rest of the paragraph, Jemma concluded that the entry had been written after the three women came to Solomon's Cross and first discovered the abundance of potent magic stirring beneath the surface of the mountains.

I feel stronger here, like I can breathe better.

I will admit that when we first arrived, I voiced strong concerns to E and J. I was, and still am, afraid of what might follow. The mountains cannot hide me from my Enemy forever.

There it was again: Enemy with a capital E as if it were a title. Jemma's hands tightened on the pages as she leaned closer. She decided it was time to switch on a lamp so she could read better.

Despite my reservations, my power has never felt more alive than it does here. We have decided to learn about the magic and manifest its power as best we can. We may never get an opportunity like this. We could tell as soon as we climbed up to some of the higher crests. The wildlife is, well, wilder here. All manner of plants—trees, mushrooms, flowers—grow faster and in far more abundance on the heights. There seem to be more animals as well.

The people of the town in the mountain's shadow have been welcoming, thinking we lost loved ones in the war and have come to make a new home. They have been kind, helping us in the ways we each needed. Although I fear staying here or anywhere for long, I believe we can use the magic brewing beneath these mountains for the good of those who have helped us.

Jemma formed a good impression of the woman whose words sprawled beneath her eyes. Although she did not understand Vesna's situation, she could sympathize with her reservations. *Who was hunting her?* she wondered. Out loud, she murmured, "Who were you afraid of, Vesna?" The woman's mention of the kindness of the town's people held Jemma's attention. These were not the words of a crazed woman who had gone mad after losing her children. That would come later, Jemma supposed.

She was jolted from her thoughts when her father appeared at the bottom of the ladder. "Going to bed, Jem. Goodnight."

"Goodnight, Dad." Jemma closed the journal, realizing how late it had gotten. Another time, she could read more. She hoped to discover the story Mama B had told her from the perspective of the journal's primary author.

CHAPTER EIGHT

When Jemma awoke and went downstairs the following morning, she found a note from her father.

We will talk when I get home this evening.

At first, she felt a pang of dread. Was her father going to make her talk about what was going on? Many thoughts raced through her head: everything from the draught Mama B had given him to make him forget almost having the life sucked out of him by a boo hag to her holler witch training to the real reason for Val's friends being sick. Then she saw that he had written something else.

Left some freshly squeezed orange juice in the fridge for you.

Jemma smiled, and the dread went away. It seemed Her father was going to let her go back to Gran's Rest. The day went by faster than any in the past week had as she anticipated her father's return. Jemma flew through her schoolwork, then went for a walk outside while the sun shone, melting more of the snow piled between trees. The moments passed with little guilt or anxiety. For the first time in a long time, Jemma felt like she was in a good life rhythm.

When her father came home with their dinner hours later, he told Jemma, "I'll let you go back to Gran's Rest soon, but not yet."

Jemma's hopes deflated. She had missed her daily bike ride up the mountain when the weather was fair. Although she could deal without virus-filled computers and boo hags, she missed Mama B too, especially after reading Vesna's journal.

"I have a work trip to go on that'll last a few days. I'm not sure how long, but I don't want you going back to work until I return," Tad told her.

Jemma nodded. It sounded fair. He grinned. "Of course, I don't expect you to stay cooped up in the house by yourself the whole time I'm gone, so if you want, you can meet up with the McCarthy kids. You just can't go to Gran's Rest." This boosted Jemma's spirits. She loved spending time with her father but was good and ready to spend time with other people.

"You can go back to work as soon as I return from my trip. I called Mama B and talked it over with her. She understands and respects my decision."

Jemma nodded again.

Tad's good spirits faded a bit. "I asked her to tell me if you came around."

Jemma was almost certain Mama B wouldn't do that if it were an emergency, but she decided not to test the woman. It would be nice to have a couple of days out of the house without going to Gran's Rest since she had almost gotten to a point where she could enjoy the mundane moments of everyday life without surrendering to guilt and anxiety.

"I'll call every night while I'm away."

"Where will you be going?" Jemma asked as she began to eat the dinner he had brought home.

"Just a couple counties over. We're supposed to run lines from there into Kalhoun County, but there's some kind of trouble. Don't know what it is yet, but I suspect I'll find out soon. I won't be too far away, but since I have to be up at the crack of dawn, it's better that I stay in a hotel." He shrugged. "Besides, the company's paying for my stay."

Jemma texted Easter after dinner was finished to tell her the good news.

Thank God. Wanna hang with Val and me tomorrow? Friday night errands? Haha.

Smiling down at her phone, Jemma replied.

As long as we can go to Harv's first.

Of course.

Tad left the following morning with a cheery farewell and a firm, "Remember what I told you, Jem. I'll be calling Mama B first thing when I get back to make sure you didn't go there."

"I promise not to go, Dad," Jemma replied with a groan. She forced a smile. "Better get going. You'll be late."

With her father out of the house for the next few days and several hours before Val and Easter would pick her up, Jemma had plenty of time to pour over more of Vesna's journal entries. She finished her schoolwork and settled down in her father's large living room chair by the window to read.

The date on the first entry she read, following what Vesna wrote about coming into the Kalhoun County area before it was called by such a name, was "August 16," but the year was blurred as if the author had shed tears while writing.

> *Something fearsome has come to us. I am shaking as I write. I cannot stop myself. I have fought hard not to allow the fear to seep in, but sometimes it finds a crack.*

Jemma could tell the hand was shaking while writing since the letters were spread apart and would have been easier to read if it wasn't for the messiness of the words themselves. The longer the writing went on, however, the less shaky it appeared. Vesna seemed to have grown more confident as she wrote.

> *Josephine and I have discovered a deep well of magic beneath the mountain that looms over the town. Not only is there a source of magic we cannot tell the depth of, but there is also a crack in its seal. Whoever sealed it must have done so long ago and then departed the area, leaving whatever festers beneath the*

surface to rise slowly back up, tapping against the seal until a crack appeared.

The next line showed Jemma that Vesna had shuddered while pressing her pen to paper.

It was night, and the full moon shone. We went there knowing there was a great source of magic but not yet aware there was a crack in the seal. I fear what would have happened without the moonlight. Jo and I stumbled upon a nest of haints, four of them sheltered beneath a large tree on top of the mountain. We battled them all night, only being able to overtake them when Eloise, sensing our distress and noticing we had been gone far longer than we had said we would be, came to our rescue. Together, the three of us were about to seal and bind the four foul spirits, but we paused to question them about where they had come from.

Cackling, one of them told us, 'From far beneath! Far beneath where foul things grow!' Cackling again, the Night Woman added, 'You'll never get us all! Never!'

Again, the author appeared to shudder. The letters slanted, and some of the words were hard to distinguish, even in the sunlight.

After we dealt with the haints, the three of us met in the light of dawn. 'We have to stay here and make sure the crack remains sealed so nothing else crawls out of the darkness,' Eloise insisted. Josephine, of course, agreed with her, as she always does. I was hesitant, for I fear staying in one place lest my Enemy follow me here. If my Enemy finds me near such an abundant source of magic, what shall they do? I want to

The paragraph ended, and there was no following page in the journal. Had Vesna stopped writing, or was a page missing?

The next entry skipped ahead a few days.

Josephine has been speaking with people in town and has heard many stories from those who have lived here much longer than us. She told Eloise and me that the town has always had strange, dark things occurring around it. For instance, there was once an old estate owned by a Mrs. Rebecca Willows on the large mountain looming over the town. The same mountain where we found the crack in the seal and the haints. Many claim the estate was overrun by ghosts who drove the woman living in it mad. The estate was eventually abandoned and left in ruins after Ms. Willows' son was found dead in his bed.

Jemma shuddered as she read these words, imagining that Vesna had done the same while writing. *I doubt they were ghosts,* she thought. Vesna had the same thought as Jemma discovered when she read the next paragraph.

It is not ghosts who tramp through the Willow Hall. Though I have not seen the house and do not wish to lay eyes upon it, it is not the nature of ghosts to kill a child in his sleep or to kill at all. I have befriended ghosts, and none would have done such a thing. Haints, perhaps, but I fear something more sinister was at work. Something—or someone—drove whatever it was back beneath the ground. *I wonder if another witch or witches have come here before us and now are long gone?*

Jemma's brows rose. She wondered what it would be like to have a ghost as a friend. *I wonder if the Willows estate is still on Kalhoun's Crest? I can ask Val and Easter if they've ever heard of it.* Turning the page, Jemma found a series of scrawled notes with dates ranging over a period of a month. These were more difficult to read, but they were brief.

Jo and Eloise tell me we must stay so we can protect the people of the town from whatever comes out of the mountain, but I fear I cannot. What if my Enemy comes? He has found me before in places I thought he might not.

A few days later, there was another short scribble.

I remember the ashes and blood. The air tasted like both. So many men dead. The bombs shook the ground, splitting houses in two. Children buried beneath the rubble. The land was full of shattered stones, and now, so are my dreams. My dreams are stained with the colors and sounds and tastes of war. I taste it every time I look at that mountain.

A day later, Jemma read that Vesna kept having dreams containing memories of her war trauma.

I awoke this morning feeling as though a hand were around my throat, choking every bit of life out of me. It was just a dream.

Another entry showed Jemma that this had continued.

I have nightmares every night. They will not leave me. I am plagued by my past.

I hear the guns and cannons and bombs.

I saw a soldier shot down in my sleep tonight. His blood created an ocean over the plain.

I remember being in No Man's Land. Gunfire all around me. I am far away from there now, but it doesn't feel like it. Every dream feels like No Man's Land.

Even with so few details, Jemma was being sucked into another time and place. At last, she read,

I dreamt last night that the war had ended again. Perhaps now that I have gone through it once more in my sleep, my dreams will depart. I hope to dream of spring soon. The mountains will be alive with wildflowers and blooming trees in a few weeks. I will gather a bouquet and bring light into my house. I love awakening at dawn. The light feels good, and no one comes to torment me. Maybe the light will one day drive away my Enemy.

The lighter mood of the entries continued, and Vesna's nightmares abated. She described pleasant spring weather, the melting of the snow, and meeting someone from town. Jemma could tell Vesna's spirits had risen by the more graceful style of her handwriting, the gentler press of the pen, and fewer tear stains on the yellowed paper.

His name is Thomas Blacksworth. He fought in the war and has settled in the mountains, saying it feels like home to him here. He is handsome, kind, gentle, and of good humor and disposition. I did not like him at first, not to say he was distasteful to me. I simply didn't notice him, but according to Josephine, he noticed me.

She took it upon herself to inform him of the affections I have that I've never felt before. Since then, he has sent me an abundance of letters, poems, and flowers. He wore me down, and I accepted an invitation for an outing. He drove us to the top of a hill overlooking the northern part of town, opposite the crest where we found the magic. He likes it there because of the view of the sky.

He likes the stars and knows all the constellations by name. During the war, when he had the chance and felt lonely to his bones, he would look at the stars and remember that he wanted to see them when it was all over. It was his way of making sure he survived while fighting for others. I teared up when he told me, for I had had the same thought many times. I did not tell him that. I tell him little of my past.

Does she fear that telling anyone about her enemy will lead him to find her? Jemma wondered.

Her eyes drifted lower on the page, and she saw a series of numbers and symbols. *A code,* she mused, brows furrowing. Not having any idea how to decode the writing and wanting to continue with the story, Jemma let it be for the time being. Turning the page, she saw several more entries describing the blossoming romance between Thomas Blacksworth and Vesna Soucek.

Eventually, she started skimming the entries, glad the

woman had had a period of her life filled with joy and less fear over what might follow her out of the shadows of her past. Jemma's smile grew as she read an entry dated a year after her wedding to Thomas.

Thomas Glen Blacksworth Junior was born today, weighing seven pounds, six ounces. He is a healthy, beautiful baby boy. My firstborn. My beloved son. I am blessed.

The entries that followed were spread over the next few years, telling of the child's growth and sharing moments of joy and pain involved in raising a child. A year later, Jemma was happy for Vesna again.

I believe I am pregnant again, for such joy has filled my body, my womb, my soul. This one feels different, and I do not know why. Perhaps I will have a daughter. I would like that very much. Thomas would too. He has always wanted a little girl.

What a delight! Josephine has just had her first child, a daughter she has named Mabel.

"There!" Jemma said aloud. Mabel Doire, the previous owner of this house. So, Josephine had married around the same time as Vesna, as Mama B had told her. Nine months later, Vesna wrote:

Today Katica Rose and Pavlina Jane are born. Katica was born first, followed by her twin sister. Katica weighed eight pounds, ten ounces and...

The rest of the entry was too faded for Jemma to make

out, but by the cheerful tone, Jemma assumed both children had been born healthy like their older brother. She wondered if the photo album contained pictures of the three.

Jemma skipped ahead several pages, landing on an entry dating five or six years after the birth of Vesna's twins.

One day, I may reveal my secrets and teach my daughters the Art. Josephine has considered the same for her daughter. Eloise thinks it is best to teach them since someone will have to someday take on our mantle. We cannot carry the magic of holler witches forever.

Jemma looked up, noting that the sun had sunk lower in the sky while she was reading. The past couple of hours had passed without her noticing. *Vesna never had the chance to teach her daughters the Art,* she thought. Dread built up within her, for she knew entries about the death of Vesna's children were to come. Reading them made Jemma feel she had known the family for years. She wondered if Josephine had decided not to teach her children the ways of a holler witch after all the tragedy that had occurred.

Despite not wanting to move past writings containing the good parts of Vesna's life, Jemma had to read on.

Strange things have begun occurring here again. Men have arrived and go up to the mountain crest, where they disappear for days. Josephine, Eloise, and I fear they will tamper with the seal we have kept closed all these years and something dark and powerful will emerge. Folks in town have questioned the men about what they are doing but only receive vague, unsatisfying answers. There are secrets there. We must find out what

The entry cut off there, and Jemma jolted at a horn honking in front of the house. "Geez, Jem, are you in there or not?" Val called from the open window of his truck.

Jemma realized they had been sitting in front of the house for a couple of minutes, but she had been too preoccupied to realize it. She closed the journal and yelled out the open window, "I'll be right out!" Grabbing a hoodie and shoes, Jemma prepared to leave with the McCarthys for a Friday night of fun.

After she climbed into the truck, Easter looked at her with a broad smile. "We're not running normal errands tonight, Jem, but special errands."

Jemma's brows rose in question.

Val picked up where his sister left off. "We're getting supplies for a trip up to Kalhoun's Crest, and tomorrow, you're coming with us."

Easter nodded. "It's high time we figure out what's going on up there." The next day, Saturday, meant no school for any of them, and Mama B, according to Easter, had given them the day off. Since the climb up Kalhoun's Crest wasn't related to work at Gran's Rest, Jemma concluded her father couldn't be mad at her for it. She didn't have school anyway.

An uneasy feeling stirred within her at the thought, however. She had just spent the day reading about the bad magic sealed beneath the mountain, a supposedly haunted estate somewhere up there, and the impending danger of company men having climbed up. *Is history repeating itself?* Jemma wondered.

She decided not to tell Easter and Val yet. She needed to process what she had read before sharing it. She forced a smile. "Sounds good, but can we get something to eat first?" The brainwork needed for deciphering the cramped writing in the journal had left Jemma starving.

Val nodded. "To Harv's, we go!"

CHAPTER NINE

Harv's Hamburgers and Hotcakes was bustling when Jemma and the McCarthys arrived. It was Friday night, so a lot of activity was to be expected. Those who didn't work on the weekend were glad to be off. Those who did were glad to have a few hours of free time before heading home to bed. The workers in Harv's diner were glad about the extra tips. School was finished for the week, and many of Solomon's Cross' teens were out for dinner.

Jemma recognized some of them. A group of teens who went to school with Easter and Val occupied a booth at the far end of the restaurant. Jemma avoided meeting anyone's eye since she hadn't been keen on making friends with the people who had either made fun of Easter for her sickness or hadn't done anything to stick up for her.

"There's one," Val said, spying an empty booth. Easter and Jemma followed him, and they had to wait for several minutes before anyone came to serve them since the place was so busy. The three got the last empty seats.

Noticing Jemma glancing at the other teens out of pure

curiosity, Easter asked, "Are you wondering what they're like now that I'm better?"

"Well, yeah, kinda. Do they treat you the same?" Jemma returned with an open expression.

Easter shrugged. "It's gotten a little better. I haven't made any close friends, but the people I work with for the play are nice enough, and I don't get made fun of like I used to." She smiled. "Jade and Cameron even say hi to me sometimes."

At the mention of the two teens, Jemma glanced at the booth once more. Sure enough, Cameron, a tall ginger with an obnoxious laugh, and Jade, a girl with a purple streak in her hair and a contagious smile, joined in the revelry with their friends. Jemma felt like an outsider when she looked at such a group. She knew Val and Easter often felt the same way. *That's why we came together,* she thought, feeling a sudden surge of fondness for her two close friends.

Val leaned forward, frowning. "Some of 'em still call us 'Witch Kissers' and some shit for working for Mama B." He shrugged. "But we know their insults come from bein' ignorant, and there's nothin' we can do about it. Besides, we have jobs, and they don't. Too many of them get all the money they want from their parents."

Some of the teens, like Jade and Cameron, lived in the adjoining town, but Solomon's Cross High was the closest school, so that was the one they attended. The adjoining town was wealthier thanks to its booming construction business and more land.

Easter grinned. "I'm just shakin' whatever they say right off."

Jemma admired them both but could see they struggled with their place among the other teens of Solomon's Cross. How could they not? Not only had Easter gotten sick and the McCarthys were poor, but they had also befriended the new girl months ago and stuck with her since then. The teens of Solomon's Cross considered Jemma as strange as the McCarthys because she had gone up to Gran's Rest one day.

And now I keep going, Jemma thought. She was considered weird for consorting with a witch. *Little do they know.* She almost chuckled.

Val caught the look of amusement on Jemma's face and opened his mouth to speak but was interrupted by the long-anticipated arrival of their waitress. Lottie looked frazzled, with strings of her dyed hair sticking out from the low bun behind her head. "Busy as bees in here tonight, kids, but I'm glad to see all y'all just the same. What'll it be?"

Having been at Harv's for a long time, Lottie seldom wrote down their orders on a pad of paper anymore but memorized them instead. Well, she *tried* to memorize. Sometimes their orders came back wrong, but Jemma didn't care. She liked everything in Harv's dinner.

Lottie's smile, though tired, warmed Jemma. The woman, who was in her late thirties, had come to treat Jemma like anyone else in this town—like she'd been here since she was born, the same as the rest of them. Perhaps Lottie had a special place in her heart for the kids who were on the outside since she showed special affection to Val and Easter as well. She especially liked Tad Nox.

"Where's your father tonight?" She chuckled. "Doesn't

wanna hang out with you young 'uns?" She laughed again and asked what they wanted to eat.

Everybody likes my dad, Jemma thought as Val and Easter gave Lottie their orders. "A grilled cheese, a couple of pickle spears if you can, and a Coke," Jemma told her when it was her turn.

"I'll have it up soon as I can." Lottie moved away from their table, and the man in the next booth signaled for a refill on his iced tea. Jemma recognized him, just as she recognized most of the people in the diner. There were new people too, pleasant individuals who had apparently come here to visit the town. Maybe they were staying at Gran's Rest. The diner had changed after the reopening of Gran's Rest, and that change, by Jemma's lights, was a good thing. More menu items, better quality food now that they could afford it with increased business, and a staff that had grown a little friendlier.

Lottie brought their food soon after, and they tucked in. Lottie came around halfway through their meal to refill beverages, and Jemma stopped her with a question. "Lottie, I was wonderin' about those businessmen you told Easter about who come in here every day. Do they ever come for dinner?"

Jemma had hoped she would see them with her own eyes. Lottie wasn't curious about Jemma's question since many in Solomon's Cross gossiped, especially when the gossip pertained to outsiders.

"It's strange, ya know?" Lottie answered as she poured more water into Easter's glass from a pitcher. "They come in for lunch, and sometimes right 'fore we close an' make us stay open 'til *they* wanna leave!" Shaking her head, she added, "Damn bastards. Sometimes, they're here at the crack of dawn, but they clear out 'fore the main breakfast crowd gets here."

Lottie was then distracted by a need at another nearby table. She was so distracted that she set the half-full pitcher of water on their table. Val and Easter, who sat across from Jemma, suppressed grins.

Looks of curiosity came over Easter's and Val's faces, and Jemma thought this would be a good time to tell them about what she had read in the journal. However, the diner's door opened and two people entered.

"Not a single seat open," a tall, hulking man murmured as he surveyed the interior of the diner. Anyone who didn't know RJ Kilmer might have considered him intimidating due to his height of six feet and four inches, as well as his wide girth. However, anyone who took the time to have a conversation with him discovered that he was a gentle fellow with a pleasant disposition and a kind countenance. "The town's Big Teddy Bear Man" was how Jemma referred to him.

RJ Kilmer wasn't the one to watch out for. That was his son Anthony Jean, who went by AJ.

AJ had come in with his father, which was a rare occurrence. The young man was normally found in a pack of other teenage boys or roaming alone. Jemma meant to look away and continue her conversation with her friends, but the sight of AJ made her falter.

He had changed quite a bit since the last time she saw him. He was dressed as always in blue jeans, an oil-stained shirt from working on his precious sports car, and heavy black work boots. He was tall and lean and had been muscular, but some of his bulk had gone away due to months of inactivity.

Other things had changed too. His normal smirk had been replaced by a grimace. His blue eyes, normally sly, were trained on the diner's tile floor and barely lifted to make contact with the people who passed.

Jemma remembered what Easter and Val had shared about AJ Kilmer in the past few months. As predicted by Mama B, AJ's behavior had been caused by the boo hag's torment, and so he had tested negative for drugs. That was a relief to his father, but AJ's strange behavior had resulted in him being sent to a mental hospital for evaluation. He'd been there for the past couple of months and must have just gotten out. Jemma watched father and son step to the carry-out counter, where RJ placed to-go orders.

The time at the mental hospital hadn't done the young man any favors. Jemma noted that he seemed meaner and colder. He was gaunt; his cheekbones stuck out, and he looked like he had lost weight. Jemma wasn't sure how to feel: angry about how he had treated Easter, Val, and others, or should she pity him since not all of it had been his fault.

Well, it was *his fault,* Jemma thought, *but being followed by a boo hag doesn't help anyone.* She remembered that when AJ's mother had died, he had changed, becoming the kind of person Val couldn't be friends with anymore. It was still difficult for Jemma to imagine Valentine McCarthy and AJ Kilmer as best buds.

Easter and Val stared as three guys from the booth in the back of the diner got up and walked past AJ on their way out. Jemma recognized them as AJ's best friends. *Well, maybe not anymore,* she thought grimly when AJ lifted his head and tried to smile. "Hey, guys..." he began, but none of them so much as glanced at him.

They're ignoring him on purpose, Jemma realized. One of the three guys recoiled as if AJ had leprosy. They headed out of the diner, laughing loudly enough to irritate Jemma and make AJ stiffen. For a second, she, Easter, and Val caught a glimpse of a version of an AJ that almost nobody saw; there was a broken look in his eyes. His shoulders slumped in defeat. Seconds later, however, his cold demeanor returned, and he dropped all pretense of wanting to hang out with his friends.

"Can we get the hell out of here, Pa?" he asked in a disgruntled tone. His hands had formed fists.

Jemma's eyes roved to RJ. The older man looked after the teenagers who had just exited the diner. He looked torn between hugging his wounded son and going after AJ's former friends to flatten them with his vengeful, shovel-sized hands. In the end, the man-mountain just stared helplessly at his son. AJ's eyes jerked away, a look of disgust on his face.

They cut past the table where Jemma, Easter, and Val sat. The three of them tore their eyes away, but it was too late; AJ caught them staring. Jemma thought he would confront them, but RJ received their orders and told his son, "All right, let's go home." Jemma felt the young man's eyes boring holes into her back as he left the diner.

"He's gone," Val told her after Jemma heard the diner door close.

Easter observed Jemma for a long, thoughtful moment. "What's on your mind, Jem? You seem bothered."

Jemma sighed and set down her grilled cheese sandwich's crust, which she did not intend to eat. "I don't want to defend AJ in any way, but a lot of people don't understand that his meanness isn't all his fault." She spoke in a low tone so no one would overhear her. The noise level in the diner was high enough to keep that from happening anyway. Everyone else was involved in their own conversations.

Easter nodded. "I know what you mean. And even before the…BH, AJ had other shit going on." In public, when talking about the boo hag, they used that abbreviation.

Val silently looked at his plate. He still had reservations and stinging wounds from AJ's behavior. Jemma didn't blame him.

"We're the only people who understand," Jemma continued. "Hell, AJ himself doesn't know what happened to him. That's got to be confusing as hell."

To a certain extent, Jemma also understood AJ's being without his mother. Once, Jemma had been close to her own mother. Then, seemingly out of nowhere, Delilah Nox had left her and her father, stating she wanted a more exciting life. However, she had stayed in the boring town they all lived in.

To this day, it still didn't make sense to Jemma. She wondered how much confusion and emptiness AJ felt since his mother was no longer in his life.

RJ Kilmer, who seemed as pleasant as her own father, had to deal with the ramifications. Jemma almost chuckled at the thought of driving Tad as crazy as AJ drove his father. *I might be taking holler witch lessons behind his back, but I'm not planning on going to jail anytime soon.* Jemma felt guilty as soon as she had the thought. The boo hag had been partially responsible for AJ's time behind bars.

"Well, what if we reach out to him?" Easter offered.

Val's head jerked up, and alarm filled his eyes. He did not, however, offer a verbal objection. His sister continued with a shrug. "Might not hurt to text him. We need to stop by RJ's anyway. Maybe he'll be there, and we can say hello."

"Yeah, but I like the idea of texting before running into him and having to, ya know, *talk* to him," Jemma replied.

Val finally spoke. "I'm with Jem. I'd rather get in and out of RJ's with as little trouble as possible."

Easter appeared conflicted but nodded. Having finished their food, Jemma flagged Lottie down for their check, planning to pay for Val and Easter's meals as a thank you for getting her out of the house. They always objected, but Jemma countered, "You pay for the gas to pick me up and drop me off. Let me cover it." The gas cost less than their meals, but Jemma wanted to help her friends. *Besides, since I do school online, I get more hours at Gran's Rest than they do.*

After paying Lottie at the carry-out counter where the register was, Jemma thought to ask another question. "Hey, Lottie, I was wondering about the pictures on the board over there." She gestured at the corkboard by the entrance to the diner, where old newspaper clippings and black and white photographs from World War Two and other significant times in the town's history were on display. "Any of them go by the name Thomas Blacksworth?"

Lottie seemed surprised at Jemma's question but answered anyway. "Why, yes." She went around the bar and to the board, then pointed out a photograph in which two men stood side by side. "It's this fine-lookin' fellow right here." She pointed at a tall, angular man with dark hair and strong facial features. He was handsome, just as Vesna's journal had stated. He was wearing his military uniform and had ribbons and medals attached to his jacket.

"He's got one family member left in this town, I believe," Lottie continued. "His niece's daughter. Still lives over on Pinewood Drive. Strange woman who don't talk to nobody." Lottie gestured at their surroundings. "Never comes in here, anyhow."

"What's her name?"

"Miss Dagwood, I think. Never married far as I know, nor had children," Lottie answered.

Jemma's interest increased. Lottie added, "Strange story, child. Mr. Blacksworth's children died in a terrible accident, and his wife went mad soon after." She narrowed her eyes at Jemma. "Why you askin', anyway?"

Jemma shrugged. "Just interested. I'm researching the war veterans who lived in this town for a school project."

Easter and Val, who had approached Jemma and Lottie as the conversation took place, gave Jemma strange looks but held their tongues. They sensed Jemma's questions had nothing to do with a school project.

Lottie seemed satisfied with her answer. "Well, you might try to talk to Miss Dagwood, then. Good luck. She don't like visitors."

Despite the dismal description of the old woman, Jemma felt hopeful about having a new lead. *It really feels like a case now,* she mused. "Thanks, Lottie."

The three left the diner.

CHAPTER TEN

"What was all that about back there?" Val asked Jemma as soon as they returned to his truck. They lingered outside of it, Val and Easter eyeing their friend with curiosity. Jemma wanted to tell them what she had found in the journal, but the sun had set, and Loretta's would be closing soon. The place closed early Friday through Sunday.

"I'll tell you after we get done shopping."

Val eyed her with equal parts wariness and curiosity. Easter was more trusting. "Let's go, then," she chirped cheerfully and led the way down the street to Loretta's. They did not need the truck to get from place to place since the main street running through Solomon's Cross had all of its prominent businesses.

At Loretta's, the three shopped for things teens in Solomon's Cross didn't normally buy on a Friday night, including gloves and weatherproof jackets for the climb to Kalhoun's Crest. They also bought food and canteens. It would take most of the day to get to the top, explore, and get back down. With the journal in mind, she wondered if they would be close to the estate once owned and occupied by Rebecca Willow.

That's another person I should ask about, Jemma thought. However, she doubted the woman was discussed anymore since none of her family was left, let alone lived in Solomon's Cross. These thoughts passed through her mind as she, Easter, and Val left Loretta's and made their way to RJ's hardware store at the end of the main street on the left side. Before they went in, they stopped at Val's truck to drop off the supplies they had bought.

They dragged their feet as they headed to RJ's. It would be closing soon, which Jemma hoped would help them get in and out quickly. As they stepped inside, she remembered her first time here. Memories of spilled paint cans going everywhere and her father wanting to knock out AJ Kilmer's teeth filled her mind.

Jemma glanced at Val's list of tools that would come in handy, not only for climbing but for "creative entry," as Val called it, into any ETRAA areas. The list included bolt and wire cutters, a small sledgehammer, and other items Jemma had never heard of. Val was the mechanical type, not her. She would stick to chemistry and spells.

The store was quiet as the three young people hunted for the necessary tools. Most of the shopping was done by Val. Easter and Jemma ambled around, discussing paint colors and wood finishes in low voices. The place was so quiet that talking at a normal volume seemed disrespectful. RJ, who was at the counter, was the only other person in the store. No sign of AJ anywhere.

Jemma was relieved. She understood Easter's desire to reach out to him, even though the girl had more reason than anyone else to hold a grudge, but Jemma wasn't sure she was ready. Val was less ready and distracted himself with his shopping.

They gathered what they needed without encountering the other teen. Jemma glanced at her watch. It was almost nine-thirty. Although her father wasn't due to return for a few days, she wanted to get home soon so she wouldn't have to lie about what time she'd returned when her father called.

She glanced up from her watch as Val set everything on the counter. The large, hulking man hadn't seemed to notice the teenagers until that moment. He looked up, baffled by their appearance. The man was clearly distracted and sad, but he mustered a smile. "Well, good evening, McCarthys." He nodded at Jemma. "You too, Ms. Nox."

The teens returned his greeting with polite ones of their own. RJ scanned the items Val wanted slower than he would have under normal circumstances. His distracted state made him scan one item twice, which Val had to correct with no small amount of awkwardness. "Oh, boy. I'm sorry," the hardware store's owner murmured. "Mighty tired today is all." There was tension in the air, and Jemma wanted to get away from it. Perhaps RJ knew they had been in Harv's diner and had seen the interaction between them and his son.

After he placed them in bags, he paused before giving him the total. *He wants to say something but can't get it out,* Jemma thought.

Easter saw that was the case as well, and being the kind person she was, asked, "Anything else, Mr. Kilmer?"

"Oh, please," the large man told her with a small smile. "Call me RJ." He considered his words for a couple of seconds longer before admitting with a deep sigh, "I'd like to ask the three of you to do something for me. A mighty big favor." He paused, fidgeting with the full bag. "Please consider buryin' the hatchet with my boy and try makin' friends with him?"

Jemma was stunned and indignant at the request, but the father's sad look and pleading eyes made her listen. "I know the three of you are good kids and good friends with one another," the man continued, "and I know you all have good reasons to dislike my son. I'm askin' you to please consider it out of mercy and pity."

No one knew how to react, so the teens were silent for a moment. To break the silence, not because she had reached a decision, Jemma forced a smile, "We'll think about it, Mr. Kilmer." Promising to think about it wouldn't do any harm, would it?

RJ's smile got warmer. "Thanks, kids. I'm mighty grateful. You just don't know what all he's been through."

We might know more than you and your son, Jemma thought, but she kept that to herself, not wanting to burden the man further. RJ Kilmer was one of the most understanding people she had ever met, but he probably would not be able to handle the thought of his son being possessed by a supernatural creature like a boo hag.

"Well, you kids have a good night, now," RJ told them after he had taken Val's payment and handed him a receipt. The man was almost in tears as he thanked them. Jemma made for the door, fearing the big man would crush them in a bear hug. The McCarthys told RJ goodbye and goodnight before leaving the store.

On their way to the truck, Val demanded, "Are you really going to think about it?" Fire could be seen in Val's eyes, even on the darkening street. Val was too loyal to Easter to be willing to piss on AJ if he was on fire.

To Jemma, AJ was like a wounded yet dangerous animal, waiting to bite and scratch anyone who came near, regardless of how good their intentions were. She also knew that nobody else could help AJ, only them. His father had looked like he was about to give up hope, and not because he didn't love his son. It was clear how much he did.

"I don't know," she answered.

Easter had a sweeter soul than either Val or Jemma. She also had the most to forgive AJ for. "We can try, and we should do it soon." She shrugged. "I might even invite him to my play. If he doesn't come, then he doesn't. At least I tried." A somber expression came over her face. "Anytime I've seen him at school in the week since he's come back, he's been alone and dismal. Doesn't wanna talk to anybody."

Val and Jemma exchanged glances that revealed equal amounts of hesitancy and wariness. With Easter's improving health came a more forgiving spirit. "What happens if we ask him…to hang out and he just sneers?" Val objected. "You know that's what he'll do. He'll know we're just doing it out of pity, and—"

His words were cut off by a look from his sister. Val fell silent, his argument making him feel petty and foolish.

Jemma didn't know if she agreed with Val or Easter. It was the same as with her calling—she wanted to give in to her selfish side, the one that followed her desires. The other side of her told her she couldn't just leave a wounded animal on the side of the road to be run over, even though it might bite.

Val sighed as he put their supplies in the bed. "I guess it won't matter anyway." He looked at Kalhoun's Crest rising into the night sky. Jemma had always considered the mountain ominous, but it was worse since she'd read Vesna's journal.

"We're going to die or end up in jail tomorrow," Val muttered.

Easter poked his shoulder and forced a goofy grin. "What are you talking about? We're the stealthiest people in this whole town. Hell, in the whole county! No one sees a McCarthy comin' out of the shadows."

Jemma, sensing that Easter's teasing was lightening the mood, joined in. "And if we do go to jail, we'll get rich exposing ETRAA and be able to bail ourselves out."

Easter laughed. Val tried to scowl, but the twitching of his lips gave him away. At last, he gave in to his amusement. They climbed into the truck, and Val played his favorite CD since the CD player and speakers had decided they would work today. As they drove back to Jemma's house, the teens sang at the top of their lungs, laughing between verses.

When they arrived, Jemma saw her father's truck in the drive and light pouring out of the kitchen and living room windows. Val's brows furrowed. "Wasn't he supposed to be gone for a few days?"

"Yeah," Jemma answered, confused. She grabbed her

things and hurried out of the truck, waving to Val and Easter. "Thanks! I'll see you tomorrow!"

"Eight o'clock sharp!" Val called. The speakers' volume increased as he drove back down the mountain.

Entering the house, Jemma found her father slouching on the couch, looking tired but happy to be home. Jemma produced her best smile, which was only half-forced, to her surprise. "Dad, you're home early."

Tad rose and pulled her into a tight hug. When he stepped away, he explained, "I came back early because of some work up the mountain."

Jemma stilled. "What do you mean?"

He dragged a hand through his hair, looking more tired than he had a moment ago. "I think it's called Kalhoun's Crest? Anyway, that big ol' mountain opposite here. There's some work going on up there. Some other corporation's doing something. Not sure what, but we can't go up and do any wiring until it's done."

Jemma tried not to show her alarm. "Really?" She went for interested. "How long do you think they'll be up there?"

Tad shrugged. "Who knows? My boss thinks it'll be another month at least. Maybe longer." He gave her a tired smile. "I don't mind, though. Just glad to be home." He looked at her seriously. "I called Gran's Rest, and Mama B told me you hadn't been up there today. I'm glad you obeyed me. Still, I'd rather you wait to go back to work after you've finished your schoolwork on Monday."

Jemma reverted to the first subject. "Actually, Easter, Val, and I are going up to Kalhoun's Crest tomorrow, if it's okay with you. Minerals and chemistry things, like I told you."

His brows rose. "That makes sense. Doesn't the creek by where the McCarthys live come down from the mountain?"

Jemma nodded, and Tad chuckled. "Very well, then. Have fun, stay safe, and learn lots!"

I hope so, Jemma thought, though she knew what she would be learning wasn't what her father had in mind.

Yawning, Tad turned to go into his bedroom. "What time are you leaving tomorrow?"

"Eight," Jemma answered.

Tad chuckled again. "You've never gotten up before eight of your own accord, Jem."

There *had* been a few instances Tad didn't know about, but Jemma didn't bother to enlighten him. She just smiled. "Go to bed, Dad. You look as tired as an old oak."

Tad chuckled once more, bid his daughter goodnight, and disappeared into his bedroom while releasing another yawn.

Jemma felt a combination of nerves and excitement. As she made her way to the loft, she realized sleep would come hard tonight. Her mind was racing, so she pulled out Vesna Soucek's journal and opened it to where she had left off.

Jemma got sucked into the tale of the coven's increasingly desperate struggle against human greed. It was a familiar one; Jemma felt like she was reading her own memories. Vesna gave much detail, drawing Jemma into a world she felt she had lived in.

She was walking in the mind of a woman who wanted to protect her children. Through the writings, she saw Vesna standing in an old cabin, the pale sunlight of early winter filtering in through handmade curtains hanging over the windows. In her hands, she clutched a handkerchief. She had a nervous expression on her face. "Jo, I think it might be best to send the children away until all is settled here," Vesna told the woman whose house they were in.

I fear for the children's safety, the journal entry stated. *I've asked Jo if we might send them away. We could tell our husbands we think boarding school might be good for a spell or send 'em to stay with family belongin' to our husbands.*

Jemma noticed that the longer Vesna stayed in Solomon's Cross, the more her writing sounded like the way people talked there. She shortened words and cared less for grammar. She read on.

Jo has thought about it and says it might be a good idea, but El thinks it would not be good.

"El," Jemma murmured, "must be short for Eloise just like Jo is short for Josephine." Vesna's hand was shaking when she wrote the remainder of the paragraph.

El says the children need to stay so they can see us be strong. She believes that one day, they'll take on our mantels. The girls will, anyway, and to understand the burden they will bear, they need to see us handle it.

I am not sure I agree. What will it matter if the girls can or cannot handle the burden of our magic if they are not alive and well? Jo and I haven't even said whether we planned on training the girls in the Art.

Every day that we are here in this town and trouble brews up on that God-forsaken mountain, I think about never telling my Rose anything about the Art. Anyhow, if I do train her, Thomas will have to learn my secret. I hate having secrets. Hate it more than anything.' But they must be kept. My Ene

The entry cut off at the bottom of the page. Jemma wasn't sure if Vesna hadn't finished the sentence or if a page had been torn out and destroyed. Had the woman written more and decided her words gave more away than she wanted? The shaky writing revealed the woman's fear. Jemma gripped the journal tighter, dreading what would come next but needing to know from Vesna's point of view.

The fateful entry met her eyes. Jemma could tell before reading it. Many of the words were smudged with tear stains. The writing was distorted due to a trembling hand. The woman who had written this part of the journal had been broken beyond what she could handle.

I was in town today and met one of the men from the corporation. He's a slimy and unpleasant fellow. He gave me a sour look, then stopped and stared as if he realized who I was. Not that he had heard my name and knew me but knew what I was. I didn't like him one bit. A sinister-looking smile grew on his face, and he gave me a knowing look. "Hello, ma'am," he said as he approached. He leaned forward. "I know what you are, witch, and I ain't gonna stand for it. Get out of our way, or you and your two sisters are going to pay."

I was scared out of my mind after that and went straight

home. For days, I was able to ignore it, but then I couldn't do it anymore. I went to Jo and El and told them what had happened.

"We have to go back up the mountain and see what is going on," El insisted. Jo and I didn't want to go. El insisted, saying the only way we'd find out how the men knew what we were and what they were doing was by going to see for ourselves.

We went that night and found the crack in the seal had opened again with all the commotion the men on the crest were making. All night, we dealt with those dreadful haints. The strangest part was that the men on the mountain didn't seem to notice or care about the Night Women. The man in town knew what I was. Does he know about the haints too?

Jemma's eyes widened. This part of the entry had been written earlier in the day. What came next was the difficult part. Her eyes snagged on the line she had just read. *Does he know about the haints too?* Her hands tightened on the journal. Did the company men then and now have an idea about the abundance of magic on top of the mountain? Her heart pounded.

The next words she read brought her a multitude of images and feelings.

Vesna screaming as she returned home and saw smoke billowing from the house. A fire had been set, and by the looks of it, it had been intentional, not an accident by one of the children. She hadn't stayed out of the way as she had been warned, and this was her punishment.

Tears formed in Jemma's eyes, blurring the page as the image bloomed bright, angry, and red in her mind. The flames danced over the house. Thomas Blacksworth staggered out, coughing and struggling to get clear of the fire.

Vesna lurched forward to retrieve her children, but it was too late. They were gone, consumed by the flames. Their final screams curdled the air, and even though Jemma couldn't hear them anymore, she felt as though she could.

Josephine and Eloise rushed forward when they saw Thomas fall to the ground outside his house. They dragged him away from the burning building as the roof collapsed with a tremendous crash. If the children had been alive when that happened, they were not now.

Josephine and Eloise had to hold Vesna back as she screamed for her children.

> *I wish they had let me go. I know I would have been killed, but I would have welcomed death if it meant I got to be with them.*

Jemma's heart broke as she read the words. *If only Mama B had let Jo and Vesna send their children away. They would have lived. This would not have happened.* Her anger rose as she continued to read. The following entries were sporadic and made little sense, but she was able to distinguish lines here and there.

> *I hate them both. I hate Josephine and Eloise for what they did. I hate Eloise most. I should never have listened to her. She doesn't understand. She's never had children of her own.*

Jemma closed the journal and retrieved the photo album containing pictures of Vesna, Josephine, and Mama B, as well as townspeople from long ago. The older photographs showed the three women standing side by side. There was one of Vesna and her husband. Vesna looked like she came from Eastern Europe, though Jemma didn't know which country. Josephine was pictured beside her husband and their five children. Only one of the five was a girl, Mabel Doire.

Vesna's children were named William, Katica, and Pavlina. Jemma didn't hate Mama B, but having read the account from the perspective of this other woman, she couldn't help but understand Vesna's tragedy.

Closing the album, Jemma murmured, "It's no wonder she went mad after all that."

CHAPTER ELEVEN

Val and Easter came to pick Jemma up before her father was awake. Jemma crept out of the house quietly, grabbing a couple of granola bars on the way.

As she climbed down from the loft, she thought about the journal. She *had* been able to fall asleep, but upon awakening, a strange feeling settled over her. She still felt admiration for Mama B, but it was stained with the hatred she had sensed in Vesna's journal entries. Jemma had been awakened from her uneasy sleep by the buzzing of her phone. Val calling.

When she got outside and into the truck, Val glowered. "Took you long enough."

Jemma rolled her eyes and laughed. "You're always in a rush."

Easter also rolled her eyes. "Tell me about it. Try living with him."

Despite their teasing, Val relaxed. The prospect of the day had put a light in his eyes. He glanced back at Jemma as he pulled out onto the road and turned left, guessing what was on her mind. "Wait, this is the wrong way," she told him. The way he had turned only led in one direction: up the mountain to Gran's Rest. A small kernel of dread took root in her gut.

"Yes, I know," Val replied. "Mama B called last night because she wanted to know why we wanted the day off. Once we told her our plan, she said to stop by this morning for supplies."

Jemma's brows furrowed. "We have everything we need."

Val shrugged. "She's the witch with a history with that mountain, not me. Besides, you haven't seen her in a week. I expected you would be excited about it."

"I am." Jemma forced a cheery smile. She *did* want to see Mama B after a week. The woman wouldn't be going with them to Kalhoun's Crest, of course, but Jemma was glad she wanted to help. She hesitated since her father had told her she wasn't allowed to go back to work until Monday. *He said I couldn't go back to work, not that I couldn't go visit Mama B*, she thought.

The visit felt disobedient despite the justification. It wasn't like she had a choice since Val now drove up to the front of the bed and breakfast.

The day was grim and overcast. Although much of the snow had melted, the sky threatened more unpleasant weather. Easter cast a rueful glance at the heavy clouds. "I hope they pass the town. I don't want to get caught in a storm."

After Val parked, the three of them hopped out. Mama

B was waiting for them on the front porch. "I began to wonder if the three of you ran off without me!" she called as they made their way over.

Easter grinned. "We would never, Mama B." Jemma decided that despite how she felt regarding Vesna's story in the journal, she needed to be her normal self. Mama B, however, would be able to see through any façade she put up. *It's for Easter and Val,* Jemma thought, *and maybe for myself too.*

Mama B shuffled over to a box on the porch swing, withdrew various items, and handed them to the teenagers. Jemma relaxed and gave Mama B a bemused look as she took the things the old woman had bought for them online. Mama B never went into town, so she could not have purchased these there. It seemed she had embraced the full scope of the online world, including shopping.

Mama B handed them ponchos in bright colors that none of them would wear, hats, rain boots that were too small for any of them, small garden shovels, bags for evidence—which were just tote bags with random company logos printed on them—and more. *We're not going to be able to carry all this shit,* Jemma thought, trying not to laugh.

"Wow, Mama B," Easter started, also trying not to show her amusement. "This is awfully generous of you. Wh-where did you buy all this?"

Mama B's face was full of excitement and glee. It was like it was Christmas morning, and she was bestowing gifts upon grandchildren. Jemma remembered that Eloise Brickellwood had never married or had children of her own, so perhaps this was her making up for that.

"Oh, well, here and there," she offered. Jemma had a good guess. She had seen Mama B on large selling platforms browsing sports and outdoor sections. What she ended up buying, it seemed, had been gimmicks rather than necessities.

"I got all this on sale!" Mama B said. Val struggled not to drop anything. Easter and Jemma exchanged looks.

Great, Jemma thought. *Looks like we've got an old woman with a shopping addiction on our hands.* She had bought multiple of everything. "In case this breaks, or you lose this, or…" Mama B was talking more to herself than to them.

She hasn't finished paying her property taxes, I bet, Jemma thought, still trying not to laugh. Playfully chiding the old woman, however, could be managed. Jemma's lips quirked as she said, "We'll be talking about your online shopping budget when we get back, Mama B. Don't buy anything else until I do."

The old woman glowered and braced her hands on her hips. "I'm not done! There's more inside—"

Val cut her off with a wide smile. "We've gotta be goin', Mama B, but thanks a lot for all…this." He looked like he wanted to get back to the truck so he could dump it all in the bed and be done with it. When Jemma had heard that they would be coming up here for supplies, she had pictured receiving some herbal remedy Mama B thought they might need. This was…well, different.

Suppressing a chuckle, Jemma thought, *She never ceases to surprise me. I wonder if she was like this when she was younger?*

Jemma wondered if Josephine Doire and Vesna Soucek

had ever seen this side of her friend. Online shopping addictions hadn't been possible back then, but had Mama B been consumed by the magical state of the world and those who would one day take the mantle from her?

Jemma stiffened when she remembered that Mama B had been the one to insist Vesna's children remain in Solomon's Cross. Mama B had told Jemma something similar. *She wanted someone to take her mantle one day. That's what she wants from me.* She swallowed hard, wondering what lengths Mama B would go to in order to keep Jemma here, even if it resulted in injury or death. Jemma pushed the thought away. *No, she regrets what happened. She won't be like that with me.* Still, fear lingered in the back of her mind.

For the first time, Jemma was able to see the woman as more than just an old witch who had lived on this mountain for longer than she had been alive. Mama B wasn't a villain, but she also wasn't the hero who saved everybody. In war, there were casualties. Mama B had foibles, weaknesses, quirks, and the potential to be as fallible as anyone else.

I can still learn from her, Jemma thought. *And I can still care for her. I can't put her up on a pedestal, though. That won't help me or her or anyone else.*

Mama B's voice broke through Jemma's thoughts. "Well, I suppose you should get going." She looked like she preferred them to come inside and see what else she had bought.

Jemma hoped she wouldn't turn into a hoarder while they were gone. She had helped clean out the inside of Gran's Rest once. She wasn't looking to do that again. She followed Val to the truck. Easter was the last to bid Mama B farewell and wish her a good day.

On the way back down the mountain, Easter twisted in her seat to eye Jemma. "You didn't talk much to Mama B. Everything all right?"

Easter knew her well and had deep intuition. Still, it often surprised her when Easter read situations so well. Jemma wondered if that ability was what made Mama B think she might one day do well in the Art. *Easter might do better with it since she has lived here all her life and has no plans to leave,* Jemma thought.

She wanted to tell the McCarthys about the journal, but she feared that would make them more uneasy about the trip to Kalhoun's Crest. She decided she'd tell them after they finished, depending on what they found.

She also didn't want them to have the same new perspective on Mama B as she did, thus creating tension. She discarded her thoughts to answer her friend's question, mustering a smile. "Yes, everything's all right. I'll fill you in on what's been going on the past couple of days later." Instead of telling them about the journal, she related what her father had told her the night before about work being done on the mountain and not knowing how long it would take.

Val and Easter's interest was piqued. "You think we'll run into workers up there?" Easter asked.

Jemma shrugged. "We'll see." She suspected they might see any number of things: workers, a haunted old estate, a crack in a magic seal. She didn't want to think about it. She did, however, prepare herself to use magic. She hadn't used any outside of training since dealing with the first boo hag.

And I was hoping I wouldn't have to again for a while, she thought.

"Fine, keep your secrets," Val quipped, though he looked annoyed. Easter was better about respecting Jemma's boundaries and gave her a reassuring smile.

They made it into town, and Val headed home. Jemma had been to their house once, but Easter and Val didn't seem to like inviting her over. For one, the trailer they lived in with their parents was cramped. Jemma wondered if they were embarrassed. They said they liked coming to pick Jemma up because she lived near Gran's Rest. She chose to believe them.

Val drove past their trailer. The trailer park along Cider Creek was as rundown and shabby as any Jemma had ever seen. Given the cool temperature that day, not many people were out, but she did see some. A couple of kids were riding bikes down the rutted dirt road that no one had ever bothered to pave. With the Tennessee government unable to collect many tax dollars from the residents in this part of Kalhoun County, they hadn't bothered repairing roads or building a school closer to the area. Kids had to go to the Solomon's Cross elementary and the combined middle and high school.

Easter and Val didn't seem to mind. Jemma had the notion that her friends liked to get away from the trailer park when they could. In addition to the two young boys Jemma saw on bikes, she glimpsed an old man wearing worn jeans and a tank top sitting in a plastic lawn chair outside his trailer, holding a bottle of beer. An old, very wrinkled basset hound lay on the ground beside him.

The day had been dismal since Jemma awoke but being here made it all the more so. The trailers looked like old men huddled together, trying to stay out of the impending rain. Jemma didn't doubt many of these mobile homes needed repairs. Beaten-up cars and trucks lined the street. Jemma remembered that Easter told her Val was a savior in their neighborhood because he often helped his neighbors repair their vehicles. In the bed of one of the trucks slept a shabby black cat. Jemma saw many other dogs and cats, both outside and through the windows of the homes. There seemed to be as many animals as people.

At last, Val pulled the truck to a stop. Jemma saw that they had reached the creek. It was like a small river running down a steep rocky slope, upon which grew pine trees and shrubs. A narrow path ran alongside the creek as far as Jemma could see up the mountain. With Kalhoun's Crest looming above her, the sun was not in sight. The sky was a pale, ominous gray.

Perfect for what we're doing today, Jemma mused grimly. She helped Val and Easter unload their things and place them inside backpacks. Nothing they would take was from Mama B. Jemma shook her head and tried not to laugh as she rifled through her pack in search of one of Val's flashlights. She didn't expect to be on the mountain after dark, but...

"Just in case," she murmured.

"About a mile up, which is as far as I've gone, we'll lose cell signal," Val told them as he tied the adjustors on his backpack across his middle.

"Great." She hoped her father wouldn't try to call. *At*

least he knows where we're going should anything go terribly wrong, she thought. Mama B knew, too. This was a comfort.

The three teens crossed the creek by stepping on large rocks that protruded from its stone-strewn bottom. Jemma's hiking boots only got a little wet. When they were on the other side, Val took the lead on the path leading up the mountain. He had been a mile up the slope with local kids in tow while teaching them how to set traps. That was where everything had gone wrong.

Jemma gripped the straps of her pack and shifted its weight so it was more comfortable on her back. *I hope we make it to the top before anything happens,* she thought. With grim determination, she took up the rear. Easter fell in between Jemma and her brother. She looked a lot healthier today than she had even a week ago. For that, Jemma was glad since the trip would be exhausting. They had allotted enough time for plenty of rests.

The temperature was in the low forties, but without the sun, it seemed colder. Jemma hoped that after climbing for a while, she would get warm.

As they climbed, however, Jemma began to lose that hope. They reached places where the incline was a lot steeper and more rock than grass and path. The trees thinned, and a cold, cruel wind cut through those that remained, ruffling Jemma's hair and attempting to penetrate her clothes. Although walking had warmed her, the wind took the heat away.

Jemma staggered to the left, hoping Easter and Val hadn't sensed her growing fatigue. Val and Easter were doing well, and Jemma had expected to be able to keep up, but a new sensation had overcome her. Finally, she had to stop and lean against a nearby oak. Easter and Val turned, their expressions concerned as they saw Jemma's pale face.

Easter rushed over. "What's wrong?" She twisted the cap off one of her canteens and handed it to Jemma.

"Thanks." Jemma took a long, grateful drink. After she swallowed, she explained, "The higher we climb, the more nauseous I feel. At first, I thought it was the altitude, but..." She shook her head. *It's close,* she realized.

Easter exchanged concerned and knowing looks with her brother. Val's shoulders tensed. Jemma confirmed their suspicions by saying, "It's the same feeling I had at the hospital when I was in Sharina's room and when I touched Mr. Stomphord's hand." The feeling she had experienced whenever the boo hag was near. She tried to regulate her breathing. Stopping had cleared her head a little.

"I hate that you're feeling that way, Jem," Val started, "but honestly, that's a good sign. Means we're getting close to finding out what the hell is going on." He tried to sound encouraging, but it didn't work.

Jemma nodded and mustered a smile. "You're right. I can keep going. Let's head out."

Her unease grew as they continued to climb. After a while, another sensation joined it. It wasn't just the kind of dread one felt when danger was near. Jemma had often sensed magic in the places where Mama B trained her. A warm thrum in the trees and ground of a healthy forest with magic that had been used for good, for instance. Here, the thrum beneath the ground was faint but dark and it trickled like shadows. She sensed the anger and cruelty that tainted the very soil beneath her boots.

Nearby, she thought. *So close*. They had walked for over two hours and were just passing the farthest spot Val had reached. They were almost there, wherever "there" was.

Jemma took a deep breath and prepared herself for what they would find.

CHAPTER TWELVE

Finally, they reached a flatter portion of land near the top of the mountain.

It was almost noon when they stopped for a break. The day had grown warmer, and the dark clouds had blown east, so the sun was out. The pale-yellow glow brightened everything around them. The altitude brought wind and chill, but the appearance of the sun made it bearable.

They were all grateful to rest, and they took lunches out of their bags. They chose to sit on larger rocks up higher on the bank from the creek, which had narrowed the higher they climbed. With the sun shining, the water glittered as it swept down the mountainside. So far, they had seen nothing unusual, not even other footprints, shoe tracks, or ruts made by tires. If a group of people was regularly coming up the mountain, they had found another way. On the other side, perhaps. The other side of the mountain was in a neighboring town and didn't belong to Solomon's Cross.

Val voiced what Jemma was thinking. "What do you think we're going to find?"

Easter shrugged. "Beats me. I was hoping we would see more than just trees, grass, and water."

Jemma considered telling them about the journal or at least sharing what she had learned about corporations having come up the mountain before. Mama B had told them the same thing, but now Jemma could offer more information. She thought about the supposedly haunted estate that had belonged to the late Rebecca Willow and wondered if they would come across it. They might not since the higher portions of the mountain were much wider than she had expected. They weren't even at the top yet.

Jemma was about to mention what she read when Val got to his feet, his eyes full of alarm as he directed his attention at the creek. Glancing that way, Jemma and Easter saw what had caught his attention. Val had heard rustling in the brush on the opposite bank. Then, the creature appeared.

A large black bear ambled out of the bushes and into the creek. It was clear that the animal wasn't healthy. Its breath rasped wetly in its throat, and bloody foam dripped from its mouth. Every few steps, the bear pawed the stones littering the creek and let out a pained moan.

Jemma, Easter, and Val froze to let the bear pass, hoping it wouldn't sense them. It did.

The bear lifted its head and sniffed the air, then turned and faced the teens. Jemma and Easter still sat on the boulder where they had been eating their lunch. Val was still frozen, unable to tear his eyes away from the animal.

Jemma's gaze went to the twenty-two Val had borrowed from his father, which was leaning against his rock. If worse came to worst, they could use it, but she hoped they wouldn't have to. Killing a bear, even if it was to save their lives, would get them in no small amount of trouble with the local government. Besides, if she remembered correctly, it would take a lot more than a .22 caliber round to kill a bear, not to mention accurate shooting.

They would have to think of something else. The bear let out a pained snarl and clambered up the bank toward them. Jemma knew what she had to do. She hadn't done any spellcasting or binding in the past few months even though she had continued training with Mama B, but now was the time. "Val, buy me a few seconds, will ya?" There was urgency in her voice, but she looked calm.

Val picked up the wire cutters, a small shovel, and a walkie-talkie he had packed in case they got separated and hurled them at the bear one after another. Most of the items missed, but the small shovel struck the bear between the eyes. The animal staggered and howled. The blow pissed it off, and it ran toward them.

Jemma grabbed jars of clover seeds and mugwort from her bag. She had to work some binding magic and fast.

"J-je-jemma," called Val's frantic voice. He reached for the gun.

"I've got it," she hissed, although she was not confident she did. The bear got closer. Finally, she had the right combination of ingredients. She whirled and tossed the seeds in front of the bear when it was ten feet from them. "Come on, come on," she told herself, trying to remain calm. Her panic and nerves made casting the spell more difficult. She muttered the words Mama B had taught her for the binding trap, and thin lines of yellow magic drifted off her fingers.

With a wet-sounding growl, the bear lunged. A net of clover sprang out of the ground, and the bear stumbled into the trap, howling as he crashed to the matted grass. He was bound; now Jemma just had to seal. The magic around her fingers faltered and began to fade. She was losing focus.

"Come on," she told herself again, hissing the words between her gritted teeth. The sealing spell would separate the supernatural thing that was inside the animal and drive it back into the ground. The bear continued to emit sounds of agony.

Easter winced. "The poor thing."

The bear let out one last moan and sank to the ground, no longer fighting the clover net. A dark, shapeless *thing* emerged from the animal. Jemma thought her eyes were playing tricks on her. It dove into the creek, and the water turned from glowing white to dark, murky green. The haint had returned to the water.

The bear's condition made sense now. It had drunk the water or attempted to catch fish and had instead caught a boo hag. The children who had waded in the creek must have had a similar experience. Jemma spun to Val, who still had the gun in his hand but no longer looked like he would shoot the bear. "Did you ever wade in the water with the kids?"

Val shook his head. "No. I stayed on the bank and watched to make sure no one fell and hit their head on a rock. Fortunately, no one did, so I stayed out." That was how the kids had gotten sick but Val had not.

The bear, finally free of the toxic spirit, shuddered and closed its eyes, dead beneath the blanket of clover. Apparently, the haint had sucked out its life. That also made sense. The boo hag had done something similar to Easter, but Easter hadn't died because she had the energy and will of a human, not an animal.

Jemma took the encounter as a somber warning. The haint was now aware of their presence on the mountain. Jemma decided to keep the clover and mugwort close.

Easter shuddered. "I wanna finish this investigation as soon as we can."

Jemma looked at Val.

"I agree. Let's get to the top of the mountain so we can head down before dark."

The sun had gone back behind a cloud as if it didn't want to see what would happen next.

A little while later, Jemma spied a pile of craggy rocks that seemed to form a barrier. They approached the rocky crown at the top of Kalhoun's Crest and saw that most of the trees had been cleared, leaving an open area.

"Jemma!" Easter hissed. A second later, the girl's hand landed on Jemma's backpack, and she pulled her down so they were concealed behind the pile of rocks. "They'll see you." Easter kept her voice low. Just before she was yanked to the ground, Jemma had glimpsed two guards standing at a gate in a fence that ran around the enclosure before them.

"They were fucking lying," Val muttered. Of course, all three of them had known that already, but here was confirmation. Jemma hadn't expected such an extensive setup. How long had they been up here?

There was a small building in the middle of the fenced enclosure. Men were going in and out of it. *A testing center?* Jemma wondered. The armed guards at the gate didn't seem concerned about keeping people out. For the most part, the men who'd invaded the mountain had been left alone. *But not for long,* Jemma seethed.

The fence had barbed wire at the top, and there were enough security cameras around to reveal that they had had issues with break-ins. *Or they were trying to keep animals out,* she thought. The bear that had died thirty minutes before had roamed the land up here before coming into contact with haint-infested waters.

"We're going to have to sneak past the guards and get through the fence to see what's in that building," Val murmured to the girls.

"And to see what they're doing on the other side," Easter added as she gestured at a mass of rock that rose up thirty feet ahead and to their right. The longer Jemma listened, the better she could hear the indistinct sounds of workers conversing and machinery, maybe trucks, on the other side of the mountain.

She nodded at the McCarthys and tried to keep the roiling sickness within her at bay. "Look." She pointed at the guards. "I think they're about to take their lunch break." The two men had left the gate and were heading toward an enclosed white van parked at the tree line several yards away. Jemma heard the van door slide open, and she peeked around the rock to see the men sit just inside the door and unwrap sandwiches. They spoke to one another, but they were too far away for her to hear what they were saying.

"Let's go while they're distracted," Val prodded.

Jemma didn't want to move, but this might be their only chance. "If we move to the right, we can get to the fence where those bushes are. That way, they might not see us."

Val nodded. Easter looked worried. Jemma took her hand and pulled her up from the ground. With a deep breath, she muttered, "Now or never."

The trio kept low to the ground. The wall of rock became shorter, but if they crouched, they could reach the bushes that adjoined the fence without being detected. At least, that was what Jemma hoped. She was glad they had chosen to wear neutral green and brown clothes instead of the colorful ponchos Mama B had purchased for them.

Jemma's heart rate increased, and she had to rest when they reached the bushes. She tried not to keel over. "It's the..." She gestured at their surroundings. "The haint or whatever. It's everywhere, and it is stronger."

Easter and Val shot Jemma worried looks, but they couldn't turn back now. Jemma wondered if the earlier witches had felt this way when they'd stumbled upon the magic teeming beneath the ground. Jemma rested her hand on the ground, and the distant hum of dark magic reached her fingers. It didn't make her head buzz and veins pulse worse than they already were. She hoped that was a sign that the magic and whatever creatures lurked beneath hadn't yet come to the surface.

A haint had slipped through the cracks. Maybe that was all. It was small comfort. Val had taken the wire cutters out of his bag. After the bear died, he had collected the items he'd thrown at it. He inched toward the fence. Sticking his hands out, he cut a hole at the bottom of the fence that was wide enough for them to squeeze through one at a time. It wasn't so large that it would be noticed right away. The cutting took longer than they had anticipated and sapped Val's energy as well.

By the time he finished, his face was strained, and the veins on either side of his head were pulsing. Easter offered him water, which he drank before replacing the wire cutters. "Now we go in," he stated after they had been secured.

Jemma's eyes flicked to the nearby security camera. It did not scan anything beyond the fence like the ones at the gate did. After they slipped past the fence, though, they would be in range. *I bet that building is where they watch the camera footage,* Jemma surmised, glancing at the large shed.

She looked at the camera again. It rotated, so if they timed their movements properly, they could slip past it. "Why don't the two of you go ahead?" Easter suggested. "I'll stay here. That way, if you get caught, I can run back down the mountain far enough to call someone."

Being the most cautious of them, Easter had suggested the best course of action. Jemma surveyed their surroundings. Yes, someone as small as Easter could hide among the bushes and not be noticed. "If we're not back in an hour," Jemma said as she checked her watch, "go get help."

Easter nodded. Val and Jemma crept to the opening in the fence. Val watched the rotating camera closely, and when it turned to the left, he veered to the right. Jemma saw him reach the building, where he ducked behind two large barrels a couple of feet from the wall. Val was skinny and could fit behind them. She waited her turn. The camera rotated back and stayed to the right for longer than it had before. Had someone inside the building heard Val run over?

Jemma spied another camera at the building's front door. Val had to run past it to hide behind the barrels. "Shit," she hissed. Neither had seen it. She hoped the only thing anyone inside had seen was a blur, and they assumed a bug had flown past the lens. Her task was now harder. She had to run past both the rotating camera by the fence and the one at the front door. At least the camera by the fence was far enough up not to see the hole in the fence.

After a few more minutes of tense waiting, the time finally came. Both cameras were turned in the opposite direction. She took off, still trying not to throw up and also trying not to make noise. She skidded to the halt at the barrels, and Val reached out to jerk her into hiding.

Since he had been here longer than Jemma, he had had time to survey the area. Jemma did the same, and her eyes narrowed. "What the hell?" she murmured.

A few hundred feet beyond the fence, the land sloped down. Shafts had been cut into the mountain's side, and large trucks and vans bearing the ETRAA's logo and name were parked nearby. People milled around, and heavy equipment littered the area.

ETRAA was doing far more than a geological survey,

which confirmed that Mr. Stomphord had lied. The men operating the machinery wore work clothes. Others stood by, arms crossed and grim expressions, wearing suits. *Those might be the men Lottie said come into the diner every day,* Jemma thought. They seemed to be in charge.

From what the teens could tell, the men had dug into the mountain's natural crags to hide their work. *It was much more than simple core samples,* Jemma thought. Workers loaded one of the trucks with rocks, and the driver started down the mountain. Other vehicles had been positioned behind ridgelines so only someone who got close or flew a drone over the place would know anything was going on.

They didn't want anyone getting close if the fence and cameras were any sign.

The longer she was near the shafts, the worse the sense of wrongness emanating from them felt. It was like the potent stink from an infected wound, as if the mountain itself had a festering sore in desperate need of cleansing and stitching. The scent was less distinct and not as concentrated as what she had smelled in Cider Creek. She hoped that meant whatever was down there hadn't fully emerged.

They still had a chance. Mama B had mentioned that her wards were connected with the life on the mountain. So far, the trek had shown that most of the animals, excluding the bear, had not been badly affected by the doghole mines...yet. That was a relief, but they didn't have time to waste. They had to get back and tell Mama B what they'd found.

Val was taking pictures and videos of the activity before

them as well as the fenced clearing. With the evidence they gathered, they could prove what the ETRAA was really doing. They could mobilize the locals to stop them, and it would also be good for Mama B to see since she hadn't been to Kalhoun's Crest in years. Jemma supposed Mama B's reasons for that lay in the tragic deaths of Vesna's children. Perhaps coming here brought her too much pain.

Even with this evidence, Jemma still had questions. Why was the ETRAA here, and why had the rep lied to them? There was far more going on. Were they linked to the haints? Did they know what they were dealing with down there?

Before they left, Jemma wanted to find the source of Cider Creek and see if anything was being put into the water that might have caused the haint to crawl out of the darkness and reside near the creek. She explained that to Val in a whisper, and he nodded before creeping out from behind the barrels. This side of the building had no cameras or windows, so they were able to slide along the outer wall to the corner.

They had to get back to the hole in the fence and go to the other side of the clearing, passing the guards and their van. Then they could melt into the trees and follow the stream a few hundred feet to where Val thought the source was. Getting back to the hole in the fence meant passing the two security cameras, but this time, they would not be able to see the one connected to the building and could not time it perfectly.

"I'll go first," Jemma told Val. "Then I'll give you a signal from the fence that tells you when both are turned away." She'd risk being seen, but it would have to do. When the camera at the fence faced away from her, she darted forward, heart pounding until she slipped through the hole. She almost barreled into Easter on the other side.

"What did you find, and where is Val?" the girl asked.

Jemma signaled for Easter to be quiet by putting a finger to her lips. She turned to watch the cameras, and when the coast was clear, she gave Val the signal. As he ran over, Jemma gave Easter a quick rundown on what they had seen.

Easter looked toward the horizon, where the sun was beginning to descend. It was late afternoon. "We'd better find the end of that creek, then."

CHAPTER THIRTEEN

This time, Jemma took the lead. She marched them back to the pile of rocks, and when the guards came back to the gate, they darted behind the van and into the wooded area on the other side.

The creek went up a few hundred feet farther, and Jemma spied the wide, dark opening of a cave. She stopped short when she saw two men in front of it, then pushed back into the trees, Val and Easter behind her. They fell in a heap, and Jemma hit her elbow on a rock. She hissed, unable to stay silent.

Val slapped his hand over her mouth as the two men drifted a little closer. "If we get caught..." was the warning in his gaze. Jemma nodded, and he removed his hand. She rubbed her elbow as the three watched in tense silence. One of the men appeared to be a foreman. He wore heavy boots and clothes fit for work. A hard hat was perched on his head, and he had gloves on his hands. He held a pickax and looked disgruntled as if his work had been disrupted by the arrival of a man in a suit.

Jemma almost gasped; she recognized the second man. They had met him in Johnson City—Mr. Stomphord, the ETRAA rep. All pretense of being friendly had been discarded. The man stared the much taller foreman down as he crossed his arms over his chest. "You and your men need to go much deeper into the mountain. You're moving too slow."

The foreman looked distressed. "Trust me, I know, boss."

"Oh, do you?" the ETRAA rep replied in a tone that was both nasal and nasty. Jemma stiffened, wanting nothing more than to run out and slap the man. If she did that, though, she might faint. Her nausea had grown stronger since she saw him. She hoped they wouldn't have to watch for long.

The foreman grunted. "Might need to consider going loud."

Going loud? Easter, Jemma, and Val exchanged looks. They assumed that would mean heavier equipment, more miners, a bigger basecamp, and using explosives. Whatever would open the mountain faster. And bring whatever lurks beneath to the surface faster. Jemma's initial reaction had been relief that the seal had not been blown wide open, but that faded. What the foreman had suggested would be bad. Jemma's concern was reflected on Easter's and Val's faces.

Thankfully, Mr. Stomphord did not agree. "We will do no such thing. You need to find another way and fast. Not an option since we had to clean up a situation with some hill brats that drank from a shit creek like the animals they are."

Jemma bristled. One look at Val told her he was about

to launch himself at the man, proving Mr. Stomphord's point. It was not a good time for that.

The foreman lifted his hard hat and scratched underneath. "I know, but diggin' any further like we been doin' ain't an option either." The ETRAA rep tried to cut in, but the foreman held his ground, swinging the pickax with one hand as if he and the tool had been one for a long time. "My men know what they're doin', sir, and they know diggin' for much longer ain't the way. So, unless you want the team quittin' on you, you'd better give them higher wages or a different way to get in."

Jemma wondered if the foreman was a resident of Solomon's Cross who had been caught up in a scheme he hadn't planned. Just a man looking for work. The building nausea within her wasn't directed at him or the other workmen but at Mr. Stomphord and others from ETRAA.

Mr. Stomphord considered the foreman's words with a pinched expression, hands balled into fists. Was he trying to come up with a way to threaten the foreman without revealing what was beneath the rock? Jemma wondered if the workers knew ETRAA's intentions. She had a feeling they didn't.

"*Fine*," Mr. Stomphord all but snarled at the foreman. "I'll run it up the chain of command and see what I can do."

Ah, so he had bigshots above him. Val's hand fell on her shoulder a second later, pulling her down as Stomphord's eyes roved to their hiding place. Then the two men walked toward the shafts but stopped and spoke in low tones. The trio stayed hidden and didn't see the men pass them. When it had been silent for a few minutes, Val peeked his head out.

"All clear. We should go hunt around that cave real quick." The sky was pinker, which told them that the sun was closer to setting.

"Let's be quick," Easter urged. The three scrambled up, and after checking one last time, they clambered up the slope to the cave's entrance.

It yawned like a great dark mouth. The closer they came to it, the stronger the effects of the haint's presence became. It took all of Jemma's focus not to keel over. Noticing her pale skin and the cold sweat on her face, Easter reached out to steady her. Jemma could feel the haint coiled up in the cave like a copperhead in its den, a venomous presence soiling the water as it slid out and down.

Other shafts had been dug into this part of the mountain, and Jemma saw the tracks of tires and boots, though none of the workers were here. The other holes could be sealed, but the cave would need far more than having dirt put back over it and a simple spell. It needed a deep magical cleansing, and they'd have to seal the haint, or there would be more damage.

Jemma wanted to go into that cave and finish the foul creature off, but she knew the task would require more power than she had and a command of the Art she lacked. She thought about bringing Mama B up here, but would the old woman have enough in her to help finish off the task after the exertion of climbing the mountain? Jemma wasn't sure. They would have to formulate a better plan.

Jemma was about to relay that to Val and Easter when the other girl's alarmed whisper reached her ears. "He's coming back!" Jemma whirled and saw that Mr. Stomphord was walking back up the path, though he had not yet noticed the teenagers. He was on the phone, telling someone in a disgruntled voice, "I'm going to touch base with the contact as soon as I..." He stopped speaking and looked frazzled, as if he were getting chewed out.

He will see us! Jemma thought, panicking. *Worse, he'll recognize us.* She thought about the past, how Vesna had been warned to stay out of the way, and the consequences she had suffered when she didn't. Jemma didn't want to chance consequences of her own.

Val took stock of the situation, and before Jemma could act, the young man had darted out of the cave and down the path and barreled into the ETRAA rep before the man knew what was happening. Val tackled him so that he fell on his face and could not see who had jumped him.

Mr. Stomphord cried out and dropped his phone. Easter stomped it with her boot hard enough to break it so whoever was on the other end wouldn't hear what happened next. Using his walking stick, Val clocked the man on the side of the head. Stomphord cowered to protect his face, which kept him from looking at them.

Jemma hurried after Easter, and they tore down the hillside. Val ran behind them. "Did he see you?" Easter asked.

Val shook his head. "I don't think so."

Despite Mr. Stomphord having not seen them, Jemma didn't doubt he would call for help as soon as he recovered. Val had not knocked him out.

When they reached the van, the sun hung low on the horizon. The dusk was seeping in, its shadows growing longer and thicker. They would be going down the mountain in the dark. They had flashlights, but it would not be easy, especially if they had pursuers. Jemma skidded to a halt by the van, but it was too late. Mr. Stomphord had alerted the guards.

"Hey!" one of them shouted, then charged them.

"Fuck!" Val hissed as he, Jemma, and Easter tore down the side of the mountain as fast as they could go without getting hurt. They stumbled past the dead bear to the path beside the creek that led down the mountain. The wind howled around them.

Behind them, Jemma heard the pop and crackle of a gunshot. *Shit!* Were the guards shooting at them? Had they not realized the people who had broken in were teenagers? Had they seen the hole in the fence? The gunshots didn't come close enough to hit them. Jemma could tell by how far away the cracks were. The gunfire did, however, impress upon her how serious this was.

Those running the basecamp on top of Kalhoun's Crest didn't want any outsiders coming up there. Jemma skidded to a halt after they reached thicker trees. "Why are we stopping?" Val hissed, then realized what Jemma was doing. She had taken out her jars of ivy seeds and nettle and scattered them on the ground before sprinting ahead, still tossing the seeds behind her.

The sounds of branches breaking as guards hurtled down the slope in the dying light reached their ears. Calmly, Jemma muttered the spell to activate the seeds. A moment later, they heard screaming and swearing when the men encountered Jemma's little surprise: a net of ivy vines intertwined with stinging nettles. It was like running into a thorn bush that enveloped them.

She kept running, Val ahead of her now and Easter just behind. She was glad to hear no more sounds of pursuit, only angry shouts from where she had tossed the seeds. After a few more minutes, they were forced to slow since darkness surrounded them. They checked for signs of pursuit before turning on their flashlights and making their way down the rest of the mountain at a slower yet still urgent pace.

They were silent until Val's truck was in sight, then, "We have to bring the fight to ETRAA," Val said. Easter chimed in, "We have to take them *down*."

Jemma was still reeling from being so close to the haint. Even here, close to the water it had poisoned, she could feel its presence. She shuddered. It was colder now, too. "What is it?" Easter asked, noting Jemma's solemn look. The McCarthys were understandably worked up about what they had seen, but Jemma had information they didn't.

It was time to tell them about the journal and the photos. "Let's get going. On our way back, I'll tell you what I've been meaning to share."

When they started back to the McCarthy home, Jemma divulged what she had learned, beginning with finding out who the true author of the journal had been. She hesitated to tell them about Mama B's insistence on Vesna's children remaining in Solomon's Cross, which had cost them their lives. She wanted to tell her friends the whole truth, but she feared they would form a distorted view of Mama B. She settled for telling them Vesna decided against it in the end without stating why.

Jemma also didn't want to mention Mama B's desire to

train Vesna's and Josephine's daughters in the Art. What would Easter think? Jemma was still trying to figure out if Mama was intentionally shaping her and Easter to be her replacements. Maybe Val too, since the three worked well together. Jemma wasn't sure if boys could be taught the Art. Val wouldn't be called a witch, but could he still learn? She shoved her thoughts aside and focused on sharing what they had heard from Mama B from the perspective of the woman who had suffered the most.

Wrapped up in the story, neither Val nor Easter asked questions until Jemma finished.

"It's like the past is repeating itself," Easter stated in disbelief.

Val's brow furrowed. "And that haunted house you talked about? Where do you think that is?"

Jemma shrugged. "The mountain is larger on top than we saw. Could be it was destroyed." She hoped it hadn't been. More secrets might be unearthed if they found it.

Thoughts about what lay outside their small town and what Mama B had said her calling was invaded her mind. She hesitated, and Val urged her to say what was on her mind. "I don't know, guys. This whole thing's got me feeling...*trapped*." Her words felt like a confession.

Easter nodded gravely. "I understand. It is hard, protecting our home and those we care for." She leaned back and took Jemma's hand. "You're strong in the Art, Jem, which makes you the most capable of protecting everyone and everything. We don't want you to feel trapped or fight for a place you don't feel is worth fighting for."

Jemma wanted to say that Solomon's Cross wasn't her

home, but she looked at Easter's face and then Val's. She had only known them for seven months, but it was hard to think about spending the coming years without them at her side. *These two are more like family than anyone except Dad,* she thought.

Easter and Val seemed to feel the same about her.

The place she had lived before coming to Kalhoun County was no longer home. She had no desire to return to Hendricks, Indiana, especially since her mother still lived there. If these two were like family, why couldn't this be her home?

They reached the McCarthy house, but Val only stopped to let Easter off since he planned on taking Jemma home.

One look at her friend showed her how exhausted he was. In addition to being tired, the three were also footsore and torn between hot food, a long shower, and a warm bed. Jemma assured Val he wouldn't have to wait longer for any of those things.

"I'll call my dad to come pick me up."

CHAPTER FOURTEEN

Tad took one look at his daughter as she climbed into his truck and chuckled. "You look beat, kid."

Jemma mustered a smile, hoping her fatigue would hide any lingering fear or apprehension about what they had discovered on the mountain.

"Find what you were looking for?" Tad asked as he pulled out of Cider Creek and headed toward the main part of Solomon's Cross.

Jemma nodded. "Yes, we did, but I'm really tired."

Tad didn't ask any more questions, and Jemma proved her exhaustion by falling asleep on the way home. When they arrived, Tad had to help her out of the truck and half-carry her inside. He laid her on the couch, and although Jemma had a blurry recollection of it, it reminded her of being a kid and her father carrying her to bed after long road trips. Life was different now, and they were both older, but their relationship had remained the same. It was a small comfort in light of Jemma's experiences that day.

As she started to fall asleep again, Jemma remembered

Mama B. If she didn't contact her, Mama B might become concerned about their well-being. She opened the email app on her phone and typed a message but then remembered Mama B's mammoth computer and that the old woman might not be able to check it. Sighing, Jemma dialed the number for Gran's Rest.

"Yes, dear?" Mama B answered when she picked up the phone. She had waited up and knew only Jemma or one of the McCarthys would call this late in the day.

"We're back," Jemma stated in an exhausted voice. "We'll tell you everything soon." She lost track of both her thoughts and words as everything from the day came rushing back. Although she did not mention what they had found, Mama B could sense that it weighed on Jemma. "I'm looking for a home, ya know? A family, I guess. I don't know what I'm talking about. So tired…"

She paused, and without being able to rein in her words, she added, "Mama B? Why didn't you let Vesna try to save her daughters?"

Mama B was silent for a long moment. "You need sleep, my dear. I'll talk to you soon. Get some rest." Her voice was gentle, but her tone was off—sad and faraway. Jemma didn't notice since she was almost asleep again.

The old woman hung up and Jemma succumbed. During the ride home, the nauseating feeling had faded, but it lingered as she fell asleep.

It tainted her dreams. She dreamt of a snake coiled up in a dark den. She saw many faces: those of Vesna Soucek from the photo album, Mama B, Easter, Val, her father, Mr. Stomphord, and RJ and AJ Kilmer. The last face that visited her was very familiar, but Jemma tried to forget it over the past few years. It was the face of Delilah Nox.

At long last, she drifted into a dreamless sleep.

When Jemma awoke the next morning, she was disoriented to find herself on the living room couch instead of in her bed in the loft. She heard her father in the kitchen and everything that had led up to him placing her on the couch to sleep rushed in. And everything after that.

Jemma sat straight up in alarm and horror. She remembered the last question she had asked Mama B before she went to sleep. *Why the hell did I think it was okay to ask that?* she wondered, rubbing her eyes. *How am I supposed to salvage this?* Mama B wouldn't quickly forget what she had asked.

She had a feeling that her fatigue hadn't been the only factor in muddling her mind. Even now, after a full night of sleep, Jemma still felt the lingering effects of being so close to the haint. A dull headache persisted behind her eyes.

Hearing her awaken, Tad ambled out of the kitchen and gave her a cheery smile. "Happy Sunday, kid. Sleep well?"

Jemma just nodded, not wanting to tell him about the murky, unsettling dreams she had experienced. "Well, good. I have breakfast ready. Eggs won't stay hot for long!" In addition to eggs, Tad had also made French toast and bought Jemma's favorite brand of apple juice. She sat down at the table, but the headache, combined with a stirring in her stomach, made her not want to eat.

Tad gave her a quizzical look. "Something the matter, Jem?"

She mustered a smile. "Not ready to eat yet. Just woke up."

"Of course," Tad answered as he scooped a piece of French toast dusted with powdered sugar into his mouth. By the looks of it, Tad had been awake for the past couple of hours. His eyes were bright, and he had a contagious energy about him. After he polished off his food, he scooted over to Jemma and opened his laptop. "Remember that I told you we couldn't do work up on Kalhoun's Crest for a while? Well, it might be much longer than we thought. Take a look at this."

Jemma's interest increased, and she leaned in to look at a press release flickering across the screen.

The Eastern Tennessee Rural Advancement Association, also known as ETRAA, announces it will be expanding its operations and is looking at projects in Kalhoun County.

I see they're keeping up the lie and pretending they aren't already doing it, Jemma thought. They had worked fast to cover their asses. By stating they would begin operations in Kalhoun County, anyone who heard or saw them working up on Kalhoun's Crest wouldn't think much about it.

Jemma sighed. "Sorry about that, Dad. I know that puts you out of some of your work for a while." The more she thought about it, the more she wanted to blow ETRAA's cover.

Tad just smiled. "It's not all bad, Jem. They've offered

me a job as their networking manager." He grinned and leaned back, folding his hands behind his head. "They don't waste time, do they? I'm considering taking it. It's better money than what I'm making now, and I won't have to leave for days on trips. All my work will be done here in the county."

Jemma recoiled in disbelief, and her heart started pounding. *No!* This was the worst possible scenario. Or was it? Could her father find out more for them? *No,* she thought. *I can't put him at risk, not like that.* She forced a smile, trying to hide her knowledge and feelings. "That's cool, Dad, but is it worth it?"

Tad's brows furrowed. "What do you mean?"

"Well, let's say you do take the job and it doesn't work out, or they don't stay around here for long," she started. "If you cut ties with the company you have a long-term commitment with, you might not be able to get your old job back if something goes wrong."

As far as Jemma was concerned, something was going to go terribly wrong as soon as she could make that happen. The last person she wanted to be caught up in it was her father. "Shouldn't give up a steady thing for a flash in the pan, ya know?" She tried to sound casual. "And the trips are good for you. Gets you out of the house and stuff."

Tad's hands dropped to his lap. "I didn't think of any of that." He scratched his head, considering. "Still, it's a good opportunity, and maybe they would keep me on after they left Kalhoun County. I could still work from here." Jemma's heart sank, but she was relieved to find that her father hadn't been won over by ETRAA. Not yet, anyway.

I have to get the word out about ETRAA quickly, and not in a way where my father can find out it was me, she mused with a renewed sense of urgency. Jemma decided to change the subject so her father would stop thinking about it. She wiggled her eyebrows. "Any luck on the dating front, Dad?"

Tad's brows rose, and he chuckled a little nervously. "I haven't given it much more thought, Jem. Why do you ask?"

She grinned, taking the opportunity to tease him. "There are some ladies down at Harv's askin' after you. They all think you're…well, 'fine' is the word they use."

"Like who?" Tad asked, not engaging in Jemma's amusement.

"Oh, like Lottie and her friends," Jemma replied lightly.

Tad laughed and rolled his eyes. "I don't think Lottie and her friends are my type." The tension broke and Jemma also laughed. She knew that, but it was fun to poke her father. The only "type" she knew her father liked was her mother. Now that Delilah had waltzed out of their lives, she wondered if Tad's type had shifted.

Tad stood, grinning at his daughter. "I'll be in my office if you need me."

Jemma distracted herself by eating some of the breakfast her father had made, then texted Easter with the update about ETRAA's expansion. She mentioned they had offered her father a job.

Yikes. Doesn't sound good. Meet us at Gran's Rest this afternoon?

Apprehension and dread filled Jemma at the thought of seeing Mama B after the question she had let slip the night before. They had far more to be concerned about, though, given ETRAA's presence on the mountain. Jemma sent her reply before Tad could ask her what her plans for the day were.

See you then.

The day was warm, so Jemma decided to ride her bike up the mountain instead of having Val and Easter pick her up. To go to Gran's Rest, she had to put in a special request to her father. "Mama B wants us to come up for tea. No work, I promise." *Not the groundskeeping work I get paid for, anyway,* Jemma added to herself.

Tad considered. "I suppose it's all right. You're going back to work tomorrow anyway. Maybe you and I can go out for dinner tonight. Been a while since we've gone out and done anything, just the two of us. We can talk more about your school and your future as well as my job dilemma."

Jemma said his idea sounded nice, but she cringed at the thought of talking about her future. Right now, what she wanted resembled what her father had in mind. *But what if my calling doesn't fit with that?*

She remembered wondering if Solomon's Cross would ever become her permanent home. She decided to put those thoughts aside until after she had spoken to Mama B.

Relieved that she wouldn't have to sneak up the mountain, Jemma grabbed her backpack and bike and was on her way.

It was early afternoon when she arrived on top of the mountain, and a couple of minutes later, Val and Easter drove up. Mama B was inside speaking with guests. Since it would look strange for the old woman to disappear upstairs with the three teenagers, Jemma, Val, and Easter lingered in the front hall with the old woman while her guests flipped through pamphlets and looked at the paintings on the walls.

"Business is booming, Mama B," Easter told her cheerily.

Mama B smiled, the look on her face kind and warm. "Sunshine brings all kinds of people out," she announced. Jemma glanced at the door. A pile of packages had just been set down by a postman who had seldom come up the mountain before Mama B's shopping binge began.

Jemma's brow furrowed, and she turned to the old woman. "More shopping?" Neither Mama B nor Jemma mentioned what had been said the night before.

Mama B gave her a sheepish look. "Well, yes."

"Now, Mama B," Easter chided in her gentle way. "You can't be ordering new things every day. Soon you'll have far too many things to know what to do with."

Mama B opened her mouth to protest, but Val poked her shoulder and teased her about becoming a hoarder. She was interrupted by the approach of a middle-aged couple who was looking to check out of their room and head home. Based on their accents, they had come from up north.

"We had a lovely time," the wife gushed with a smile. "And my back feels so much better after what you gave me."

Easter and Jemma exchanged knowing looks. Mama B grabbed a small glass jar from the check-in desk in the front hall. "Here, take this. It is an herbal body wash that will assure my help will last."

The woman thanked her, and they checked out. The couple left, which allowed the old woman and her teenage employees to talk. "Tell me, child," Mama B stated, her attention directed toward Jemma. "I can tell you've been near that foul haint."

Jemma had been feeling better all morning, especially after eating and an invigorating ride up the mountain in the warm early spring air. Nevertheless, a dull headache made itself known, so she followed Mama B into the kitchen. The old woman brewed the tea she had made before, and as Jemma drank, Val and Easter told her what had happened the day before.

Val began with the bear, and Mama B's brows rose in both surprise and admiration when he explained that Jemma had made quick work of binding and sealing the bear, thus driving out the foul spirit within it. Easter described what they had seen at the top of the mountain near the fence and the security building. Val told her about the workers and what they were doing inside the mountain.

Mama B turned to Jemma. "What did you feel when you saw that?"

"Darkness stirring beneath the surface," Jemma replied as she finished her tea. "But it was indistinct enough to tell me it hadn't gotten out yet."

"But it won't be long," Easter added woefully.

Val talked about following Cider Creek up to the cave

and what they had overheard between the foreman and Mr. Stomphord.

The longer Mama B listened, the more concerned she became. "I think they're doin' things now that they know they've been discovered," Val finished with a sigh.

"We don't think they saw our faces, though," Easter inserted.

Mama B nodded. "Good. I fear what they would try if they knew who was spying on them."

Jemma stilled. Was Mama B remembering the tragedy of Vesna's children dying in a fire?

Mama B looked at her worn hands. "I would have never allowed the three of you to go up there if I thought you would be chased and shot at." She looked up and met each of their gazes in turn. "I'm sorry."

Jemma felt that the apology was genuine, and the tension in her shoulders eased. She shared that her sickness had gotten stronger the closer they got to the cave. "I'm sure the haint was in there. Maybe it has moved in."

Mama B nodded. "Those foul creatures do like dark, wet places."

Jemma told Mama B what she had informed Easter and Val of that morning: that ETRAA was covering up what they were doing by announcing that they were "expanding their projects" across the county.

"It might be best to send the photos and videos we took anonymously to a local news source and hope that will trigger a real investigation," Jemma suggested.

The others agreed. Easter offered, "I can get on that. I know just who to go to." Jemma didn't know who she was referring to, but she figured Easter had connections from growing up here.

Mama B turned to Val. He looked ready for action, not like the shaking leaf he had been when his young friends had first gotten sick. "Find out from the parents of the children in Cider Creek if and when they are coming home so Jemma and I can make something to treat them with. If they cannot be treated at home, we will find a way to go to the hospital, but I would rather avoid that."

Jemma agreed. She wasn't keen on running into Doctor Falksworth again since she believed he wouldn't allow the three teens in the children's wing again after what had happened.

Val nodded. "I'll let you know what they say."

"Good," Mama B answered. "You and Easter can go do your parts today while Jemma and I make the brew." Jemma remembered what she had made for Easter when she was sick. It had helped keep the boo hag away. The children wouldn't be relieved of their torment, but the treatment would keep them from getting worse. *That will buy us time to deal with the haint and whatever else lurks on that mountain,* Jemma thought. *Hopefully.*

Jemma dreaded Easter and Val leaving because it meant she would be alone with Mama B. As soon as they were gone, however, Mama B went into the cellar, where no one but she and Jemma were allowed, and set about gathering what she needed for the herbal tonic. They would have to make an extra-large batch to treat all seven of the hospitalized children. Jemma followed her down and, under Mama B's instruction, gathered the few late-fall apples still stored down there, plus cinnamon and cloves.

"These are the same ingredients I used for Easter," Jemma mused as she looked at what was on the kitchen table. The cook had left for the day, so they had the time and space to make the herbal tonic.

Mama B winked at Jemma. "Yup. I've already got the tonic made up, but we'll flavor it with what we have here." She gestured at the apples and spices. "A cider tonic for the Cider Creek children! We'll be ready with enough tonic no matter what Val reports." A look of glee came into the old woman's eyes. It had been a long time since she had cared for so many children.

Jemma smiled. "This feels like the old days to you, doesn't it?"

Mama B hesitated, her hands stilling over the apples as she began to shave off the skin and cut up the fruit. Then she nodded, and a small smile crept across her lips. "Yes, it does." Despite the grievous circumstances, Jemma was glad to see the old woman finding joy in her work, as small as it was.

They fell silent, and Jemma focused on the rustling of the gentle breeze in the pine needles just outside the kitchen window. She looked forward to the following day when she could begin working again and finally plant the seeds she had stowed away for the garden. The longer the women were silent, however, the harder it was for Jemma to bring up the question she had asked the night before.

After a while, Jemma heard a soft sniffling. She turned and saw that while Mama B was still cutting up the apples, there were tears in her eyes. Jemma dropped her dread and rushed over. "What's the matter, Mama B?"

"Oh, it's nothing," Mama B tried. Jemma wished Easter

was here. Her friend was better at drawing troubling thoughts out of people in the form of words. Jemma decided she would just have to figure out how to do it herself. Besides, she knew Mama B better than anyone else at this point in the old woman's long life.

At last, Mama B set the knife down. "Well, it's this. I didn't mean to wrap the three of you up in the same fate as I have, but it's happened. I knew I would train you as soon as I met you, my dear, but not involve you like this." A tear drifted down her cheek. "I've made many mistakes in my life, but I fear this is one of the worst."

Jemma felt for the old woman. She understood making mistakes, and she understood Mama B's fear. She couldn't imagine how long this old woman had spent her life alone, holding in all the secrets she carried. And yet this was her home. *Can I be the same way without having to be alone?*

For the first time since she'd started to work at Gran's Rest, Jemma saw how much she and Mama B had in common. She gave the woman a reassuring smile despite not feeling confident about their situation. "Whatever the case may be, Mama B, we need each other." She picked up the knife and finished cutting up the apples. "That means we'd better figure out the best way to work together. Whatever troubles come our way, we'll figure them out."

CHAPTER FIFTEEN

Jemma hadn't been to Harv's diner with her father in weeks. They had gone all the time when they first moved here, but after both became busy with their jobs, they had slacked on the weekly tradition.

It was Tad's suggestion, and Jemma was glad he would not be cooking, so she agreed. After their conversation that morning, Tad seemed eager to discuss "their futures" further. The notion made Jemma groan inwardly, but she knew she couldn't avoid it forever.

"Guess what, Dad? I am going to be a witch when I grow up" would not go over well. "Well, I'm already a witch, and I'm not sure I even want it," was the follow-up.

When her father picked her up from Gran's Rest in his truck, she put on a smile. Tad and Mama B conversed at length, as they normally did after Jemma finished work. It was like they were much older friends than two people who had become acquainted six months ago. That was how they both were; each knew no strangers. That normally would have been endearing, but...

I'm starving, she thought. She headed to the truck, a silent signal to her father that she was ready to go. It took him some time to pick up on it since he was enjoying himself talking with Mama B. "Jemma tells me she's helping you pay your property taxes. That's a wise thing to do, Mama B," Tad stated with a grin.

Not wanting to spend another hour here and watch Mama B and her father get into an argument about whether or not Mama B owed taxes to anyone, Jemma turned on the truck and beeped the horn. "Jemma's hungry!" Tad declared with a smile.

Mama B asked him to help her take packages inside first. Jemma groaned. Tad carried in what the postman had brought up the mountain that day.

When at last he returned, he gave her a wry smile. "Mama B sure does buy a lot online these days, doesn't she?"

"Don't even get me started," was Jemma's reply.

Tad just laughed and switched on the radio. They heard only static. "Guess we're too high up the mountain." He waited until they were closer to the bottom of the winding road before trying again, only to hear more static.

Jemma grinned at her father. "Looks like your radio's shot, Tad. Maybe Val can come over and fix it."

Tad frowned, shaking his head. "It can't be! It worked when I came to pick you up. Must be somebody tampering with the radio signal somewhere. Gotta be a tower on one of the mountains around here."

Jemma started. Were there radio towers up on Kalhoun's Crest? If so, was what ETRAA doing disrupting them? Since he was driving, Tad didn't spare a glance at his daughter and thus didn't see the alarm in her expression. He shrugged. "Oh, well. Guess you'll just have to deal with my singing, Jem." He winked. "I should have tried out for one of those singing competition shows we used to watch when you were younger." He dove into one of Jemma's least favorite Tad Nox performances. *"She'll be coming round the mountain when she comes! She'll be coming round the mountain when she comes!"*

Jemma couldn't suppress her grin as he told her, "Come on, Jem, sing the 'yee-haw' part! *She'll be coming round the mountain when she comes! Yee-haw!"*

Thankfully, they were at the bottom of the mountain and driving onto the main street running through Solomon's Cross by the time Tad suggested that. Jemma considered it a mercy. Tad was still humming the tune as she climbed out of the truck. At least he was in a good mood. For that, Jemma was thankful.

Harv's diner was as busy as always, and Jemma put aside her thoughts to focus on finding them a table. There were none, so she and Tad took stools at the counter, where they could see into the kitchen. "Lookin' for somebody, Jem?" Tad asked after Jemma had glanced at the corner booth at the end of the restaurant a couple of times. She did not see any of the businessmen Lottie had mentioned.

She picked up the menu and shook her head. "Nope."

A moment later, Lottie came over, smiling more broadly at the sight of Tad than she did when it was just Jemma or the McCarthys. "Evenin,' Noxes. Coffee for you, Tad, and orange juice for you, Jemma? Decaf on that coffee, given how late in the day it is?"

Both nodded, and Tad grinned. "Might not even have to decide what I want to eat, Lottie. You know me better than I do."

Jemma looked up from her menu and saw a flush on the older woman's cheeks. Lottie winked, and Jemma cringed inside. "I know just what you'd like tonight, Tad." She turned to Jemma. "And you, dear?"

Jemma chose to forego her usual grilled cheese sandwich with dill pickle spears and ordered a burger and fries instead. "Why don't I throw in a milkshake too?" Lottie chortled. "Strawberry, your favorite."

"Sure," Jemma replied. She had the notion Lottie was putting it on more than normal on account of her father. Jemma glanced sideways at Tad. He hadn't seemed to notice.

Lottie walked away, but as she made their drinks at the nearby coffee maker and juicer, she kept stealing glances over her shoulder at Tad. Jemma's father was oblivious. Jemma almost laughed. Many women in town had a crush on Tad Nox, and many thought he liked them back since his easy charm and friendly manner were often mistaken for innocent flirting. *I'll have to talk to him about that,* Jemma thought as Lottie returned and set their drinks on the counter.

She lingered for a moment, even though there were other customers waiting for her, and asked Tad about how his job was going. He perked up. "My job is going just fine, Lottie, but I am looking at maybe taking a different one."

Lottie's smile widened. "Hope it's better for ya and will bring you into the diner more often. Been a few weeks since you've come in. Course, Jemma's in here all the time."

Tad replied, but Jemma had stopped paying attention. In her effort to not show her wariness about her father taking a new job, she had allowed her attention to drift around the diner. Her eyes snagged on a figure walking past the windows outside.

AJ Kilmer walked with the arrogance she had always seen in him, but unlike before, his head hung low, and he kept his eyes trained on the sidewalk. He seemed to be in a hurry. Maybe he didn't want anyone to stare. Just then, AJ's eyes drifted from the ground to the window. He stopped for a second and noticed Jemma was looking at him. He glared and stalked off.

Caught again, she thought with a sigh. She remembered the promise she had made to RJ. *We have to take care of that soon*, she decided with no small amount of dread. She just didn't know how to go about approaching a wounded animal who wanted to bite her head off.

Jemma's thoughts were interrupted by Lottie's voice. She looked up and found Lottie and Tad gazing at her with inquisitive expressions. Realizing she had been asked a question, Jemma replied, "Sorry, I was distracted. What did you ask?"

"That's all right," Lottie returned. "I asked you how your school project was going and if you'd had a chance to visit Miss Dagwood."

Tad's eyes widened. Jemma had made no mention of visiting someone in town as a part of a school project. She kept her attention on Lottie until she finished replying. "I haven't, but Val and I plan to go tomorrow."

Lottie wiped the counter with a rag and shook her head. "Best of luck to ya, Jemma." She started to say something else, but the cook hollered from the kitchen. Rows of plates lined the counter, ready to go out to hungry customers. Jemma noted that the diner was short-staffed this evening. Lottie had her hands full, but that didn't stop her from paying Tad extra attention.

Once she was attending to other customers, Tad gave Jemma a quizzical look. "What school project?"

"It's for Val," she responded hurriedly. "He has to write a paper about something historical in town." She motioned at the bulletin board with the WWII clippings and decided she wasn't going to keep the whole truth from her father. "One of the veterans who used to live in this town has a distant relative we're going to visit tomorrow and interview." She paused and considered holding her next words back, but she let them slip out. "The veteran's wife was a dear friend of Mama B's."

Tad did not sense the significance of Jemma's words. He nodded and gave her a smile. "I am glad you want to help out your friends, but remember, your schoolwork comes first." It was a gentle warning.

"Yes, Dad. I know."

Their food came. After he had had a few bites, Tad asked, "Things are going well at Gran's Rest, I take it?"

Jemma nodded. Tad listened with kind interest as she explained their plans for the grounds and preparations for springtime activities with guests. "Seems like you and Mama B have become good companions. Not the kind of close friend I thought you would make when you moved here, but she makes sense for you," Tad commented when she had finished.

Despite the burdens weighing on her from the events of

the past couple of weeks, Jemma smiled. "I feel the same way."

She could tell her father was trying to come up with a way to broach the subject of his potential new job again. After a moment, he said, "Look, Jemma, I know how you are. You examine everything from every angle to make sure we can get the best possible result for our lives." He smiled. "I appreciate that about you, but sometimes, we need to take risks. I think taking this new job will be a good risk."

If only he knew what she did. Jemma tried to keep that thought from showing on her face. At this point, bringing up the problems she faced would look like a desperate attempt to keep him from the job. They would have to get what they knew to the news outlets immediately. Her father could decide if he still wanted the job after that. Jemma gave Tad whatever smile she could muster. "Okay, Dad. Do whatever you think is best."

Tad laughed and gave her a playful jab in the ribs with his elbow. "Since when have you been on board with what I think is best without having an opinion?" When she didn't reply, Tad knew she still had reservations, but he didn't pursue the subject.

After they were done eating, Jemma suggested they pay quickly since she didn't want her father and Lottie having another long discussion. Outside, Jemma couldn't keep herself from glancing down the street at RJ's hardware store. She stalled on the sidewalk beside the truck, and Tad noticed. "Everything all right, Jem?"

She nodded. "RJ's is closed, that's all." It was strange to see the hardware store closed before its normal time since

RJ was one of the most consistent men Jemma had ever come across. She got into the truck, and after buckling herself in, she looked up to see a well-maintained car pull up to the building. A man in a business suit climbed out, looked up and down the street, and disappeared into the hardware store.

Jemma frowned. Was he from ETRAA, and if so, why was he going into RJ's? Surely, they had all the equipment they needed already up on the mountain. Tad didn't seem to notice and pulled the truck away from the diner before Jemma had a chance to examine the car. She was eager to visit Miss Dagwood the following day.

Val picked Jemma up after school. Jemma climbed into his truck, knowing Easter would not be joining them since she had a rehearsal. "Good news!" Val announced as he pulled out of her driveway. "The kids in Cider Creek will be coming home in a few days." The relief on his face reassured Jemma.

"I'm glad. Mama B and I can give them the remedy we made to help them heal faster once they're back."

Val filled Jemma in on what the doctors had told them, and they concluded the doctors were full of shit and were bluffing to make it seem like they had handled the situation. Jemma couldn't blame them, though. How could she expect the doctors in Johnson City to be aware of a witch who had dabbled in dark magic hanging around the children? She redirected her thoughts to the task at hand.

Miss Priscilla Dagwood lived on Ardenwood Lane, a

part of Solomon's Cross where the houses were larger, and every lawn had neatly trimmed hedges and gardens full of flowers. There was a beautiful fruit tree just beginning to bloom on Ms. Dagwood's front lawn, but not much else since it was only early spring. The house was much smaller than its neighbors and seemed rundown, which made sense given how old the woman was and that she had no family in the area. Jemma had checked before coming.

"No one else," Lottie had told her. "She's the only one left in her family." Jemma wondered where the rest of Thomas Blacksworth's family were. Had any of them come to Solomon's Cross with him?

"How the hell are we going to do this?" Val asked as he parked the truck.

Jemma didn't know. She had brought Vesna's journal and inner trepidation but little else in the way of preparation.

They made their way to the door and, finding the doorbell hanging by its wires, Jemma announced their arrival by using the brass knocker. Silence followed. She knocked again, and a sour voice within said, "No solicitors!"

She knocked once more, and when no reply came, Jemma called in a pleasant voice, "We're not trying to sell anything, Miss Dagwood. We just want to ask a few questions."

Silence reigned for another moment, then the door creaked open. A short, hunched woman with wisps of white hair and large round glasses appeared. She frowned at the two teenagers on her front porch. "Questions? What questions?" A mangy-looking cat appeared at her feet.

Jemma introduced them with her brightest smile. "My

name is Jemma Nox, and this is Valentine McCarthy." She decided to stick with the same story she had told her father and Lottie. "We're interviewing people around town for a historical project for school. We're wondering if we could ask you questions about Thomas Blacksworth, who served in World War Two. He was a relative of yours, correct?"

Miss Dagwood frowned but nodded curtly and opened the door wide enough to let them in. The interior of the house was dingy, and a chilly draft came in through an open kitchen window. The TV was on, set at a low volume. It showed a midday game show where winners received boats and pool tables. Jemma looked around.

Miss Dagwood hobbled over to a faded rocking chair and sat down. Jemma and Val took seats on a nearby loveseat since it seemed polite, not because they wanted to sit on furniture covered in cat hair. The loveseat, like the rest of the room itself, emitted a strange smell—a mixture of pet odor, cigarette smoke, and something sour.

Jemma decided they would keep the visit as short as possible. By Val's stiff posture and the wrinkling of his nose, she knew he wanted to do the same.

She took out a notepad and the journal she had brought with her. "I first saw Mr. Blacksworth's name in this journal. It was written by his wife, a woman named Vesna Soucek—" She extended the book toward Miss Dagwood as she spoke, but the woman waved it away.

The old woman cut Jemma off with a sharp look. "No one in my family dares utter that damned woman's name."

Jemma and Val exchanged glances. Jemma wanted to pursue the topic of Vesna but had to do so with discretion.

She backtracked. "Can you tell me how you and Thomas Blacksworth are related?"

"I never met the man. Died before I was born," the old woman responded. She didn't seem to care about him, and Jemma couldn't blame her. She had several family members she had never met. "He was my mother's uncle. I heard all kinds of stories about him in the war. Seen plenty o' pictures, too."

"Any pictures of his wife and children?" Jemma ventured.

Miss Dagwood stiffened. "Yes, they took many photographs." She didn't elaborate.

Val tried next. "Did he marry after coming home from the war?"

"That's what I've been told." Miss Dagwood eyed them for a long moment. Jemma pretended to write something on her pad. She felt she had to do something since the old woman's stern, sharp gaze made her skin crawl. She wondered if coming here had been a mistake.

Miss Dagwood sighed. "I admit that while I was growin' up, I did a lot of wonderin' 'bout that woman. My mother was like a daughter to her uncle. He lost all his children in a fire while they were still young. He and my mother were close. Anyhow, after all that happened, no one in the family ever did talk about that mad woman if they could avoid it."

Jemma could see that she and Val weren't going to learn much. "Do you have any photographs of Thomas Blacksworth that we could see? There's one in his war uniform in town, but are there any more?"

Miss Dagwood laboriously pushed up from her seat and went to a dust-laden mantel. She retrieved a photo album and leafed through its contents until she came to an old photograph. She handed it to Jemma, and Val leaned forward to look at it over her shoulder. "Keep it. None of us really wanted the picture anyway. It was never any of ours. It was sent with a box of memorabilia years ago by someone I did not know."

Jemma saw why no one in the family wanted the photo. It wasn't just a photograph of Thomas Blacksworth alone or with his family. Vesna stood beside the former soldier, with their three children in front. To their right was another family: an adult man and woman with brown skin and their own children, including a pretty little girl Jemma assumed was Mabel Doire. Her eyes snagged on the last figure.

"Mama B," she murmured. Val gasped. The young, eager face of Eloise Brickellwood gazed at her from the sepia-toned print. It struck her that everyone looked happy and content.

Before everything went to hell, Jemma thought. She looked up and thanked Miss Dagwood. Seeing that the old woman was tired and wished to be alone once more, she suggested to Val that they leave. Miss Dagwood led them to the door, and although she did not smile or bid them goodbye, she wished them well on their school project.

Val took the photograph from Jemma as they walked to the truck. "Funny to see Mama B looking so young. Hard to believe she ever was."

Jemma agreed.

"Shame we didn't learn anything," Val murmured as they climbed into the vehicle.

They had only learned that Vesna hadn't been well

regarded by Thomas Blacksworth's family. Jemma retrieved the photograph and turned it over. Her eyes snagged on the inscription in the corner. The photograph was bent, and the pencil inscription was faded, making it difficult for Jemma to decipher.

"I can't believe it." Val leaned forward. "Do you see that?" she pointed.

Val frowned. "Can't tell what it says."

"I swear it says 'Willow.'" Her mind reeled. Could the photograph have come from Rebecca Willow? Had Vesna and the others met her?

Val's brows drew together. "I don't see it, Jem. Interesting, though. You should hold onto that." His doubt showed on his face as he drove away. Even if the writing said "Willow," it was not necessarily connected to the woman who had once lived on Kalhoun's Crest. Miss Dagwood had said the photograph didn't belong to anyone in the family. Someone she didn't know who'd sent it.

Jemma put the photograph into the journal for safekeeping. The sun was going down. She had to get home before dark and complete her homework before her father had dinner ready for the two of them.

"I'm going to find a magnifying glass later and get a closer look," she decided aloud.

CHAPTER SIXTEEN

It was Wednesday, the day after Jemma and Val had gone to visit Miss Dagwood. Jemma had slept but awoken many times in the night to turn over the events of the last several days in her mind. Everything from what they had seen on the mountain to her father thinking of taking a new job to their sleuthing with Miss Dagwood made an appearance.

All night, she thought about the back of the photograph. She had used a magnifying glass, but the pencil marks were too faded for her to make out the word. *I know!* Jemma thought before going back to sleep. *I'll ask Mama B tomorrow if she remembers who took the photograph.*

The following day, however, gave her no opportunity to get Mama B alone.

Since it was the middle of the week, there were few guests, but Mama B found plenty to be talk about. Those who had never even heard of Solomon's Cross before coming here learned some of the town's history. Although they attributed Mama B's knowledge to her age, they had no clue just how long she had been here.

Jemma and Easter were at Gran's Rest finishing up work as the golden hour blessed them with radiant sunlight. It was a warm day, which allowed both of them to begin planting flower seeds in the beds behind the bed and breakfast. They had begun their work in layers of clothing. By the late afternoon, they had shed their outer garments, leaving a small pile of sweatshirts and scarves on the bench near the backdoor.

Val had not joined them. Easter had told Jemma he was at home, eagerly awaiting the arrival of the children from Johnson City. Two kids who had had milder symptoms were coming back today, and the rest were to follow later in the week. Once they were all home, Jemma and Mama B would take their brew over.

Jemma and Easter finished their work and made their way inside to let Mama B know they were done for the day. They found the old woman chatting with a young man at the front desk and could see the conversation would not be over anytime soon. They smiled and waved their goodbyes before making their way to their bikes. Jemma promised herself she would ask about the photograph later. As far as she was concerned, an investigation of Rebecca Willow and her home wasn't necessary at the moment.

They had secured their bikes to a tree near the bed and breakfast's mailbox. As they reached the bikes, they were met by the postman. He stuffed mail into the box and turned to the girls. "Mind helping me take some packages to the porch?" Jemma and Easter agreed, and the postman handed them several boxes, all containing things Mama B had ordered online.

"How often do you have to come up here now?" Jemma asked the postman.

The man sighed. "Almost every day. I used to come up once a month with letters, but now…" His words trailed off, and he shook his head at the sight of all the sealed cardboard boxes. "I gotta tell ya, I'm worn out."

"We'll take everything inside. No need to worry about it," Easter offered.

The postman thanked them and drove off. Jemma said in a dry voice, "If we don't stop her, poor old Mr. Henry is going to break his back *and* his mail truck coming up here every day."

Easter grinned and gathered a couple more boxes from the ground. "We'll have to stay on her like an addict fresh to sobriety."

Jemma rolled her eyes but couldn't help grinning. "First, she'll need to learn what sobriety is."

After they had dropped the boxes off on the porch, they returned to their bikes and left. They had errands to do in town, then Val would pick them up, take Jemma home, and return to his house with Easter. Jemma hoped they would hear a good report about the two children who were brought home that day.

As they made their way down the mountain, Easter asked, "What happened with Miss Dagwood yesterday? Val was too tired to tell me last night and went straight to bed."

Jemma explained that Miss Dagwood had given them very little to go on. "She mentioned 'that mad woman' her family refused to talk about."

"Do you think they ever found out she was a witch?" Easter wondered.

Jemma shrugged. "Could be they were angry because Vesna went crazy. Miss Dagwood knew the children had died in the fire but not how or who set it."

Easter gasped. "Do you think her family suspected Vesna killed her own children?"

Jemma wasn't sure. "It's possible. We'll never know." She felt sorry for Vesna again. The woman had fled an unnamed enemy, only to end up in a town that, years after she was gone, might still blame her for the death of her children. *While the responsible person is on the mountain,* she thought. Jemma shoved her negative feelings toward Mama B away. She knew she shouldn't blame the old woman. Mama B was many things, but an arsonist wasn't one of them. Whoever had set Vesna's house on fire was long gone.

Easter blew out a long breath, then gave a shaky laugh.

"What is it?" Jemma asked.

Easter shook her head and pumped the brakes on her bike. She came to a stop, and Jemma halted too. "It's just that I never realized how many secrets this town had until you came along, Jemma. Of course, I knew it had history."

She shrugged. "But nothing like what I'm seeing now. It all started with me getting sick. If the boo hag hadn't gone after me, I don't think I would know what I'm learning." She seemed conflicted. Easter loved to learn, and anything she unearthed was a treasure to her, but had getting sick been worth it? Jemma thought about the Cider Creek children, and she wasn't sure. Life wasn't as black and white as it had been when they were younger.

Jemma looked around and realized they had stopped in the exact location where the two had first met. They grinned at one another. "Gosh, Jem, it feels like so long since we met," Easter remarked with a smile. "Seems like we've known each other forever."

Jemma felt the same way. She pedaled off on her bike a little faster than before. "Let's get into town before the sun goes down."

Easter suggested they stop by Harv's for a quick bite before heading to the pharmacy, where they would ask to have Mama B's tonic included in the medicines assigned to the children by the doctors from Johnson City.

"Whatever the doctors prescribe won't work anyway," Easter grumbled as they made their way down the street to the small drugstore. "The meds the doctors gave me when I was going there for appointments did jack shit. If anything, they messed me up more."

"Maybe they gave these kids something stronger since a lot of them couldn't even breathe on their own," Jemma responded in a somber tone. She had thought a lot about why Easter had done much better than the children. Had the boo hag gotten stronger, or had Easter McCarthy always had a magical gift that allowed her to fend off attacks to some degree? Mama B had mentioned Easter's potential as a holler witch to Jemma on many occasions. She wondered if it was desperation on the part of the old woman and her desire to find a replacement or if Mama B just saw something special in Easter.

Easter shrugged, and Jemma's thoughts drifted away. "Maybe." Easter didn't say another word until they entered the pharmacy and went up to the counter.

They had put the glass jars with the brew concocted by Mama B in the basket of Easter's bike. They brought them inside in Jemma's bag. Jemma spied one worker—a pleasant-faced woman named Linnea Strang—behind the counter. She had kind brown eyes and soft waves of brunette hair around her oval face. She smiled at the two girls. "Good evening, ladies. What can I do for you?"

Easter smiled back and explained to Ms. Strang that many of the children in her neighborhood had become sick. "I'm sure you have received prescriptions from their doctors and parents."

"What are their names?" the woman asked.

Easter told her, and Linnea pulled them up. "Yes, right here. Have you come to pick them up?"

It struck Jemma how unusual it would be in any other place for one person to pick up medical prescriptions for a whole neighborhood. However, Ms. Strang and the McCarthy girl were well-acquainted, and on top of that, the pharmacist knew she could trust Easter. Easter shook her head. "No, I've come to ask you to include something with them."

Linnea paused, lifting a brow. Easter explained that she had had the same sickness months ago. "My friend Jemma here helped me by giving me an herbal brew Mama B made."

"I work up at Gran's Rest," Jemma inserted quickly. She was glad to see Ms. Strang did not have a strong prejudice against Eloise Brickellwood.

"Anyway, the brew made a world of difference and helped me heal a lot faster," Easter added without mentioning that a boo hag had been dealt with after. "It's all-natural, too."

"Well, I don't see how a natural herbal remedy would

do the children any harm," Linnea replied with a soft smile. "We need more of that for all of us, especially the children. Might ease their symptoms, at the worst."

"We have them with us," Easter told her, which prompted Jemma to unload her bag. Linnea's eyes widened at the sight of the glass jars.

"You put quite a bit of effort into this."

Jemma shrugged, smiling. "It helped Easter. I just want to make sure the kids get the same help."

Linnea's smile grew. "Your father must be so proud of you."

Except he doesn't know, Jemma thought. The statement, however, made Easter perk up. A new light entered her eyes. "He *is* proud. Jemma is a lot like her father, you know."

Linnea's eyes did not move from Jemma. She tilted her head. "I haven't seen him in a while. How is he? Still considering that new job?"

Jemma started. Her father had only told her about the new job a few days ago. How did Linnea know about it, and why would her father have seen her? As far as she knew, Tad didn't make many trips to the pharmacy. *Well, news does travel like wildfire in this town,* she thought. She mustered a smile. "He's doing well. Still considering the job."

"Well, whatever he decides," Linnea told her, "I'm sure will be best for you both."

It struck Jemma that Linnea Strang had the same brand of hopeless optimism as her father. She was a gentle, kind spirit, and Jemma didn't want to leave her presence. "All right, I'll add the brew to the list and send it home with the parents when they come to pick it up tomorrow," the pharmacist told them. "What should I call it?"

Jemma gave the woman the official name, thinking it wouldn't hurt, then she and Easter left the building. When they got outside, the sun was almost down. Easter nudged Jemma with her elbow and wiggled her eyebrows. "What do you think, Jem?"

"Think about what?"

Easter rolled her eyes. "You're not as oblivious as your father, but sometimes..."

"What?" Jemma demanded.

Easter laughed. "Well, *I* think Tad and Linnea would make a cute couple. She'd be a good match for him."

Jemma was taken aback. The idea of her father dating had been a joke since he would never look twice at Lottie and the others in town who had crushes on him. But Linnea? Easter was right; the woman would be a good match for her father. Jemma wasn't sure how she felt about it.

"Did I go too far?" Easter asked. She now appeared concerned instead of amused. "Did I blindside you?"

Jemma shook her head. "No, you're fine, E. Just haven't thought about it, is all."

"Maybe that's part of the problem," Easter ventured.

Jemma stiffened, but knowing Easter meant well, she replied, "Tad's a good man and was a good husband to my mom." She sighed. "Could be there's still a part of his heart that needs to be filled. I've just spent so much time trying to move past my mother, ya know?" She'd had to hide a box of memorabilia from his marriage when they'd first moved so he would stop dwelling on the past. "I just didn't think he would move on this soon."

Easter slung her arm around Jemma's shoulders. "Might not happen. It was just a thought." She smiled, and the look was contagious. Jemma decided not to give the matter too much thought, not while they still had Kalhoun's Crest and ETRAA to deal with.

The girls retrieved their bikes and decided to go to Harv's to wait for Val. Easter sent him a text, and they made their way down the street. The evening was warmer than any of the recent days, and the sky was tinged pink by the setting sun. A soft wind blew past, ruffling their hair and clothes. Jemma felt lighter now that she didn't have a backpack full of herbal brews.

As they rode down the street, Easter shared what she had been doing for the past few days after rehearsals were over. "I anonymously submitted the videos and photos you and Val took to the newspaper here but also to the main newspaper in Johnson City. I sent them to the radio broadcasting services and a television station too."

"Hear anything back?"

Easter shook her head. "I don't think I will. For one, the radio doesn't work anymore. The tower up on Kalhoun's Crest is down for some reason. Funny timing, huh?" She gave Jemma a knowing look.

Jemma nodded, remembering that her father's radio had suddenly gone out. It hadn't been a mechanical malfunction in the truck. "Anyway, I think the newspaper here will release it since there's so little hot news to put out these days. If the county thinks it is worthwhile, which they might, they'll put it out on the local TV station."

They reached Harv's and dismounted their bikes once more. Jemma was thirsty and winded from the exertion. "Well, let's hope for the best. Wanna grab something to drink before Val gets here?"

Easter grinned. "He asked us to get him an iced tea as payment for picking us up."

The following day, Jemma completed her work at Gran's Rest by late afternoon and went home to finish her schoolwork before having dinner with her father. While she was doing homework, her phone rang. She jolted out of her concentration on a Spanish exam and picked it up.

"What's up, Easter?"

"Turn on the news." Easter's voice was grim.

Jemma switched on the old television, which her father had dug out of storage months ago. It was from his college dorm room days. Only a few channels made their way this far up the mountain, and to Jemma's relief, one was the local news station for Kalhoun County. A female newscaster with short blonde hair wearing a red blazer was on the screen. Across the bottom of the screen were the words:

The Eastern Tennessee Rural Advancement Association spreads its operation across Kalhoun County.

The newscaster repeated the message with slightly different phrasing. "The Eastern Tennessee Rural Advancement Association says they are beginning phase one of their work in Kalhoun County with the intention of making sure the land on top of the mountains is safe and suitable for later development. Sources say this happened after seven sick children in a nearby trailer park neighborhood got sick. Their case caught the attention of the hospital in Johnson City, its medical professionals, and the ETRAA."

Jemma waited with bated breath.

"However, newly received photo and video evidence from an anonymous source shows that the ETRAA began their work long before they released that statement," the newscaster continued. "How long has ETRAA been at work on our land without the taxpayers' knowledge? Tomorrow, we will be speaking with a representative from the association to hear why this has happened."

Several of the photos and videos Jemma and Val had taken were shown: the shafts in the mountain, the equipment, and the profiles of some of the workers. None of ETRAA's personnel, only the workmen they had hired.

Jemma had forgotten Easter was on the phone. She only remembered when her friend spoke again. "I've checked the newspaper in Solomon's Cross. They're taking it seriously and have made claims that ETRAA, like a lot of government-funded programs, is hiding something."

"Send me pictures?" Jemma requested.

A moment later, her phone *dinged*. She opened an image of the newspaper's front page. The headline read:

Secret Work Taking Place on Kalhoun's Crest.

One of the pictures Val had taken was below the headline. Easter said dubiously, "The picture will make some people suspicious, but I bet ETRAA already has a clever way to cover it all up."

"Yes," Jemma mused, feeling defeated. "They'll be embarrassed, but I don't think this is going to cause the full stop we were hoping for."

"That's what Val said," Easter agreed.

"We're going to need more," Jemma added. "Especially now that ETRAA is trying to make everyone like them by giving them good deals and jobs." As she said that, Tad ambled out of his office. He hadn't heard what Jemma had said, but he stopped short when he saw the news on the TV. He frowned, crossed his arms, and watched as the newscaster repeated what she had said a moment earlier. She finished speaking about ETRAA and moved on to pet adoptions at a newly built animal shelter in a neighboring county.

"Gotta go," Jemma told Easter and hung up.

Tad snapped out of his daze and looked at his daughter. "An anonymous source, eh? Did the three of you see anything when you were up there?" The narrowing of his eyes told Jemma he was wondering if she'd had any part in it.

"Come to think of," she replied, "we did see vans and men and a fence." She didn't go further. That was true. She didn't want to lie, but she also didn't want her father to know the full scope of their problem yet.

Tad sighed. "Maybe I'll rethink it." He shrugged. "Then again, they might have a good reason. Don't want the press all up in their business until they know for sure what they're doing."

"Yeah, I know, but it's strange that they didn't just say they'd already been working. Why lie about the timeline?" Jemma asked. She had part of the answer, but she wanted to deter her father from taking the new job.

The TV was now showing the nightly weather and traffic reports. She switched it off, and Tad suggested they have dinner. She made her way to the kitchen as her phoned *dinged*. It was Easter.

> **Forgot to tell you while we were on the phone.**
> **I texted AJ and asked if he wanted to go to Harv's with us tomorrow. He said yes.**

Jemma stopped between the living room and kitchen. The beep of the microwave and her father pouring something from a plastic jug into cups were background noise. *Great,* she thought. *I get to spend my Friday night with AJ Kilmer.*

More than dread, she felt surprise. AJ Kilmer had agreed to hang out with them? She sat down at the table as her father brought over their drinks. Jemma concluded AJ had said yes because he was lonelier than any of them had realized. She ignored the negative feelings that cropped up as AJ's face lingered in her mind. They could all start over. He had been a jackass because of a boo hag, after all.

CHAPTER SEVENTEEN

As was their Friday night custom, Val picked Jemma up at her house around 5:30. Knowing where she would be going and with who, Tad gave his daughter a cheery smile. "Have fun, Jem. See ya later."

Jemma felt different as she stepped out of the house. The McCarthys seemed to as well. Easter was her normal cheery self, but it felt forced. Val didn't even say hello to Jemma. He just gripped the steering wheel until his knuckles turned white and kept his mouth shut. Since the nearby radio tower wasn't working, they didn't have any music to listen to on the way down the mountain. They sat in solemn silence, turning over in their minds what might happen with AJ.

Jemma focused on the sound of the wind in the treetops, which were just beginning to sprout new leaves. The wind scattered loose rocks and dirt over the road as Val's truck swept past. Jemma fidgeted with the zipper on her hoodie. *Why the hell am I nervous?* she wondered. It wasn't that she expected AJ to make a scene; she just didn't know how to act around someone she didn't like.

When they arrived a few minutes later, there was no sign of AJ, so the trio headed into the diner. AJ sat alone in a booth, his focus on the drink before him. "Oh, good!" Easter said cheerfully. "He's already here." She went over to him.

Val and Jemma stayed behind, exchanging looks, then reluctantly followed so as not to seem like they wanted nothing to do with him.

AJ looked up at the sound of Easter's voice and did his best to smile. It was more like a grimace. At least he didn't glare or snarl. That was a start. Easter slipped onto the bench opposite AJ, and since Val always sat by his sister, he slid in after her. Jemma lingered for a second by the booth. *Shit, I have to sit next to him.*

She sat down, feeling as stiff as a log. As she sat, Lottie caught her eye, and they exchanged looks. The waitress lifted a brow, bewildered by the addition to Jemma's and the McCarthys' Friday night group.

Easter's voice brought Jemma's attention back to the table. "What'd you do today, AJ?"

The boy beside Jemma muttered a response that Easter had to ask for again. "Sorry, didn't catch that."

AJ shrugged. "Worked for my dad. Fixed my car."

Easter smiled. "That's nice. What's wrong with it? Val works on his truck all the time. Maybe he'll know…" She was cut off by a sharp look from her brother.

AJ, however, relaxed a bit.

No one ever asks him questions about himself, Jemma thought.

"Rear axle's out of whack. I'm gonna have to replace it." He related that with very little enthusiasm, but Jemma could tell that it was the closest they would get to him opening up.

They were interrupted by Lottie, who came over to take their orders. She sensed the tension at the table too. AJ was less tense, but Jemma remained stiff.

Val...

Jemma wondered if he would break his jaw, he was clenching it so hard. He stared at the menu as if he were studying for the exam of his life. After taking their orders, Lottie asked Jemma, "How's your father?" Jemma thought the question would come with a twinkle in Lottie's eye and a deepening of the pink on her cosmetically blushed cheeks. Instead, Lottie had a dubious expression. "I saw him here in town last night," the waitress added.

Jemma's brow furrowed. She didn't remember her father leaving the house. "Oh, he was just with a friend."

Lottie chuckled. "With a friend. That's what he's calling it?"

Jemma's confusion was evident on her face, but she didn't have a chance to ask Lottie what she meant. The waitress was called away by a customer asking for a refill. AJ chuckled at Lottie's response, and Jemma actually looked at him. His eyes were on his hands, which were lying in his lap, but his lips bore a genuine smile. When he saw his companions looking at him, the smile vanished. His head snapped up, and he glared at them.

Easter swept in with another attempt. "I haven't seen you at school, AJ. Do you—"

His brusque answer cut her off. "I'm doing school

online right now." He bent to take his straw into his mouth and drink.

"Oh, neat," Easter answered. "That's what Jemma does. School online, then works full-time."

"Too bad I don't have a car to fix up, or any car, for that matter," Jemma added, trying to sound like she was interested in the conversation. Val, even though they had ordered and he knew the menu by heart, kept staring at the laminated booklet. Jemma guessed Easter might have done some sisterly blackmailing or bribing to get him to come here.

"Why not?" AJ asked Jemma, turning slightly to eye her. Part of his wall had come down.

"Why don't I have a car?"

"Yeah." He straightened. "Aren't you sixteen?"

"Almost seventeen."

"Then get a car."

Jemma's answer popped out of her mouth before she could think to keep it in. "Not all of us can afford to get a car." Realizing how sharp she sounded, she attempted to soften the words by adding with a shrug, "I like being driven around in Val's rust-bucket anyway."

Val's head popped over the menu. "Hey now, don't talk about her like that." That eased the tension. Easter and Jemma laughed. Val remained rigid, but Jemma saw AJ's lips twitch into a smile out of the corner of her eye.

He played with his straw and didn't look at any of them, especially Val. He didn't know what to say or do. None of them did. Jemma checked her watch, sure that at least twenty minutes had gone by. *Only seven!* Dismay filled her. At least they served food fast here. AJ caught Jemma glancing at her watch, and his brows drew together. He looked away before Jemma could catch his eyes. *He's really observant,* she thought.

Their food came a moment later. After Lottie set down their plates and refilled AJ's drink, the door to the diner opened. Jemma wouldn't have looked up, but the four guys who came in were laughing raucously and pushing one another around.

Great, AJ's friends. AJ's head snapped up from his plate as they sauntered in, then he lowered his head and looked at his plate. His shoulders tensed, and he leaned over his plate. He looked like he wanted to disappear.

The tallest of the four spied the teenagers in the booth by the window and smirked. Jemma's expression hardened. She didn't doubt that he would come over to them.

The jock—he made sure people knew he was a jock by wearing his varsity football jacket—ambled over. "AJ, fancy seeing you here!" he exclaimed. He called to the other boys, "Hey, y'all, look who's here." He braced his hands on his hips.

AJ kept eating and didn't acknowledge his presence.

Val's sharp eyes moved upward. Easter looked helpless. Jemma wanted to punch the guy like she had punched AJ the first time she'd met him. The other three sauntered over, snickering.

One of them sneered. "Way to go, AJ. You sittin' with the town freaks now? I guess it makes sense now that you're a freak yourself."

That was it. Jemma bounded to her feet. "Jem…" Easter cautioned.

Val's face flushed a deep crimson.

Another kid chortled. "Even these freaks don't like you! That's how much of a freak you are!"

"Leave. Us. Alone," Jemma warned in a cold voice.

The tallest one crossed his arms and stared down at her. "Whatcha gonna do, new girl? Punch me?"

Jemma rolled her eyes. "That the best insult you can come up with? 'New girl?' I've been here for seven months."

"'I've been here for seven months,'" he mocked in a high-pitched voice, sending the other three into fits of laughter. "New Girl, Sick Girl, Freak Guy, and…well, you used to be cool, Valentine."

Val looked like he was about to boil over. Luckily for all of them, Lottie stomped over. "Get the hell out of the aisle and stop heckling perfectly good customers. Go sit your asses down or get the hell out of here." The boys made their way to the other end of the diner and sat in their usual booth.

Jemma sat down, fists clenched. Lottie sighed. "Don't worry about it, kids. They come in here and make trouble all the time. You're not the only ones they make fun of."

Yeah, but they probably have the most fun with us, Jemma thought. She picked up her fork and held it so tight, she thought it might snap in half. A deep sigh from beside her caught her attention.

AJ lifted his head. "Look, they're right. I know y'all are only doing this," he gestured at the table and the food, "because my old man asked you to. It's humiliating, but…" He sank back against the booth, shoulders slumped. Jemma had never seen such an open expression on his face. "I guess I deserve it." He looked up, and his eyes met Easter's and then Jemma's. Finally, he did his best to meet Val's eyes. Val, for once, looked at AJ. The redness in his face was just beginning to fade.

"I treated all of you like shit," AJ confessed. "And yeah, I'm still pissed off at y'all for everything that happened. I know that's stupid, and I should just let it go." It was the most AJ had spoken since they arrived. Jemma didn't know how to respond.

"Yeah, well, that anger is left over from the bad shit the boo hag gave you," would not help, so she didn't speak. Her silence was reinforced by a warning look from Easter. "Your father did ask us to," Jemma finally answered, "but we could have said no. We didn't, and we're glad you agreed." She found that she meant the words.

Easter gave AJ a smile. "We've been busy, or else we would have asked you sooner."

AJ tensed again, sensing he had opened up too much. "Yeah? Busy with what?" Jemma wondered if he had only asked so he wouldn't have to hear the laughing from his old friends at the other end of the diner.

Easter hesitated. "We've been doing a lot of hiking."

AJ lifted his head, frowning. "Ain't it too cold for that?"

Easter shrugged. "Some days."

"Say, you guys still live in Cider Creek?" AJ gestured at Easter and Val. "Heard about what ETRAA is doing up on the mountain? Have y'all seen anything?"

The answer was yes, but Easter and Val shook their heads. "Heard, yes," Val answered, still not looking at AJ.

"They've been caught lying about the timeline of their work," Easter stated. "Some people still want to partner with them, though."

AJ nodded and leaned back. "I know."

Jemma, who had been eating and listening during this interchange, went on high alert. She glanced at AJ. "What do you mean?" The young man held her gaze for a second before looking away.

"Well, my old man, for one, is still gonna work with them."

Jemma's heart sank. Kind, gentle-hearted RJ Kilmer was in ETRAA's back pocket. It was the final nail in the coffin. AJ went on, "They're getting us discounts on brand name goods in exchange for supplying what they need for the mines."

Easter, Val, and Jemma did their best to hide their displeasure, but it didn't work. AJ's eyes narrowed. "There's something weird going on. Y'all are thinking the same thing, and you don't want me to know about it."

Jemma tried to play it off. "We went and saw the kids who got sick in Cider Creek. We're afraid ETRAA's mines will add more harmful metals to the water they play in." It was partially true.

AJ shrugged. "Don't let kids play in the creek."

Val started to voice a sharp objection, but Easter's hand on his arm stopped him. AJ set down his fork. "Look, I'm not dealing with this anymore. If y'all wanna be mad at my father for doing what's best for me and him, so be it. But I don't have to stand for it." He glared at Jemma long enough for her to figure out that she had to slide out of the booth to let him go. AJ threw a twenty-dollar bill on the table and left the diner.

Jemma leaned back, sighing.

"It makes sense," Easter remarked in a soft voice. "The

one loyalty he has left is to his father, and I think he sometimes feels unworthy of RJ's love."

"So, he's going to defend his father no matter what," Jemma added, then nodded. "I can't blame him." Still, she felt the frustration and weight of their failure. Things with AJ had started to seem…bearable. Now he was gone, and the tension he'd left behind was palpable.

"We need to get back to that mountain and deal with the haints," Jemma heard herself say. "We can't depend on people's suspicions to drive ETRAA away from there." And if they didn't work fast, more of the mountain would be opened up. Who knew what would come crawling out of there? The thought made Jemma shudder.

"I plan to go to Gran's Rest tomorrow," Jemma stated after Easter and Val nodded. "Not for work, but to let Mama B know what needs to happen. I'm going to ask her for a couple more witch lessons before we go."

The trio finished their food in silence and used the twenty-dollar bill AJ had left to pay for their meals, even though they felt guilty about it. Having little cheer left, Jemma asked Val to take her home, even though it was only eight o'clock. When they got there, Jemma started at the sight of the empty driveway. Her father wasn't home.

Val and Easter left a moment later. Jemma was thankful she had a key. Once inside the house, she got something to drink from the kitchen. She spent her evening tidying the living room and kitchen, then played a video game until she heard the crunch of tires on the drive. Tad entered the house a moment later and started in surprise at the sight of his daughter on the couch. He grinned. "Didn't think you'd be home so early, Jem."

She mustered a smile, not wanting her father to realize she had heavy matters on her mind. She didn't mind her father knowing about their efforts to befriend AJ. She just didn't want to relive the evening right now. "Where were you?" she asked instead.

"Went to hang out with a friend," Tad answered. Jemma remembered the funny look Lottie had given her when she spoke of her father and his friends. Tad had buddies from work, but none of them lived in Solomon's Cross. Before she could ask who he had hung out with, Tad sank onto the couch beside her. "I rented a couple of our favorite movies. Whaddaya say to a father-daughter movie night? Hope you're not too tired."

Jemma smiled. "Sounds good. I'll make popcorn." She got up and made her way to the kitchen while her father turned on the TV and popped in a DVD he had rented. It felt like the old days in Jemma's childhood. She placed a bag of popcorn into the microwave.

She figured she'd better enjoy these moments while she could.

Before this whole town went to shit.

CHAPTER EIGHTEEN

Jemma stood in the forest on the grounds of Gran's Rest six days later. Over the last week, she had come here every day after finishing her homework to train with Mama B. For weeks, she had avoided training, but knowing where they would be going and why, she felt she needed more preparation.

"I'll be goin' with you young 'uns," Mama B told her after hearing what had happened with AJ Kilmer. Jemma had gone to Gran's Rest the next day and reported that the children from Cider Creek were doing better now that they had Mama B's brew, but they needed to move fast before anything worse happened.

ETRAA had come out with a statement apologizing for the mix-up in their timeline and promised the listeners or readers that they had simply been trying to make sure everything was in order before making any public statements. Although suspicions and questions abounded, they were assuaged by the association's ability to make deals and give businesses and workers great perks for working with them.

Tad Nox was still considering going to work for them. When Mama B heard that, she shook her head and *tsked*. "Tricky world we live in when greedy men like that scuttle out of the shadows like the cockroaches they are. We know they're cockroaches, but nobody else will recognize that 'til they're dealt with."

Today, Jemma was in the forest with a light late snowfall beneath her feet. False spring had left them, and the last of winter gripped the region once more. Jemma was sure it would only last a week or two before the warm weather returned, but of course they got the cold weather this week. How convenient, she thought dubiously.

She had said as much to Mama B, but the old woman didn't catch the girl's sarcasm. She just gave her a pat on the hand and said, "Fret not, my dear. The weather doesn't know what we'll be doing."

In a way, it did. Jemma sensed magic around her, and it changed with the weather. When it was cold, the magic felt like a trickling stream she had to keep from freezing by manipulating it. She looked forward to warm weather when the magic would flow beneath her touch.

The magic was also different at Gran's Rest than it was on Kalhoun's Crest. Here, it was close and binding like a strong, warm hug from a loved one. On the mountain, however, it was elusive and dark like a shadow lurking in a corner, sliding away when one turned to face it. When would it strike her? Would she be able to bind it?

The plan was to make the trek up the mountain Friday

night under cover of darkness. Jemma was still working on the excuse she would give to her father. Mama B would join them since she knew how much magic would be required to "bind a whole nest of them foul creatures." That level of spellcasting was beyond Jemma's skill and ability. Still, both the older and the younger witch thought it best that Jemma learn the ritual for binding a large number of haints.

Jemma stood shivering in the forest as Mama B explained. "There are some spells within the Art that can render the stone of a mountain so stubborn that even the full might of technology will struggle to conquer it." She chuckled. "And since greed drives them, they will lose interest when the earth itself defies them." She shrugged. "There is no profit in struggle." Mama B seemed to be speaking from experience.

Little had changed, it seemed. Jemma could see it, clear as day. How many times would history repeat itself in this small, worn-out town?

Mama B planned to carry out the ritual, but it wouldn't hurt for Jemma to know it in case anything went wrong. The ritual included words uttered in the right order, depending on what needed to be sealed. There were different words for the binding and sealing of haints than for closing off the section of earth from which they had come. It would take a lot more energy than ridding a bear or a water source of a foul spirit.

Mama B instructed Jemma to close her eyes and block out external input. She was to focus on the pull and tug of magic within her body. "Now, sense the danger and where it is. Push your magic toward it. Move your fingers the way your magic needs to move around whatever is binding it."

Jemma didn't sense any danger, not here or now. After drawing the magic from her body, which was easy since she had been doing it for months, Mama B instructed her to do the same but with her eyes open. "This time, do not shut off your senses. Take everything in and use it to your advantage." This was necessary since if she was in a high-stakes situation, it would be difficult to shut out the chaos erupting around her.

She practiced for some time. The lesson was difficult, but she was finally able to complete it. Mama B, thankfully, had become a more patient teacher in the past few weeks. Oftentimes, she forgot how long she had had power and that having it for so many years had made her one with it.

Jemma, on the other hand, was not as connected to her power. She needed more time, and the older woman sometimes did not remember that.

Jemma spent the nights leading up to the event poring over the journal to find out how Vesna, Josephine, and Eloise had bound and sealed the mountain the first time. She found scribbles here and there but not many. Vesna avoided talking about spells and focused on herbal brews and remedies. As far as magic went, the journal was more like a recipe book than a spell tome.

To Jemma's surprise, much of what they needed for their second hike up the mountain was available at Gran's Rest, courtesy of Mama B's online shopping spree. Instead of purchasing colorful, over-bright clothing to wear in the rain, the old woman had been meticulous in her purchases this time.

It was an improvement to their plans, if not the old woman's budget. Jemma wasn't fond of the idea of becoming Mama B's bookkeeper *and* groundskeeper. After they sealed the mountain, she would propose that the task went to Easter, who was as thrifty as they came.

On Thursday, Jemma rifled through the recent packages, glad to see there had been fewer today than on previous days. The postman she had met the previous week had stopped, replaced by another. Mama B had scared the first one off.

Jemma was just glad she wouldn't have to spend money on supplies, though she still needed to talk to Mama B about her shopping addiction when they got back.

During their training, the old woman had been preoccupied. Jemma often caught her gazing through the trees with a wistful look in her eyes. Jemma didn't doubt that painful memories weighed on her employer's mind.

She recalled Vesna's journal entries. It had been many years since the women came to Solomon's Cross and sealed the crack on the mountain. Much tragedy had occurred, and Mama B probably avoided thinking about those times.

Once the supplies Mama B had purchased were sorted and loaded into their packs, Jemma and the old woman selected the clothes they would wear. Jemma had requested Val and Easter bring their clothes over too. "Don't put a weird spell on them, okay?" Val had told her while handing her his best pair of jeans, his heaviest shirt, and a waterproof jacket.

Jemma had winked. "No promises." Now, she saw what Mama B had in mind.

The old woman scuttled onto the porch with a jar full of pressed flowers, some thread, and two needles. "We'll sew these pressed-flower charms into the garments. Then we'll be warm, sure-footed, and hard to see."

Jemma smiled. The longer she trained with Mama B, the more she learned, and much of it was unexpected. "You might as well get your little surprises together," Mama B encouraged Jemma when they had finished sewing. Jemma went to the cellar to collect the herbs and other ingredients she would need to create nets and beehives from seeds.

She'd need more than a couple of nets and a few stings to get rid of a nest of haints, but it was a start. Val would be bringing the McCarthy family's hunting rifle, but everyone knew that would be their last resort, considering how outgunned they would be. They wanted to be as quiet as possible and go unnoticed.

Mama B also requested that Jemma bring her father's baseball bat. Jemma wasn't sure how the old woman had known about it, but she agreed. She just hoped her father wouldn't notice it missing.

She watched in wonder as the old woman took the bat and spread her hands over it before muttering an incantation in a low voice. Gradually, glowing blue sigils appeared on the old wood and chipped paint. Mama B tapped the bat after she finished. She had combined the magic with an oil rub of pressed nettles. "Now this simple bat will pack a good wallop!" she announced.

Despite all of their preparations, from training to pressing flowers to making bats glow, they still needed a few things from RJ's, like a crowbar and another pair of bolt cutters. They had lost their first pair during their mad flight down the mountain.

After she finished working with Mama B that evening, Val picked her up. The teens went to RJ's hardware store. As Val drove, Jemma explained what she and Mama B had done to prepare. She stopped mid-sentence when she saw RJ's shop. He had changed the exterior, and the new appearance made her jaw drop.

The large glass windows that faced the street were covered with signs put up by ETRAA. "That's one way to declare your campaign against a whole town," Val muttered as he put his truck in park. They could hardly see into the store.

Jemma was grim. "It's like they're moving in and plopping their asses down wherever they want." In solemn silence, the trio climbed out of the truck and made their way inside. It was busier than usual, which, under normal circumstances, would have made Jemma happy for RJ. Instead, it seemed to have everything to do with the ETRAA. Due to the discounts the association provided, RJ could purchase the name-brand items his customers wanted, and they were buying everything they could get their hands on.

Val mumbled something about making a point and buying bolt cutters that were *not* a name brand. He disappeared into the back of the shop. Jemma and Easter waited near the front door, trying to stay out of the way. They watched RJ as he scanned items and took payments. "He looks like he's in good spirits," Easter murmured.

Jemma nodded. It was true. There was a light in RJ's

eyes. He laughed with the customers, many of whom were longtime residents of the town and old acquaintances or friends. Jemma knew many in Solomon's Cross had gone to neighboring counties to purchase their hardware supplies after what had happened with AJ. "First RJ's wife dies, then his daughters move away, and now his son's become a delinquent," was the kind of thing Jemma had overheard.

She felt sorry for the hardware store owner and for AJ. "I'm glad he's busy again," she told Easter, "even if it's for a reason we don't like." Val appeared a moment later with a new pair of bolt cutters, and they had to wait in line to pay for them.

When it was Val's turn, Jemma realized no one else had come into the store. They were now the only ones there. RJ was weary but in excellent spirits. He laughed as Val handed over the bolt cutters. "This is the second pair, son. What'd you do with the first, lose 'em or break 'em?"

"Lost 'em," Val replied, trying to smile.

"Well, since you are such loyal customers," RJ continued, "we'll just pretend you broke them because they were faulty. These're on the house."

Val had too much pride for that. He took out his wallet and slid several bills across the counter. "No, Mr. Kilmer. It was my fault, and I should pay for them."

RJ just waved a dismissive hand. "No, son. I'll take care of it."

Val gave him a hard look, then leaned over, opened the register, and placed the bills inside. RJ stared for a moment before relenting. He handed Val the cutters, along with his receipt.

"Business doing well, Mr. Kilmer?" Easter ventured.

RJ nodded, and his smile grew wider. "Boomin'." He waved a hand at the signs cluttering up his window. "All because ETRAA helped me out. Good people, I think, no matter what's been said about them on the news."

Jemma, Easter, and Val exchanged disparaging looks. RJ Kilmer, one of the nicest people in town, was wrapped around the slimy finger of whoever was in charge of work on the mountain. "W-well, we're glad to hear it," Easter managed.

RJ leaned forward on the counter, his massive arms taking up almost all the space. "They've got summer internships for teens, ya know. You three might wanna think about joining. I've already looked into it for AJ." He fished around behind the desk and pulled out a pamphlet that he handed over.

Val took it and frowned. "Interesting."

RJ didn't seem to notice Val's dubious reaction. His smile had faded. "Thank you for what you did for AJ. When he came home, I could tell it hadn't gone well, but I don't blame none of ya for it. I thank ya all the same for tryin'."

Easter, their spokesperson, forced another smile. "We were happy to do it, Mr. Kilmer, and we'd be happy to do it again if AJ wants to."

RJ beamed, but then his light faded. He shook his head, sighing. "I'm just not sure what's goin' on with him these days. Since he got back from bein' with y'all, he's gotten worse."

That was interesting. Jemma stepped forward. "What do you mean?"

"Doesn't wanna work or even fix up his car no more,"

RJ responded. "He just sits in his room all day. I'm sure he's not even attending school online, but I ain't got the heart to make him. He's been through so much." His face hardened. "Then again, I'm his father, and I can't let 'im get away with that."

The conversation extinguished RJ's good spirits. Easter smiled again, and it wasn't forced. "It'll all work out in the end, Mr. Kilmer. AJ's going through a rough time, but it won't last forever." She spoke with more confidence than any of them felt.

As they walked away from the counter, Jemma had a feeling that AJ's increasingly worse disposition wasn't just the result of hard things happening to him in everyday life.

Those haints might have found a way to torment him again. As that crossed her mind, she glanced over her shoulder and spied a figure standing in the doorway of RJ's office. AJ glared at the three. He looked thinner and paler than he had been the week before. Jemma stopped short. AJ had heard everything they'd said. AJ's eyes were ice-cold and menacing.

Something else was present in those eyes. Jemma didn't like the look of it.

The three friends exited the store, and once they were underneath a streetlight, Easter asked to see the pamphlet RJ had given Val. Jemma read it over Easter's shoulder. The summer program listed many outdoor activities such as swimming, hiking, canoeing, archery, and camping. It appeared that ETRAA wanted children to go up the mountain for extended periods of time, days or weeks. Future job opportunities in "rural arrangement and planning" were mentioned.

"Whatever the hell that means," Jemma mused. It seemed like another way for the association to get deeper into the pockets of the people of Solomon's Cross and then spread their tentacles elsewhere.

Tomorrow couldn't come fast enough.

CHAPTER NINETEEN

The four determined they would need to approach Kalhoun's Crest in the dark to limit the risk of being seen. Jemma surmised that fewer workers would be present then. "Means colder winds and not being able to see as well," she mumbled as she packed a bag.

"Spending the night at the McCarthys'?" Tad asked when he spied his daughter's overstuffed backpack.

She zipped it shut. "Yep. I'll be back tomorrow." *Hopefully,* she thought. She was glad Tad had asked the question so she could give a simple "yes" and not have to lie.

"Any special plans?" Tad prodded as he leaned casually against the doorframe between the kitchen and the living room. Jemma had just taken some granola bars out of the cupboard and put them in her bag.

Jemma stilled. *Looks like I'm going to have to lie anyway,* she thought with a sinking heart. She turned to her father. "We're going to check on the kids in their neighborhood. The ones that came back from the hospital." That part was the truth. "And then, you know, movies and such."

"Well, have fun," Tad urged.

"Fun" was the last thing Jemma expected to have. Her dad headed toward the couch but turned back, his brow furrowing. "I ran into RJ in town this morning. He seems to be doing a lot better. Said business was booming, thanks to ETRAA. I think I'm going to take the job, Jem. It could do both of us a lot of good."

Jemma nodded and forced a smile. "Whatever you think is best, Dad."

Tad smiled, but it didn't reach his eyes. "You're still not thrilled about it, and I can't see why." He sighed. "But keep your reasons to yourself if you wish."

Jemma didn't reply. All she knew was that they had to clean out the nest of haints tonight, or everything would become a lot worse. She checked her watch and saw that it was 7:30. Val would be here any moment to pick her up. Outside, the sun hung low on the horizon and was blocked by the trees on the mountain, so all Jemma could see was the pink sky. She headed to the door but stopped before she reached it. She suggested, "If you get bored tonight, Dad, you might think about going to the drug store to pick up stuff for the medicine cabinet."

Tad's brows rose. "Running low on some things?"

Jemma listed generic medicines. They weren't running low, but he trusted her enough not to check. She hoped he'd run into Linnea. Jemma still wasn't too keen on her father dating, but if he was going to woo any woman in town, Jemma wanted it to be someone who was level-headed, didn't gossip everyone's ear off, and was her father's age. Besides, Jemma liked Linnea Strang. It was better than having the diner women all over him.

"I don't know, Jemma. I'm pretty tired," he replied as he dragged a hand through his hair. Jemma appraised him. Her father didn't *look* tired.

"Okay, Dad. Sure." She laughed, but she could tell he was holding something back. She didn't bother to pursue the subject.

"Fine. I'll go, Jem. Who knows when I'll be down there next?" Jemma's heart sank. If her father took the new job with the ETRAA, he would be working longer hours, which would leave little time for drug store runs and family nights.

The light honking of Val's horn followed the crunch of his truck's tires on the gravel drive. Jemma bid her father goodnight and practically dove out the front door, barely remembering to close it behind her. She bounded to the truck and found Easter in the back seat. Mama B would take shotgun.

When Val's truck rattled up to Gran's Rest, the old woman awaited them on the front porch.

"Still not sure bringing her is a good idea," Val murmured as he caught sight of Mama B's overstuffed bag, a hat that looked like it had been dug out of an ancient tomb on the other side of the world, and long, dusty robes. If she hadn't seemed like a witch before, she did now. Jemma knew the robes and hat had pressed-flower charms sewed into them to keep the old woman warm and surefooted.

"She's a lot more capable than she looks," Jemma commented. "And she might not be fast, but she'll endure longer than we will."

Val's doubtful look deepened.

Easter gave his shoulder a playful punch. "When you're as powerful as Mama B, we'll consider not bringing her along."

Val mumbled something under his breath as the old woman waddled over and tossed her things into the bed. Jemma hopped out to help her into the passenger seat. "Haven't ridden in one of these things in years!" Mama B announced as she leaned back. Easter had to show her how to fasten the seatbelt, which Mama B denied needing.

"Trust me," the older McCarthy encouraged. "You will want it." In his eagerness to get back to Cider Creek and get the affair over with, Val had driven to Jemma's house with his hands clenched around the steering wheel and his eyes a little wild.

"Drink this before we go, son," Mama B suggested as she handed Val a teacup. Jemma hadn't seen the woman bring it into the truck with her, but there it was. Val raised a brow but obeyed. Jemma assumed the drink would have a calming effect on their driver.

She was proved correct when he pulled out of the drive at Gran's Rest. He was much calmer. Mama B took the teacup back, and it vanished.

Jemma wanted to live long enough to learn how to do that. She exchanged looks with Easter. Neither of the girls in the back seat said a word until they were off the mountain and in Cider Creek.

They made short stops at the homes of the sick children. Mama B had brought them more of her brew. Some of the parents were thankful for her help, while others were wary. Some weren't home. The stops took about forty-five minutes, during which Jemma kept urging them to get to the bottom of Kalhoun's Crest before it was dark.

They reached the part of the neighborhood where the creek went up the mountain at long last. The shadows were long, thick, and blue. "Shit," Val muttered as he pulled his truck to a stop.

Jemma leaned around him to see what had caused his dismay. She uttered the same word. The path up the mountain before them was barricaded, and a "no trespassing" sign was posted on a fence that looked like it had just been erected. Concertina defended the top of it.

"Guess we won't be going that way," Easter muttered. The disappointment and disdain in her voice matched Jemma's feelings.

Val swiveled to face Mama B and Jemma. "Can't the two of you brew up a spell to bring it down? Or we could use the tools we brought. We have to—" He was cut off by Easter pointing ahead. Everyone looked in the direction of her finger and found there were two figures walking down the mountain.

"Guards," Jemma heard herself say. "Makes sense. It's dark, so they're probably coming down for the night shift."

"Well, what the hell are we going to do?" Val demanded, his agitation clear.

"First, let's get this truck under cover," Jemma suggested. Val was still rattled but fired it up. While they drove back to his house, Jemma formed a plan. "We can go around the mountain to the neighboring town. Think about it; they've put up the fence here because the guards saw us run down this way. They won't suspect intruders on the other side."

"Could be true," Easter responded. "It's worth a try, but we have to go *now*. We've wasted enough time already." Mama B and Val agreed, and they set off. Easter had to pull out her GPS to give him directions. She led Val into a state park, which they had to enter without being seen since it closed at dusk. No one manned the guard shack, so they drove through without being stopped.

"If anyone approaches us," Easter said, "we'll tell them we're campers who came in too late." The path up the mountain was much narrower on this side and was surrounded by dense stands of pine trees and thorn bushes. They would have to be much more careful going up this way.

They flicked on their flashlights as they began the climb. This side of the mountain wasn't as steep, and they did not have to contend with the rushing water of Cider Creek.

They would, however, have to find the water source once they reached the top of Kalhoun's Crest. Otherwise, finding the cave would prove difficult. Jemma was grateful for the charms sewn into their clothing as they hiked up the mountain. A chill wind whistled through the trees but didn't bother the travelers since the charms kept them warm, as well as keeping them from tripping over jutting roots and loose rocks.

The last light of day leaked between the trees as they climbed. The sun sank at last, and they were swathed in darkness. All that could be heard for several minutes was the heavy breathing of the four hikers, the wind in the trees, and their boots crunching over fallen leaves and pine needles. The last snowfall had yet to melt and added to the sound. Instead of softening the ground, it had hardened it.

Mama B was largely silent. Val and Easter made occasional remarks about how narrow the path was, or that they hoped the moonlight wouldn't be too bright at the top tonight, and how they hoped they would not run into any bears. Jemma quietly agreed.

Mama B kept a close eye trained on their surroundings. Jemma came up beside her. "What's wrong?" She could tell the old woman was troubled. Did it have anything to do with her past? Mama B hadn't been up here since the last sealing.

Even though Jemma hadn't been there, she felt like she had. She didn't like thinking about what had happened to Vesna's children while she, Josephine, and Mama B were here. It made her think about her father. She just hoped he wasn't at risk while she was gone.

Mama B shone her light around. "Look, Jemma. See how bare it is here?" The higher they climbed, the more desolate the land was. The trees were sparser, and no other life made itself known. The owls and insects that would have made themselves known near Cider Creek were absent here.

Jemma swallowed hard. She didn't need Mama B to explain why it was like this. "Can't blame the winter," the old woman muttered. The nest of haints had sucked the life out of this land, their efforts enhanced by ETRAA's meddling. "Life was driven out of here," Mama B added.

Easter came up beside them. "They haven't driven out all the life on the other side of the mountain. Not yet."

"But it's leaving," Jemma added. Mama B and Easter

nodded. Val was the only one who didn't seem to sense it. Jemma was glad. Val didn't have to deal with nausea. Mama B had it the worst. It was a dark undercurrent pulling at her magic.

The pull on Jemma's magic was lighter but still present.

To Easter, it was like catching glimpses of fleeting shadows but nothing else.

Jemma was immersed in her thoughts until she heard twigs cracking behind her. She whirled, but in the darkness, she couldn't see anything. She shone her flashlight on the path behind her. Still nothing. Must have been a squirrel. Still, she felt as though she were being watched. She wondered if she heard someone breathing, but the wind erased the sound.

She whirled at a sound from up ahead. A low, alarmed cry left Val's lips, and the thud when he fell brought all three women to his side. "Tripped on a damn rock," he muttered as he got back to his feet. Jemma's gaze swept the area. They had reached the top of the mountain, and the land was clear in front of them. Fallen stones were strewn about the area, and Val had tripped over one of those.

"Looks like this was once a stone wall," Easter murmured.

The four stepped carefully past the stones. They kept their flashlights aimed low. Up here, with the half-moon providing light, they could see better.

They walked on for some time, then Jemma's breath caught in her throat. Everyone stopped dead. "What the hell is that?" Val asked, his voice trembling.

Ahead, spirals of iron rose into the air. They looked like jagged claws.

"Looks like an old cast iron gate," Jemma mused. She stepped forward and skimmed her fingertips over the rusted metal, confirming her theory. She also saw iron shards strewn around. This had been a gated estate. She had a good idea of where they were, but she was afraid to say it out loud.

Mama B, on the other hand, was not afraid. "This is what remains of Mrs. Willow's estate." The old woman released a long, shuddering sigh. "My sisters and I suspected the opening was here. We were never able to investigate, though, and after fixing the seal, we thought our work was finished."

Jemma tried to make out the distant house, but in the dark, with trees shrouding the entrance to the estate, none of them could see far. Val shivered. "I'm not sure I wanna go near it anyway."

"Me neither," Easter agreed.

Jemma suppressed a shudder of her own.

They decided to bypass the estate. Beyond it, they would reach ETRAA's worksite. Mama B lingered behind long enough for Jemma to turn back. The old woman had bent over and was shining her flashlight on the ground. Jemma stooped to see what she was examining. In the flattened grass, dark sigils had been pressed into the earth.

"The haints were here but moved on," Mama B explained grimly. "They had no more life to torment here, so they went to the other side."

That made sense. It was only a matter of time before the mountain was bare and dead.

The wind coursed around them harder up here, and their clothes did very little to keep them warm. "They've beefed up security, that's for sure," Val said moments later when they glimpsed lights in the distance. He lifted his binoculars and looked at that area. "I see six guards around the perimeter, a couple vans, and…" He paused. "Shit, they've got ETRAA reps up here. I don't see any of the workmen, though."

"They'll be here in the morning," Jemma responded.

"There are more cameras, too," Val stated a second later.

Jemma's stomach knotted. This was going to be much harder than they had thought. Six guards didn't seem like much, but that was only on this side of the worksite. How many more were in vans or on the other side?

To reach the cave, they would have to veer to the right and go downslope. That is, if they were where they thought they were. They would have to pass a van, a least one camera, and two guards at the minimum to get into the woods on the other side of the fenced area.

With bated breath, the four crept forward until they were concealed behind some bushes. Easter's alarmed face alerted them to a figure pacing inside the fence a few yards away. Mama B had sensed his presence and stopped short. They could see he was one of the suited ETRAA reps, though not Mr. Stomphord.

In a nasal voice, he spoke into his phone. Jemma couldn't hear everything he said, but she caught sentences here and there. "Damn construction work is too slow. Don't know how to hurry the fuck up." The man scoffed. "Everything's rundown. Their single diner, for one. And their hardware store is the most poorly supplied place I've ever seen."

Jemma bristled. *Then go bother some other fucking town,*

she thought. She wanted to take her father's bat and bash the concept into the man's brain.

"This one's special, though, I tell ya," the rep continued. "Town just don't know it yet, and we're doin' everything we can to make sure they don't find out." He turned against the wind and lit a cigarette as whoever was on the other end replied.

Jemma froze. Did these men know something about the mountain and its magic? While his back was turned, the four scuttled away from the bushes and veered to the right, where they found two guards leaning against posts. They spoke to one another in low tones. Once in a while, one of them would laugh.

Jemma stilled when one of them muttered, "...them damn teenagers we chased all the way down. Strangest thing, I tell ya. Like gettin' stung by bees all of a sudden. I didn't even see the hive."

"Gotta be careful in these mountains." The other guard laughed. "Nature will eat ya."

A hand shook Jemma's shoulder. She looked at Val. He pointed to the right, and she saw that the fencing had been expanded and went down the slope. *Great.* This meant they would have to cut through the fence to get in and then cut again to get out near the cave.

Quickly, they made a plan, and Mama B crept forward, her hands in front of her. The guards saw her but didn't have time to react before her net caught them. Then they had to be kept quiet. Jemma and Easter bolted forward and leapt on the fallen guards. With cloths soaked in a brew Mama B had made, they covered the men's faces. Seconds later, both men fell asleep. It would keep them out for a couple of hours and not do them any harm.

While this was happening, Val had disabled the security camera, hoping no one inside saw the guards suddenly fall to the ground. Then he moved to the fence and cut a hole.

Jemma's heart thundered as she crawled through after Val. Easter was behind her, and Mama B brought up the rear. They scrambled to their feet and darted behind an outhouse on the edge of the fenced area. They had to squeeze together to fit behind it. Here, there were no lights or cameras. If they moved down the fence a little, they could cut another hole and get out. Trouble was, there were lights along the rest of the fence.

If only we could set up a distraction elsewhere, Jemma thought.

Her wish came true.

A second later, an alarm blared. Light poured out of the building in the center. Heavy boots pounded on the ground. She froze. Had they been seen? Her heart thundered so loud, the sound almost drowned out the blaring of the alarm. The lights around the site had gone from bright white to red.

A cry nearly sprang from Easter's lips. Anticipating it, Val slapped a hand over her mouth. Mama B's eyes narrowed. The guards were not coming for them; they were running in the opposite direction. They were chasing something. *Someone.*

The figure was tall. Whoever it was, he fled toward the fence and clambered up its side, but it was too late. Armed guards took him down.

AJ Kilmer! Jemma realized. How the hell had he gotten

up here? The realization felt like ice sliding down her bones. *He followed us! How the hell did I miss it?* The sounds she had thought she made up *had* been someone following them. How had he gotten in? He had run, but maybe, just maybe, he had wanted to be caught.

It was clear that he didn't know what he was doing. He wasn't in his right mind. AJ wasn't acting of his own volition.

The guards yanked AJ off the fence and threw him to the ground. One pulled a gun. *No!* Jemma wanted to scream. Were they going to put a bullet in AJ's head?

More figures emerged from the building, and Jemma's eyes snagged on one she recognized. The ETRAA rep they had met before, Mr. Stomphord, still bore bruises and bandages from Val's attack. He lifted a hand, signaling for the guards to stop. One of them hauled the young man to his feet.

"Explain," Mr. Stomphord demanded.

Jemma had to listen hard to catch AJ's response.

"I was only coming up here to let y'all know I followed a group up here who came to mess things up." He put his hands up in defense. "I wasn't with them. Just followin', I swear. I'm not tryin' to cause any trouble."

Stomphord didn't buy it. "Then why run when we saw you?"

AJ trembled. "I saw guns. The alarm sounded. I didn't know what to do."

The ETRAA rep sighed. "I suppose seeing armed men would make anyone run. Sorry about that, young man. Thank you for the warning, but you shouldn't be up here."

She couldn't believe AJ Kilmer was selling them out. He

couldn't be in his right mind. Something had a hold of him. Unless they got rid of those haints, he would work against them. That didn't mean they had to forsake him, though.

When she turned to the others, she saw Easter swallow in fear. Val's face hardened as he watched his old friend give them away. Mama B looked grim.

"Take him inside to be questioned," Stomphord ordered two of the guards. AJ was snatched by his arms and hauled off, protesting and squirming. Jemma had a feeling they wouldn't just be asking him questions in there. "Take him to the Contact!" Stomphord shouted after them.

The Contact? Who the hell was that? Jemma felt sick. She was inclined to believe this "Contact" was someone higher up with a lot more power and authority. Her heart sank when the guards began searching the perimeter. They would be found in moments.

And our mission just got more complicated, was her next despairing thought. Not only did they have to bury the nest of haints and harden the mountain while guards were looking for them, but they also had to rescue the person who had sold them out.

CHAPTER TWENTY

Their only option was to run.

They couldn't risk darting down the fence to where they would have a shot at reaching the cave. They would have to crawl through the fence behind them and flee.

Val was already at work, but his hands shook as he attempted to cut through the fence. The guards' shouts rang through the night. Their booted feet pounded on the ground. Jemma wanted to scream at Val to hurry, but her throat was too tight, and Val was working as fast as he could.

Val scrambled through the hole, which was just large enough for him to fit through. Easter went next. Val continued cutting from the other side. Jemma slipped through, leaving pieces of her clothes and strands of her hair on the fence.

A guard called, "Over here! I see them!" Jemma whirled. Mama B was almost through. The beam of a flashlight swept over the four of them, then shone in Jemma's face.

She couldn't see the face of the guard who held it. He

shouted again. "Four of 'em! I found four of 'em, just like the boy said!"

"Run!" Jemma screamed. She yanked Mama B to her feet, and they tore down the hillside, narrowly avoiding trees and stumbling over loose stones and roots. There was no clear path, and branches and thorns tore at their clothes as they whipped past. The slope was steep, but Jemma hurtled down it. She wasn't sure she could stop herself from colliding with a tree when she reached the bottom.

Pain lanced through her limbs. Scratches from the fence and branches covered her face. No longer did she feel cold, though. There was still a bitter wind ripping through the branches above her, but their flight had warmed her up. Sweat glided down her brow and back. They had been seen, and she could hear the guards pursuing them.

They had bought time since the guards could not go through the fence. They'd had to go around the enclosure and find a way into the woods. Now they were staggering down the hill, the beams of their flashlights scanning the ground.

A low cry rang out ahead of Jemma. Easter had tripped and fallen on her face. Without asking her friend if she was okay, she yanked the girl up by her arm and held on for dear life. They continued to run. Val was ahead of them, bolting like a rabbit out of the road before a car runs it over.

The bottom of the slope was in sight, and darkness loomed ahead of them. Jemma did not know where they were or how they could figure out how to get out of this mess of trees and brambles. It wouldn't matter if they were dead or taken captive.

Mama B was behind the three teenagers. Jemma glanced back and saw that the woman was moving at a much slower pace. She *was* very old. Of all of them, Mama B could handle her captors the best, but her current pace made her the least likely to get away.

Jemma slowed and considered turning back to help Mama B, but when the old woman turned toward the guards pursuing them, Jemma saw that she was laying traps. She was pulling ingredients out of her bag and mixing them.

"Easter, help me," she hissed. Her friend held a light as Jemma worked. How Mama B could tell what she was doing in the dark, Jemma did not know. Years of experience, she guessed. Finally, Jemma had a few traps ready. She threw them on the ground, uttering the incantations Mama B had taught her.

Mama B finished laying her own and headed toward them. Jemma and Easter started running as well. Val was ahead of them. If she, Easter, and Mama B were captured, Val had a chance to get away. He could go for help.

Behind her, she heard the guards shouting, but that changed to alarmed screams as they encountered the magical traps Mama B had laid. Nets sprang up and snared their pursuers. A cloud of bees rose up from nowhere. The guards were swarmed and stung. Jemma jolted when she heard gunshots and assumed the weapons had gone off by accident when their bearers encountered the traps.

Still, her blood ran cold, and her pace increased. Easter had reached the bottom of the slope but was still running.

She couldn't slow down after the steep descent. The gunshots had apparently missed all four of them. Jemma could hardly believe this was happening—armed men were chasing three teenagers and an old woman, two of whom were witches. Their magic had given them more of an advantage than she could have hoped.

Another sound filled Jemma with equal amounts of relief and dread. The rushing water relieved her because it meant they were close to the cave. She felt dread because she knew they hadn't yet dealt with the worst of their enemies. The hardest part was still to come. As she realized this, the overwhelming, nauseating sensation of dark magic hit Jemma. She kept running but staggered and felt like she might pass out.

The cave was ahead.

Val had reached it and halted. Easter was right behind him. Jemma was third, with Mama B only a few yards behind her. She was a spry old bird.

As Jemma reached the dark opening, the miasma of the foul magic within intensified. She had to go in, but that was the last thing she wanted to do. "Jemma!" came Val's cry. She spun and saw three figures coming down the slope opposite them from where Cider Creek flowed down the mountain. There were two more guards and a suited figure—Stomphord. The ETRAA rep had a wild look in his eyes, and he thrashed toward them as if he had lost control of himself.

Val and Easter sprang into action. Val raised the bat, which glowed with the blue magic of the sigils Mama B had imbued it with. He hit the first guard running at him across the chest, and the man fell to the ground. The sigils stunned the guard and knocked him out. Seeing his fallen comrade, the second guard shot at them. Jemma screamed at Val, and the young man ducked. The bullet whizzed over his head and pinged off the cave's entrance where the rock curved over Jemma's head.

Val bolted forward and swung the bat at the guard's knees. The wood hit the man's shins, and he staggered back with a cry of pain. That gave Val the opening he needed. He hit him across the stomach to knock the wind out of him.

Easter had run up the opposite side of the creek toward Stomphord. She leveled her family's hunting rifle at him and yelled, "*Stop!*" For a moment, they thought the man might run past her. The haints must have taken control of his mind. The man had let it happen, and for that, Jemma would blame him, but his current actions were not his fault.

Stomphord skidded to a halt. Easter commanded him to sit down on a rock beside the creek. Val jumped over to them since the guards were no longer a threat—for now, anyway. They had to work fast. Mama B finally reached the cave's entrance.

THE ETRAA rep let out a low cackle, which skittered along the ground to Jemma. It penetrated her bones, filling her with an icy sensation. It wasn't just the man laughing; whatever was inside of him that had taken control of his every movement. The man twitched and lifted a shaking finger. He laughed maniacally as he pointed at the cave. "You'll never save him!"

Save who? Jemma whirled and clicked on her flashlight. She had sensed something dark and horrid stirring, and now she saw it. She froze, horror sluicing through her body.

Val, Easter, and Mama B also peered in. Each saw something different. To Val, it was just a black shape like shadows gathered together. Easter saw the same dark presence, but it was writhing and teeming with life. Where Val might have thought his eyes were being tricked, Easter saw a form. She knew she was not being deceived.

Jemma and Mama B saw the same thing: a creature with a slimy black body. It might have once been a woman, but if so, she'd succumbed to the dangerous side of the Art. Now it was a distorted thing with five heads and twice as many arms with long fingers and longer fingernails. One head was larger than the rest, and long strings of oily black hair hung from it.

The dark monstrosity had crawled out of the poisoned depths of the earth. Was this what Mama B and her holler witch sisters encountered all those years ago? Was this what they were keeping Solomon's Cross from being consumed by?

All the heads were bent over something in the center of the cave. What lay there let out an ear-wrenching scream, and a white hand flashed out.

AJ!

Jemma's mind spun. How had they gotten him here so fast? The flight down the hill to the bank of the creek hadn't seemed so far, but it had been. She could see that now. And what about AJ being taken in for questioning? Was the haint the "Contact" Stomphord had spoken of? Did this mean the men operating on the mountain knew what lay beneath it, or at least about the dark spirits in the cave?

The haints had coalesced into a hive mind. "My name is Legion, for we are many," Jemma heard Mama B say in a breathless voice. The old witch's eyes were filled with horror as she took in what was happening before her. Mama B was quoting something, but Jemma didn't know what.

The old woman snapped out of her daze. "Hurry, Jemma! Help me!"

They hit the haints with magical herbs to drain its power. Jemma tossed some in and heard the haints hiss when they touched their flesh. Then they spread herbs over the ground. The creatures shrieked and withdrew into the cave. Going into the cave meant walking knee-deep into the part of the stream that flowed out of it. The water was ice-cold. Jemma gritted her teeth and kept walking. Now that they had herbs in the water and on the ground within the cave, Mama B began marking the walls with sigils and wards.

"Do this on the other side!" she called to Jemma.

Jemma leapt out of the water and went to the wall opposite where Mama B worked. Her fingers and lips trembled as she attempted to get the right words out and the proper symbols on the wall. She had to spread herbs from her jar on the damp stone. Gradually, the sigils glowed into life, deep blue filling the cracks in the wall.

The haints shrieked in agony as the light streamed down on it. It shrank back from the body it had been feasting on. AJ collapsed. Jemma could see claw marks on both sides of his face. His face was pale, his body frail and weak.

Mama B ventured closer to the haint, which hissed as the witch approached it. It was like a wounded animal but far larger and more frightening. Its fingernails, dripping with some oozing substance, could cut Mama B in half.

"No!" Jemma choked out, stumbling toward the old woman. Mama B kept going. She put her hands before her, and tendrils of light drifted from her fingertips. She uttered the words for sealing. The haint writhed as if it already felt the pain sealing would cause it.

Mama B drew on the power in the earth around them. There wasn't much. It was cold and barren, both from the winter and the dark spirits roaming these parts.

Her eyes went back to AJ, and she sensed something stronger and more bitter. The wounds inflicted upon him went deeper than body and mind. They reached his very soul, tugging it apart and unraveling him. His body was still here, but if Jemma could look inside it, she thought she would see only the traces of his shredded spirit. Whatever hope AJ had had in his young life had been taken from him.

Deep pity welled up. Jemma felt like her heart might crack. The darkness within AJ's body left his fallen form and reached for her. Her mind clouded, and her head became heavy. She swayed and had to brace herself on the cave's wall to keep from passing out. *Stay focused*, she told herself. That was difficult since lights and then shapes filled her mind. *Memories*, she realized. *But not mine.*

First, the pale face of a woman. Jemma was certain she was dead. The woman bore a striking resemblance to AJ. She wasn't seeing her own memories, but…

His. I'm seeing what they took from his mind!

Other images followed. She glimpsed a gravestone with the words Kilmer and beloved wife and mother. She could not see the years. She saw broken bottles. A wrecked bedroom. A blazing fire and heavy smoke in the air. She saw a series of tragedies from AJ Kilmer's young life. Her heart pounded. *Why am I seeing this?*

It was the magic. Something about it and being a witch allowed her to see it. She could see—and feel—other people's pain. She hated it. *Make it stop!*

On pure instinct, she reached into her bag and pulled out a bottle that, when shaken, created a confusing mist. When inhaled, it caused short-term confusion. If drunk, it blotted out memories. *The least I can do is save him from remembering this,* she thought as she stumbled toward him. She landed beside him on her knees and pulled his head up, then forced his mouth open. He was limp, and it took all her effort to pour the liquid into his mouth.

His pain-wracked expression changed, and the lines on his face softened.

She hoped she had done the right thing.

CHAPTER TWENTY-ONE

AJ slumped against Jemma. She looked up at the sound of a straining cry and found Mama B's hands braced in front of her as if against an invisible wall. Looking closer, Jemma could see a shimmering veil of translucent magic—Mama B's magic. It wavered like a candle going out in a strong wind. The old woman's magic was weakening. Mama B would not be able to stand against the nest of haints for much longer.

An agonized look came over Mama B's face. The veins on her temples pulsed. She gritted her teeth and cried out against the dark magic reaching out for her. Mama B was strong and powerful, but this haint had had years to grow strong on this mountain while the old woman—out of fear and regret—had stayed away from it.

Jemma scrambled to her feet, determined that she would not regret anything that happened this night. Faces filled her mind. Her father. Easter and Val. Even AJ. For them, she needed to do this. For Mama B and herself. For Solomon's Cross. It didn't feel like home to her yet, but it was still worth saving. This creature would grow stronger if it was allowed to roam free.

Jemma straightened and summoned her power. It welled up within her like the warm current of a river rushing through her veins. Her skin glowed. She gathered the light in her hands, tendrils at first, then a globe like a small sun between her palms. With a cry, she threw the globe at the wall of dark magic. It went through and hit the many-headed haint like a cannonball. The creature slammed into the wall, and the cave shook.

Cords of golden light clamped down on its arms, hands, and heads. The creature shrieked and thrashed. Jemma heard the sizzle of her magic on its slimy flesh. The creature was bound, but sealing it would require even more focus. If it slipped for even a second, the haint would break the net of power, and Jemma's magic would unravel. Starting over would do her in.

She fought the nausea that came from being in the haint's presence. *Pull from the earth around you,* she told herself, repeating the instructions Mama B had given her. It was more difficult here than in her training. The mountain she'd trained on was full of life. Here, the earth was tainted with the haint's foul magic.

"Hold it in place!" Mama B shouted.

Jemma gritted her teeth and pushed. She imagined her power was a wall of light, straining against a wall of dark shadows that reached out to snatch her and dig its claws into her mind and soul as it had done to AJ. For a better life for him, for herself, and her friends, she would complete this. There was no other option.

At long last, Jemma felt the wall of darkness weaken.

Give in. The haint shrieked again, and the sound ricocheted off the cave's walls. Then the creature disappeared, leaving only a pool of oozing liquid and its foul stench.

Jemma took a second to suck in a breath, then rushed over to the old woman and helped her stand. She wasn't sure how she did it since she felt like she would collapse. "We have to get out of this cave and far away from here," she managed to tell Mama B.

A commotion at the cave's entrance made her halt. She turned in time to see a wild figure running toward the mouth of the cave where Val stood. *Stomphord!* Jemma realized. The haint might be gone, but the man still had a crazed look in his eyes. Its magic must still linger in his body.

"Val!" Jemma screamed, but it was too late. Stomphord lifted a short log and smacked Val's head. The teenage boy groaned and collapsed, dropping the bat. The ETRAA rep snatched it, and a spike of fear went through Jemma.

Given the lingering magic in his body and the madness in his eyes, she wasn't sure what he would do with it. What he was *capable* of doing. This man had apparently been under the haint's control for a long time. Months, maybe even years. The operation on the mountain, Jemma realized, had been planned for a while.

Val moaned from the cave's floor. He wasn't unconscious. Jemma started forward, but she didn't need to. Easter ran toward the cave, holding her family's rifle. Stomphord heard her and turned, bat in hand. A snarl ripped from his lips. Easter leveled the gun and fired once, then again. A stunned look came over her face. She had just shot a man. Perhaps killed him. She had acted to save her brother, but she had done something she would never have done if they weren't in this situation.

To Jemma's horror, the ETRAA rep staggered but did not fall. The magic within him must be keeping him on his feet. Did that mean she *hadn't* sealed the haint? Stomphord advanced toward Easter. The girl was rooted to the ground in her shock and panic. Val, however, managed to get to his feet and lunge at the man. He pulled the bat from Stomphord's grip and swung it into the man's head. The heavy *thwack* filled the air, and at last, with the magic imbuing the bat against the lingering darkness within Stomphord's body, he went down.

Out for good, Jemma hoped. She rushed forward with Mama B hanging onto her and got the old woman out of the cave. Val caught Mama B and helped her up the creek's bank. Jemma stayed behind. "Come on!" Val shouted.

"AJ!" she cried instead. She couldn't leave him behind. She had to drag his unconscious but hopefully living body out of the cave.

Jemma was about to turn back when an alarmed look on Easter's face made her stop. The girl looked up the bank and the slope of the mountain. She heard or saw something Jemma could not. After listening hard, Jemma knew. The shouts of guards filled the air. Their boots crunched on the slope. The guards had torn out of the traps Mama B had laid for them, and they had been joined by more. Six came into view.

Shit, shit, shit. What was she supposed to do now? Mama B sagged against the cave's entrance. Val's bat and Easter's rifle had saved them, but those would not take out six armed guards.

This is it. We're going to die.

This wasn't the worst feeling. As this thought came to Jemma's mind, she sensed shadows stirring behind her. She turned to see that the oozing black liquid on the floor of the cave was taking form again. From the slick, damp walls protruded a hand. Claws scraped the stone. An agonized shriek rang out. More hands dug out, then a head. Then several more. Jemma stumbled back, leaving AJ's body exposed. Her heart pounded. *No, no, no!*

She hadn't sealed the nest of haints after all. The creature, being clever, had simply retreated, making it look like it was sealed when it was not. The guards had reached the bank. Easter and Val were in danger of being shot. Jemma and Mama B would be next. What would the guards do with AJ after they were dead?

Jemma whirled back to the creature, which was snarling. Nausea hit her again. *Kill two birds with one stone,* was the thought that came to her mind. *Pit your enemies against one another.* She just had to work fast.

She summoned her power once more, but instead of pushing the haint away, she pulled it forward and *twisted* to warp it. Crying out as sweat slicked her body, Jemma sent it surging out of the cave toward the guards. The wall of shadow and terror flew out of the cave, and the guards fled.

Jemma thought the haint would pursue them, but once outside the cave, it wavered. Hesitated. Then turned back to her.

Panic filled Jemma's mind. The haint wouldn't leave the cave. Here, it could keep its power. It needed to stay close to the earth it had come out of until it was stronger. That meant…

It was going to try to possess her. The thought made her recoil. *She* could give it the power it needed, not the guards. It wanted *her*, not them.

"Wards!" Mama B shouted. "Use your wards!" She stepped up beside the girl and lifted her hands once more. Jemma did the same, straining to put up a wall of magic. Outside the cave, the haint wouldn't be able to live for long. It had nowhere else to go. They had to cut it off from its sources of power—the cave and them.

"You won't get us!" Jemma shouted as she pushed. The haint thrashed against their wards, trying to break through it. The longer it struggled, the weaker it became. She had to endure.

She hoped Easter and Val had had the sense to get far away from the many-headed creature before it turned on them in a last desperate attempt to steal power. The thought sent fear spiking through her. The haint might be able to sense the power within Easter and try to possess her. One of its kind had done so and become stronger by pulling the life out of Easter. Jemma was determined not to let it happen again.

The haint screamed, then dissolved into thin wisps of black smoke as the last of its strength beat against Jemma and Mama B's hardened wards. "Now!" Mama B cried. They let the wards drop but did not release their power. They sent their light plunging toward the smoke and drove it into the earth, sealing it for good.

One last step. They needed the mountain, the earth, and everything around them to work for them. *Become one with your surroundings,* Mama B had instructed her. It had been the first lesson Jemma had been taught. The same was true for Mama B and all the holler witches who had come before her. That truth had been passed down from witch to witch, so things like the binding and the sealing could be done.

Jemma flung out her arms and pleaded with the mountain. "Remember your strength!" she called. "Fulfill your old oaths!"

The mountain's response came almost at once. Kalhoun's Crest shuddered. Its response was eager but violent. She heard a crash behind her, and when she turned, she saw the cave collapse. Stones fell around the body she had left behind.

"No!" She let go of Mama B, who she had clutched for support, and sprang toward AJ. She put her hands under his arms and attempted to drag him, but he was heavy, and she had used up most of her energy while sealing the haint. She groaned as she tried to pull him. "Help!" she managed to yell.

Val was there in a moment despite the bleeding bump on the side of his head. He helped her haul the unconscious AJ off the ground, and each of them placed an arm over their shoulders. Heavy stones fell around them. They had to move fast, or the cave would bury them.

They reached the entrance just as the ceiling hit the floor. Stomphord still lay outside. He had come to and was seizing and jerking and shriveling into a husk.

The last of his humanity would thank her for letting him go. His last cry filled the air before rocks poured out of the cave entrance and buried him.

Jemma stood panting, with AJ leaning against her. The mountain had fulfilled its ancient oath. Jemma just hoped the cave's collapse meant the entrance was sealed forever. The rest of the mountain would need to be warded, but there was no immediate danger. They had to get off this mountain and take AJ to a hospital.

CHAPTER TWENTY-TWO

For a moment, Jemma, Mama B, Easter, and Val just stared at one another in disbelief. The earthquake continued, closing the shafts drilled by ETRAA. The construction workers were out of a job. *Oh, well,* she thought. *It was for the best.*

At last, the shaking of the mountain ceased, and the four could hear themselves panting, the wind whistling above them, and the quiet rushing of the creek. Jemma noticed that the sky had changed from dark blue to a soft gray. She checked her watch. "Shit," she murmured. It was 4:30 in the morning. They had been out all night, but it didn't feel like it. Time felt slow and fast all at once.

Jemma's companions appeared worn almost beyond recognition. All were covered in blood from scrapes and cuts, as well as dirt and bruises. Mama B and Jemma were smeared with black slime from the haint.

Jemma couldn't believe it. They had done it. They had sealed the mountain. She still felt defeated, though. The creature had been far smarter than the boo hag she had dealt with months ago. She shivered. The charms sewn into their clothes had either torn off or worn out. It was much colder.

Jemma wondered if this was how Vesna, Josephine, and Mama B had felt when they dealt with the haints. One look at Mama B's troubled eyes told Jemma the truth. Memories haunted the old woman. Mama B shook her head in disbelief. "It wasn't as hard last time." She sounded breathless. "Then again, I was younger. Three full-blown witches working together did the trick."

Still, they had done it—a woman who had been a witch for decades and a teenage girl who had only been training for a few months.

Jemma came out of her daze when a groan from right beside her reached her ear. AJ, whom she and Val were still holding up, was coming to. He needed medical attention.

As Jemma had that thought, the group heard and saw police vehicles approaching on the road that ran parallel to the stream. All the group had to do was hike a short distance through the trees, and they would reach the road. The flashing red and blue lights cast everything in a strange glow. The sirens blared.

"Let's go," Jemma told the others. It would be better to meet the police and control the story instead of running away. The guards who had escaped had run into the officers. Jemma just hoped the police would listen to her and Val and Easter and Mama B.

It would help that Mama B had known the sheriff since he was born. She shook her head; she was trying to be optimistic. She had just dealt with an ancient, powerful magical creature. The police from Solomon's Cross would be much easier to handle.

As they approached the road, she tried to shape the story. They couldn't say a word about magic or haints. They broke through the trees. Easter supported Mama B, while Jemma and Val continued helping AJ. He won't remember anything, Jemma reminded herself. Thanks to the mist, he wouldn't be able to tell his side of the story. Disoriented and confused, AJ moaned as they carried him to the road.

The sheriff stepped out of his vehicle. There were two other cruisers, and two officers emerged from each a moment later. The sheriff's eyes widened at the sight of an old woman and four teenagers. "What in tarnation is going on here?" he demanded, eyes roaming from Jemma and Val as they held AJ to Easter and Mama B as they hobbled forward.

Mama B glowered at the sheriff. "Can't you see we need medical care?"

The old woman didn't want any medical care she couldn't provide herself. She was covering for them, giving them time. AJ, on the other hand, did need medical attention, and it didn't seem like they would be going to Gran's Rest anytime soon. Besides, Mama B was too exhausted to minister to him.

The sheriff faltered as he tried to come up with a response. His frown passed over the teenagers. "What in hell happened to him?" He gestured at AJ.

"Hit his head," Val answered quickly. He paused as the sheriff's brows rose in question. "Real bad."

The sheriff sighed. "All right. You kids scared off the

guards up here. Can't see how, but I've never seen a grown man so scared." He shook his head and sighed again. "Come on. Let's get all y'all down to the station for questioning." Jemma was relieved to have more time to formulate their story. AJ was placed in one cruiser, Mama B and Val in the next, and Jemma and Easter in the third with one of the deputies.

The ride down the mountain and through Cider Creek went by in a blur. Jemma sat in the back of the cruiser in a daze. Never had she imagined that she would be escorted to a police station at five in the morning. Easter reached for Jemma's hand and squeezed it. "What you did back there…" Her voice trembled, and she couldn't finish her sentence.

Jemma nodded and returned the squeeze. "You too."

An ache welled up in Jemma's chest. She was glad to have the friends she did. She knew she couldn't have saved anyone or anything alone. Everything caught up to her, and tears flooded her eyes. The police station came into view, and with a hasty swipe of her hand, she wiped them away. She then realized how filthy she was and how bad she smelled. The last thing she wanted was to be questioned by the police.

A bath, a meal, and her bed sounded much better.

That was going to have to wait, though. The officers escorted the girls inside, where they saw AJ with an officer. He would be questioned later. They would think AJ was crazier than ever and might even put him back in the mental institution. The kind of help he needed would not be given to him there. That would just worsen his condition. Jemma would talk to RJ about it and convince him to keep his son home without telling him why.

The sheriff turned to question the remaining trespassers. His mouth opened, but before he could get a word out, Mama B wagged a finger at him. "I can do whatever I want. You can't hold me here."

The sheriff sighed. Having dealt with Mama B's antics before, he seemed exhausted by the whole ordeal. He put his hands up in defense. "It doesn't matter, Mama B. Trespassing is trespassing."

She folded her arms across her chest. "Well, you don't need to be askin' any of us questions."

The sheriff's eyes moved from Mama B to the teenagers occupying the chairs on the other side of his desk. "The trespassing charge involves those three teenagers whose parents, I have no doubt, don't know where they've been."

Jemma's heart sank. *Oh, no.* The last thing she needed was for her father to hear about this. *I'm so grounded for, like, ever. I can say goodbye to my friends and my job.* It was a blow, and Tad wasn't even here yet. No defense from Mama B was going to help her. Not now, not ever.

"So, before we call your parents," the sheriff continued, "how about the three of you tell me what you were doin' on the mountain tonight?" The sheriff seemed to realize that they had dragged Mama B along instead of the other way around, regardless of how willingly the old woman had gone.

Jemma, Val, and Easter exchanged looks. They had talked about this. Jemma would tell as much of the truth as possible while leaving out any mention of magic. "It started with the kids in Cider Creek getting sick. Val's real close to them, you see." She related their visit to the Johnson City hospital a few weeks ago and how they had met the ETRAA rep there. "We knew something was up. We just knew it." She shrugged. "We figured no one would believe us."

"So we took matters into our own hands," Val added, his expression hard.

"We hiked up the mountain and saw what they were doing," Easter interjected.

The sheriff nodded. "Ah, so the anonymous source was the three of you." Despite his disapproval, he seemed impressed.

"Technically, our first hike wasn't trespassing," Jemma stated, then shrugged. "How were we to know they wanted their work up there kept a secret?" The sheriff's brow furrowed as he thought the question over. She continued, "When the ETRAA came out with lies about the timeline of their work, we knew we had to get a better look."

"So, you went up at night," the sheriff stated dryly. "Not easy to see in the dark, is it?"

"Well, no," Jemma agreed.

"What about AJ?" the sheriff demanded.

"He followed us," Val answered. "And then hit his head."

"How?" the sheriff asked.

"We tried to get a closer look," Easter said. "The guards saw us. They ran at us, firing their guns."

The sheriff straightened. "They fired at you?"

All four nodded.

"You're sure?"

"Positive," the teenagers stated in unison. Mama B just

stared grimly at the officer. He didn't bother to glance at her since she wasn't helping him.

"Okay, so you ran. Then what?"

"We hid in a cave," Jemma answered. It was true. "It was dark in there, and AJ hit his head hard."

"The guards said they heard a gunshot and chased y'all to the creek where the cave was," the sheriff inserted. "What was that?"

Easter swallowed hard. "I thought I saw something. A bear, maybe, and I got scared, so I shot."

"How many times?" the sheriff asked.

"Twice."

The flush in Easter's cheeks told Jemma that her friend was having a difficult time lying. So far, though, they were keeping it together.

"Now, what I can't figure out," the sheriff continued, "is what the hell scared the guards but none of you. Mind explaining?"

All three shrugged. "We don't know."

Jemma wasn't sure the sheriff could tell they were lying. His eyes at last moved to Mama B. "Do you know?"

"I ain't got a damn clue," the old woman answered, her voice cold and resolute.

The sheriff sighed. "Well, then I don't have any more questions. For now." He scribbled something on a piece of paper, then instructed his deputy to put some information into the computer system. After several minutes, the sheriff turned back to the old woman and the teenagers. "You will each be charged with misdemeanor trespassing. That will be reported to the ETRAA, but we doubt they'll press charges." He winked. "Hopefully, this will tell them to get their asses off our mountain and out of our town."

Jemma almost breathed a sigh of relief. Where ETRAA was concerned, the sheriff was on their side. "You'll have to appear in court in a few weeks," the sheriff added. He glanced at Mama B. "You, too." He paused again and looked like he might ask another question. Instead, he shook his head. Like them, he was trying to wrap his mind around it all. "Wait here. I'll call your parents."

The following moments filled Jemma with dread. How the hell was she supposed to explain where she had been and what she had been doing? At least she hadn't lied. She had been with the McCarthys overnight. Jemma glanced down at her dirty, torn clothes. She didn't look like she had been at a sleepover, and how was she supposed to explain Mama B's presence? Jemma could tell her father the same story they had told the sheriff, but Tad wouldn't buy it. He always sensed when there was more going on.

At last, the sheriff returned and informed the youths that he had not been able to reach Mr. and Mrs. McCarthy. Easter and Val had expected that since their parents worked the third shift and would not be home for another hour or so.

Fifteen minutes later, however, two of the parents showed up. RJ Kilmer came in first, looking harried and haggard and worried to the bone. "Where is he? Where's my son?" he demanded, desperation in his voice. He barely gave the teenagers and Mama B a glance.

"We're taking care of him right now, sir," one of the officers told him. "He hit his head, or so we've been told.

He's awake, and you can see him in a moment." RJ turned to the doors as Tad Nox entered. He wasn't alone.

Jemma gasped. Why was Linnea Strang here with her father at five in the morning? They came in hand in hand. Jemma and Easter stared at each other. Apparently, something had been going on between the two before Jemma had suggested to her father that he go to the drug store. *That was why he'd acted weird about it,* she realized. Tad had assumed that Jemma knew.

Feeling blindsided, she fixed her eyes on Tad and Linnea. She felt betrayed. Why had her father kept this from her? *And it's five in the fucking morning,* she thought indignantly. *That means they've been together the whole night.* Tad, it seemed, had taken advantage of his daughter going to a sleepover to have one of his own.

RJ went up to him. "I am so sorry, Mr. Nox. I assure you that it was not your daughter who got herself into this mess. AJ must have talked the good kids into doing something bad. They went along with it because I asked them to try to make amends with my boy. I just..." He rambled on, but Tad's eyes had locked with Jemma's.

Easter and Val hurried to RJ to make sure he knew none of this was his son's fault. Tad wasn't buying it anyway. He gave Jemma a long, hard look before turning to the sheriff. "What happened?" The sheriff repeated the story he had been told. Tad listened with equal parts rapt interest and grim detachment. He was relieved that his daughter was all right, but he was angry too.

Yep, totally grounded. She might have had the power of a holler witch, but she was still a kid. She hated how powerless she felt. She glanced at Linnea. The kind woman had pity in her eyes.

"I'm sure there's a lot more to the story, sheriff," Tad remarked coldly after he heard the full account. He glanced at Jemma. "I know how my daughter operates. It's my fault I let her out for so long this evening."

"Not to worry," the sheriff responded. "No one got hurt. Well, not too badly hurt, anyway." Jemma and Easter silently swore never to confirm how Stomphord had died. The earthquake was the answer if it was ever discovered. No one needed to know that it was Easter who had shot him twice in the chest.

Tad held Jemma's gaze for a long time. Mama B rose and attempted to appease him, but Jemma's father brushed her off. "There's something weird going on here." His eyes flashed at Mama B. Jemma almost never saw her father like this. "I know she works for you, Ms. Brickellwood, and I know the two of you have become good friends, but she's still my daughter. You didn't have permission to take her anywhere without my knowing."

Hurt flickered in Mama B's eyes. Tad's hot temper and the use of her formal name instead of "Mama B" hit her hard. She sank back into the chair, shoulders slumping in defeat.

They were interrupted by the reappearance of AJ. He had a bandage around his head, and although he still looked dazed, he was walking on his own. RJ crushed him in a giant hug. Jemma's heart ached at the sight of it. As the Kilmers headed for the door, AJ's head turned toward Jemma. Their eyes met, and for a moment, his bore a startled look. Jemma felt a heated pull. Did he know she had seen his memories? So much shit had happened.

She was taken aback by the sudden sadness that appeared in his eyes the next moment. "Come on, son," RJ told him as he held the door open. AJ tore his eyes away from Jemma's and left with his father.

"I'll go home and let the two of you have time together," Jemma heard Linnea tell her father. Linnea kissed him on the cheek. Jemma gaped. "I'll call you later."

Tad just nodded and let go of the woman's hand. His eyes were still fixed on his daughter. He was too angry to speak.

"We'll take you home, Mama B," Val told the old woman. He helped her up and gave Jemma a look that said, "Good luck, friend," as he, his sister, and Mama B left the station.

Their parents were going to be disappointed. Anyone at their school who learned about it would be relentless about making fun of them. The McCarthys were hanging out with a witch again. The McCarthys were getting in trouble again.

Jemma sighed, on the verge of tears.

Tad just jerked his head toward the door, signaling that it was time for them to go.

They arrived home as dawn broke. Tad gave his daughter time to take a shower and eat a little something before he demanded she sit at the table in the kitchen. The drive home had been almost unbearable. Apparently, Tad had used the time in the truck and while Jemma was cleaning up to decide what he was going to say.

For a long, dreadful moment, Tad paced, fuming. Jemma had never seen him this angry. Finally, he stopped short and turned to her. "You need to level with me, Jemma Anne Nox, or you will never, *ever* go back to Gran's Rest as long as I have the power to stop you."

Jemma couldn't imagine life in Solomon's Cross without being allowed up to Gran's Rest. She couldn't bear the thought of never seeing the woman again. She sighed, the sound seeming to shred every last bit of reservation and secrecy. "Okay. I'll tell you everything. It's a long story, though."

Tad pulled out a chair. "I've taken off work today. I have time." His voice was still firm. Jemma wondered how much worse it would get.

Tad stayed quiet and grim the whole time she spoke. She began with how, when she first got to know Mama B, the old woman seemed to know things when she shouldn't have. She explained the boo hag and Easter's sickness. She spoke of Mama B's training. When the word "witch" came out of her mouth for the first time, she expected her father to roll his eyes and tell her she was crazy and to cut the bullshit and tell him the truth. He didn't. His expression just hardened.

"So, she began training me, and it was a good thing she did since we were able to stop the creature from tormenting Easter. We got rid of it, and for months, everything was normal. Then the kids in Cider Creek, Val's friends, got sick." She told him about their trip to Johnson City and the horrible feeling she had gotten in Sharina's room. She described how strange the doctor and Mr. Stomphord had acted. She spoke of their decision to go up to Kalhoun's Crest and find out what was going on.

"Val and I took those videos and pictures you saw on the news. Easter submitted them anonymously for us. You might be wondering how I knew to go up there. Well, I read about it." She shared what she had discovered from Mama B's story and the writings of Vesna Soucek. "That was why we went to visit Miss Dagwood. It wasn't for a school project. We were trying to find out more."

She shrugged. "I don't think it helped, though. After that, things got worse. You were offered a job with the company we knew was doing bad things. Very bad things. RJ Kilmer made a deal with them. We knew it was only a matter of time before ETRAA took over the whole town. No one would believe us if we said there was magic involved, so we had to go back up and handle it ourselves."

She explained their hike up the mountain, only leaving out the details she had forgotten about in the chaos. She chose not to tell her father two things. First, that she had seen AJ's memories. She had no clue what it meant for her, and she didn't want anyone but Mama B to know for the time being. She also didn't tell her father that Easter had shot Stomphord. "He acted crazy, and we couldn't get him out, so he got buried." That was true.

She sighed. Her eyelids were very heavy. "Then the police came, and we were taken in. It's over now, though. That part, anyway. We don't have to deal with the haints anymore." She gave her father a weak smile. "I know you hate me for what I did, but I won't apologize for it. I saved my friends. I saved us." She laughed brokenly. "Hell, I saved the whole fucking town." Strangely, her language didn't make her father spring up and shout at her.

He remained still and silent. Was he *that* mad at her? Was her story too overwhelming for him to handle? It was wild; she knew that. It was the craziest shit that had ever come out of her mouth, but it was the truth.

The silence stretched.

She had some questions of her own. Why the hell had Linnea Strang been with him? She decided that wasn't as big a concern right now, though. She could deal with her feeling of betrayal after she had gotten a lot of sleep.

Finally, Tad sighed and slapped his thighs with sweat-slicked hands. Jemma couldn't tell what he was thinking, but his thoughts seemed to be cycling at a rapid pace. "Well, I'll admit I was afraid this day would come."

Jemma's heart sped up. What did he mean? Why was he so calm?"

Tad laughed roughly. "I should have known this would happen, given the family history. I guess I thought coming here would prevent it."

Jemma could hardly believe what had come out of his mouth. Voice shaking, she asked, "Dad, what are you talking about?"

Tad looked his daughter dead in the eyes and shrugged. "I should have known. But then again, it shouldn't have come as a surprise since your mother was such a potent worker of the Art."

AUTHOR NOTES - MICHAEL ANDERLE

MAY 20, 2022

Thank you for not only reading this book but these author notes as well!

Small towns and wonderful food

My background is varied. I grew up on the far northwest side of Houston, TX, but my parents both lived in an area between Houston and Austin bounded by Moulton, Shiner (known for the beer), and Hallettsville (known for being the location that the movie *Best Little Whorehouse in Texas* was filmed with Dolly Parton and Burt Reynolds.)

A LOT of Germans and Poles and Czechs immigrated to that area of the state, including my family. Anderle is a German surname, and my mom's maiden name was Castecka.

The original pronunciation is a mouthful.

I presently live either in Henderson, Nevada, or Cabo San Lucas, Mexico. NEITHER of these places has some of the food I grew up eating in Texas, so when I get a chance to eat something similar, it brings up all kinds of nostalgic memories.

Like yesterday.

Here in Las Vegas / Henderson, there is a BBQ place called L2, which is short for Larry and Larry. The restaurant claims they are a Texas BBQ place. It's a good claim since their BBQ (especially the sausage) is dead-on what I remember eating as a child.

So, back to yesterday. I was eating some leftover sausage and mashed potatoes (yes, I added extra butter). The smells were like quarters placed in the memory strip video player for re-living the huge picnics that occurred in those small towns.

The adults would be drinking. We kids (and usually our cousins) would be getting into all sorts of trouble with the fishing, snakes, frogs, and trees. Well, the guys would. I frankly don't know what the girls did since I was young and wasn't interested in girls at the time.

Boy, would *that* change over the next few years.

As I ate the sausage, the pork/beef and spices jolted my memories. The times with my mom (who has passed) came back, and my appreciation for those times swelled.

I've lived in the suburbs for most of my life. However, for many weeks each year, either my father or mother would take us kids to the grandparents' house, and we witnessed milking cows, picking peas and cotton, and fishing in the tanks.

There is much peace when one lives in a smaller town. Yes, everyone often knows your business, but you know that you are KNOWN. The larger cities push the individual to the background, and when I was younger, it was more important to me to be known.

Now, I have a small amount of fame, and I appreciate my (almost) anonymity. Hell, in Cabo, I'm just another *gringo* for the most part. In the restaurants I frequent, the waitresses and waiters remember me, and it provides a sense of *Cheers* (the tv show), where everyone knows your name.

Which, in essence, is what a small town provides. For me? Yeah, that's just enough.

Talk to you in the next book!

Ad Aeternitatem,

Michael

If you want, you can read a couple of short stories I am sharing from my STORIES *with Michael Anderle newsletter here: (No requirement to sign up.)*

https://michael.beehiiv.com/

BOOKS BY MICHAEL ANDERLE

Sign up for the LMBPN email list to be notified of new releases and special deals!

https://lmbpn.com/email/

For a complete list of books by Michael Anderle, please visit:

www.lmbpn.com/ma-books/

CONNECT WITH THE AUTHORS

Michael Anderle Social

Website: http://lmbpn.com

Email List: https://michael.beehiiv.com/

https://www.facebook.com/LMBPNPublishing

https://twitter.com/MichaelAnderle

https://www.instagram.com/lmbpn_publishing/

https://www.bookbub.com/authors/michael-anderle

www.ingramcontent.com/pod-product-compliance
Lightning Source LLC
LaVergne TN
LVHW041906070526
838199LV00051BA/2526